HUNT·E D

MEAGAN SPOONER

HUNTED

HARPER TEEN

An Imprint of HarperCollinsPublishers

HarperTeen is an imprint of HarperCollins Publishers.

Hunted

Copyright © 2017 by Meagan Spooner

ISBN 978-0-06-242228-6 (trade bdg.)

Typography by Sarah Creech and Erin Schell
17 18 19 20 21   PC/LSCH   10 9 8 7 6 5 4 3 2 1

First Edition

To the girl
who reads by flashlight
who sees dragons in the clouds
who feels most alive in worlds that never were
who knows magic is real
who dreams

This is for you.

BEAST

We always know before the change comes. When a storm approaches, we feel it in the thickness of the air, the tension in the earth awaiting the blanket of snow. We feel the moment the wind changes direction. We sense a shift of power when it is coming.

Tonight there is hunger in the air. The forest waits for something. We pace, our steps stirring the early snows. Our frustration vents in growls and grunts. Each of us could read the change to come, neither hindered by the other. We could track it, or we could run with it. But we are trapped, and we can do neither.

We always know before the change comes— but we never know what the change will bring.

ONE

YEVA WATCHED THE SKY over the far-off forest, listening to the baronessa with one ear. The air was heavy and unfamiliar. *A storm?* she wondered, inhaling the strangeness. In the distance the treetops swayed as if in a gust of wind, but the rest of the forest was still.

She leaned forward, abandoning the sewing on her lap so she could nudge the glass-paned window open a fraction. The air outside was frigid, especially for Yeva in her finely embroidered dress, but she didn't mind—the glass distorted the distant woods, and she'd rather see clearly than be warm. *How large must a creature be to cause movement like that?* Larger than anything an arrow could bring down, unless the shot was beyond lucky. Here on the edge of the wood, there shouldn't be anything larger than a bear skulking beneath the canopy. Her father used to tell stories of larger, stranger things that hid in the heart of the wood, but she'd outgrown stories long ago. If only that sign of movement would come again, perhaps she'd be able to—

"Yeva, darling!" The baronessa's voice cut in, the world snapping back to the present. "You'll get your death in that draft. Close the window before we all catch a cough."

Yeva reached for the latch to pull it closed, trying to look less rattled than she felt. "Sorry, my lady. I thought I saw bad weather approaching."

"Not another storm," moaned the baronessa, clutching her fur wrap more closely about her shoulders. "It's too early for such snow, I don't know what we'll do this winter."

"Do you really think a storm is coming?" asked Galina, one of the baronessa's other ladies.

With her attention mostly on the far-off forest, Yeva noticed with a start that Galina had been speaking to her. "The air smells of it," Yeva replied, eyes shifting from Galina's face to the baronessa's.

Galina turned to whisper to the lady next to her, forgetting herself. The baronessa scarcely noticed, though, too busy wringing her hands. "Oh, what shall we do?" she murmured, not bothering to look outside herself, but staring around at the faces of her ladies.

Yeva glanced back at the window. There was still no sign of bad weather on the horizon, but uneasiness lingered at the back of her mind. The parlor had erupted into whispers, and with creeping dread Yeva realized that she could be here all night.

"My lady," she said, adopting for once the gentle voice she was meant to be cultivating, "perhaps the other ladies and I should retire, if we are to get home to our families before the storm arrives." A number of heads lifted among the circle of women.

"And leave me alone?" cried the baronessa as though Yeva had proposed taking her out into the storm and blindfolding her.

The baronessa was fairer skinned than most, claiming some

Varangian blood in her ancestry. Other nobles would have hidden those roots, but she owned them with pride, attributing some romantic hot-bloodedness to them. Combined with her plump face and bow-shaped mouth, it gave her a youthful appearance, childlike and sweet. For all her silliness, Yeva could not help but feel a twinge of pity for the woman. She wasn't that much older than Yeva herself, not even twenty yet, with her husband more than three times her age. The company of the wealthy ladies in the town was all she had in the dark months of the year.

Yeva smiled at her, for once not having to search for the expression. "The baron will be home soon, and of course Machna and Lada will be here." The two sisters were guests of the baron's household, visiting from the city.

The baronessa chewed at her lip, casting a glance for the first time at the tiny window. Yeva had secured the spot by being the most junior of the women in the baronessa's circle, and thus taking the coldest seat—but she preferred it to any other, with its view of the forest beyond the edge of the baron's property. Yeva felt impatience strum at her insides. She hated the indecisiveness of people in town, how they waited to make decisions, took weeks or months or years to settle, until the decisions were made for them by inaction.

"Oh, very well," the baronessa said finally, waving her hand in a sad, dismissive gesture. "If the snow has not marooned us all by morning, will you ladies return tomorrow afternoon? If it snows my husband will not be hunting, but he will be so cross that I would rather have company when facing him."

Yeva felt a sluggish stirring of dislike in her stomach. Only a nobleman, whose idea of hunting involved sitting high on a spotlessly decorated stallion while half-starved hounds did all the work, would be turned away by snow. *The snow is a canvas,* her father would say, *upon which the beast paints his past, his home, his intentions, his future. Learn to see the picture and you will know him as you know yourself.*

"Of course we will come back tomorrow," Galina replied, saving Yeva from having to formulate an answer. "Thank you, my lady."

The girls all stood, tucking their sewing away, preparing to leave until the next afternoon. Yeva hurried to follow suit, shoving her embroidery into its basket. She'd learned in her first few days that the baronessa often snared the last of the girls to leave, drawing them into conversations that could last for hours. It wasn't so much that Yeva disliked speaking with the baronessa, but rather that she'd prefer to reach home by nightfall.

And before the storm, if one was coming.

They left the baronessa mournfully describing her husband's hunting exploits to the hapless sisters from the city, and rushed to bundle up in their winter gear.

"Thank you," whispered Galina as she caught up to Yeva, jogging her elbow a little and casting her a smile.

Yeva shook her head, the corners of her mouth twitching. "I was only thinking of our safety, traveling in the weather."

One of the baronessa's ladies, overhearing Yeva, laughed. "We knew exactly what you were thinking of, Yeva. What time is Solmir meeting you?"

Yeva's smile vanished. "Solmir?" she echoed.

"Don't think we haven't seen how much attention he pays you at the baronessa's dinners." The lady raised an eyebrow. She was one of the older members of the baronessa's inner circle, soon to be engaged to a man in the baron's hunting party. "Don't give me that look. That is the point of this all, no? For us to see, and be seen."

Yeva looked over at Galina, who was watching quietly as she laced the ties on her cloak. Finding no answer there, Yeva could only shrug in response.

Galina fell into step beside Yeva, and they walked in silence through the high doors of the house and onto the street. Galina was the second-newest addition to the baronessa's collection, and somewhat more understanding of Yeva's peculiarities. She had never once blanched at the accidental mention of weaponry.

"Was it true?" Yeva broke the quiet as they passed the church.

"Was what true?" Galina looked up, brown eyes blank.

"What they said about Solmir." Yeva glanced behind them, checking that no one was near enough to hear. She felt her cheeks warming despite the cold. "About his attention to me."

Galina smiled. The expression was always sudden and unexpected on her small, solemn face. She was a relatively plain girl, but her smile was beautiful. "Yeva, you silly thing. You can't say you haven't noticed. They tease you only because they feel certain there is an understanding between you."

Yeva stopped short, abruptly enough that slush sprayed up onto the hem of her skirts. "An understanding?" She had tied her cloak too tightly—her breathing felt labored, uncertain.

"I am sorry to be the one to tell you," said Galina, dimming her smile with clear effort. Her expression was still brimming with amusement. "See you tomorrow," she added, before turning at the corner to make her way toward her own father's house, in the opposite direction. Yeva stood stirring the slush with the toe of her boot.

Solmir? He was nothing, barely more than a name in her mind. No, that was unfair; he was more than that. One of the baron's hunting party, he was without land or title, but his family was wealthy nonetheless. His father had been a respected cooper and manager of the baron's wine cellar until his death, at which point Solmir had become the baron's ward. Rumor had it that the baron, childless after two previous marriages, might confer his lands and titles to Solmir if the new baronessa failed to produce him an heir.

Yeva tried to picture Solmir in her mind, conjuring up hazy memories of dinners past. They'd always been a trial for her. The afternoons with the baronessa were one thing; they kept Yeva—for the most part—from longing for the forest trails. The dinners, however, were another. She'd always counted the moments until she could be back home again with her father, feeling like one of those ragged birds at the market beating halfheartedly against their wicker cages. The only image of Solmir her memory provided was of friendly hazel eyes and a soft voice that made her cheeks flush all the more. She recalled him broaching the strangest subjects, though she preferred his bizarre company to the dull conversation of the other gentlemen.

How long had the other ladies been talking about them, with Yeva completely unaware?

She tried to ignore how warm she was under her furs. It was not quite cold enough for full winter gear but she wore it anyway—a blizzard could rise swiftly and without warning, even this early in the winter. Sweat started to form between her shoulder blades and trickle down her spine; she set off down the road toward her father's house.

They lived toward the edge of town not because Yeva's father couldn't afford to live at its center, but because he, like Yeva, felt more comfortable with a house that bordered on nature. He'd given up life as a hunter to marry Yeva's mother, using his wealth to start a career as a merchant, but he couldn't wholly give up the need for the woods and the snow and the wild tang of the beasts.

Yeva felt a tension draining that she hadn't realized she was carrying. She liked the baronessa, and she appreciated having been taken into her circle, but some part of her still longed for the freedom she'd had even a year ago. Her father used to take her with him, training her, teaching her what he knew of hunting. It was all in fun, because what harm was there in teaching these things to a child? Echoes from a past life; things his own father taught him. Sharing them was the only way of keeping them real. Being a merchant held no passion for him, but it was safe, and it had made his wife happy until she died when the girls were young. It was only recently that her father had noticed Yeva's age, and thought that she ought to be a lady now, and no longer his wild little Beauty.

It was time to join her older sisters in society—such as it was.

The houses became smaller and more spread out as she trudged along, the laneways connecting them covered with snow once more instead of the slush churned up by many feet and carriage wheels. Yeva could see her father's house on the ridge and hurried her steps.

The sky was growing darker, though the hour was too early for the sun to set. The clouds were thickening. Perhaps there would be a storm after all. Yeva felt no shame at the fiction— there *had* been something in the air—but she would feel better able to face the baronessa tomorrow if some kind of weather came in the night.

The hill was steep enough to make Yeva's breath puff white in the cold air, and she sputtered an oath. Such terrible shape for a hunter to be in. She used to be able to run for hours, uphill or down, blood coursing through her and urging her onward. But then, she was not a hunter anymore. The roundness of face and limb she saw in the washbasin each morning, the sleek deep red of her hair, the full lips, the lazy gaze—every day she was more a lady. Every day less herself.

Yeva hurried through the door, trying to still her panting breath so no one would see her winded. One of the servants met her at the door, his lanky arms outstretched to receive her furs.

"Thank you, Albe," she told him with a smile that made him blush and duck his head. Albe had been with them since he was a boy, but lately he'd been inching around Yeva and her sisters as if they were made of glass.

All the merchants' daughters were spoken of as beauties. Yeva would have preferred to be admired for her skill, but she'd suffered the great misfortune of having been born a girl. And so no one would ever know. When she was younger, she used to dream of a husband who would love her all the more if she could hunt with him, side by side. But age, and time spent with the baronessa, had worn away that imagined future.

She could remain unmarried, but to do so would make her a financial burden to her father. To marry would be to leave the wood forever, surrendering what little freedom she still had.

But Solmir is a hunter, whispered a sinuous thought. *And a good one. If anyone were to admire your skill in the forest, it would be him.* . . .

"Your sisters are in the kitchen, mistress," said Albe, head still bowed. Yeva could see a flush on the back of his neck and the tips of his ears.

"Thank you," she repeated, and left the poor boy to recover.

As she headed down the hall, a thumping, clattering, wild noise exploded from the back corner of the house. Laughing, Yeva crouched down so that when a pair of dogs came barreling around the edge of the hall, they hit her square. Less painful than letting them catch an arm or a leg. Doe-Eyes whined eagerly, burying her face in the fold of Yeva's hip, while Pelei sniffed her all over, circling and circling and snuffling his aggravation at her collection of the day's scents.

Pelei was the scent hound, thick and shaggy and red-brown, named for the clay he so resembled. Doe-Eyes was the runner, slimmer and lighter built, less armored against the biting cold in winter. They were her father's hunting dogs, but any time the subject arose, he delighted in moaning about how his youngest daughter had stolen them from him, how they betrayed him every day they ran to her. But he loved to see them love her, and always spoke with a twinkle in his eye.

Yeva ordered the dogs back to their corner of the house, sending them reluctantly away, and went to the kitchen. She found Asenka and Lena kneading bread together, moving as one, each leaning down into the stroke as the other folded. They were closer in age to each other than Asenka was to Yeva, and so alike as to be nearly twins. Asenka's hair was two shades darker than Lena's chestnut brown, and her cheeks fuller and pinker, but from a distance the two were indistinguishable.

"Yeva," said Asenka warmly, looking up but not halting at her work. "You're home early."

"The ladies thought there might be a storm coming," Yeva replied, "and the baronessa dismissed us early."

"The ladies?" echoed Asenka, a smile lurking behind her black eyes.

Yeva grinned and lifted one shoulder delicately. "My seat is closest to the window—why shouldn't I notice incoming weather first?" She reached for the laces on her dress and tugged them loose, drawing in a long breath. Her blood was still pumping from her uphill walk.

"Oh, Yeva." Lena's voice was heavy with weary scolding.

"What are you doing? Father will be home soon—what if he should see you?"

"Father has seen me head to toe in men's clothing," Yeva reminded her, "and half covered in boar's blood. I don't think he will die from the scandal."

"But you were a child then," said Lena delicately. "Now you are grown. And anyway, what if Albe were to come in?"

"Then he shall probably explode on the spot."

Asenka let out a strangled laugh before turning her head aside to hide her mouth against her shoulder. Lena glared at her, the expression quickly dissipating in favor of a rueful smile. "Service to the baronessa was supposed to tame you, Beauty, not teach you new ways to torment us all."

Yeva smiled, turning away before Lena noticed her mistake. Yeva had been Beauty all through her childhood. Her father had named her on the day she was born after the old goddess of beauty, as he'd named her sisters after light and grace. Every few years, the holy men from the west came through to perform weddings and naming ceremonies, and the townsfolk would hide their heathen accoutrements, as the priests called them, and hang up their crosses.

The merchant's youngest daughter was renamed Yeva, after the temptress in the garden. She would have preferred Beauty, for at least there is beauty in all things, not only temptation, but Yeva she was to be. Her mother enforced the name as strictly as a warden minding his charges, but she died when Yeva was only five years old, so there was no one after that to insist her father use her proper name.

She had always been Beauty when they hunted together, always Beauty when he tucked her in at night. He called her Yeva now, because she was to be a fine lady someday, and her proper

name was the one society knew. And yet there was always a half
second's pause before he said that name, a tiny catch in his voice
that was all that remained of who she'd been before.

Though the servants were responsible for preparing dinner,
Yeva and her sisters often helped. The three spent their days
apart—Yeva with the baronessa, Asenka at the leech's shop
tending the sick, and Lena managing the household and spending
time with her fiancé, Radak, whenever he was in town. He was a
merchant like their father, and was both very much interested in
merging empires and very much in love with Lena.

The evening was their time to be together, in the brief hour
before their father returned, and they had little taste for sewing
and gossiping as ladies were meant to do. Preparation of fresh
bread to accompany the meal was tradition.

Yeva busied herself fetching herbs down from the racks,
crumbling them between her fingers and breathing in the scent.
Seasoning had been her job when she was too little to knead the
bread, and so it remained even now she was old enough. Asenka
shaped the dough, and Yeva rolled it in the crumbled herbs until
there was a light crust coating the loaf. Then Lena wrapped it all
in a cloth and tucked it close to the hearth to rise. She pulled out
the risen loaf prepared the night before and slid it carefully into
the oven, then she and Asenka washed their hands in the basin,
pulling their aprons off, chattering.

Yeva drifted into the next room, preferring to leave the aroma
of herbs on her skin. She took up her spot on the floor by her
father's chair, crossing her arms on the footstool and resting her
chin on her hands. The smell of herbs mingled with the smell
of the bread as it warmed in the oven, and she closed her eyes.
At some point her sisters joined her, still chatting and laughing.
Lena helped Asenka into her chair before taking her own. It

wasn't until a name caught Yeva's attention that she opened her eyes and lifted her head.

"Do you think there's any truth to it?" Asenka's voice was low, with the strange wobble in it that showed she was thinking intensely about whatever she was saying.

"It's everywhere. I can't see that there wouldn't be at least a grain of truth in the telling, if everyone is telling it. Yeva, have you heard anything at the baronessa's?"

Yeva swallowed. She'd heard the name, but not the context. "About what? I had my eyes closed."

They were used to her tuning out their chatter—Yeva was the quiet sister. Lena leaned forward, her face shining with interest. "There is a rumor that Solmir is going to speak for one of Tvertko's daughters." Her eyes sparkled as she spoke their father's name.

Yeva's heart seized. But before she could answer, Lena turned back to gaze at Asenka, whose own face carried a delicate pink flush. "Oh, it must be true. You've admired him for years, Ashka. And if he asks—why, then we can be married together! Think of it, a double wedding in the spring when the snows melt."

Asenka bowed her head, covering her face with her hands. "Stop that!" she protested. "My face will fall apart from the smiling. It's a rumor, nothing more. Leave it be, will you?"

Yeva kept silent, her stomach roiling. She prayed they wouldn't ask her again what she knew, for she couldn't lie to them. But how could she tell them that it was the youngest sister, not the eldest, who had caught Solmir's eye? How could Asenka bear to see her sisters spoken for, when no one had cast an eye in her direction?

Asenka always sat so that her twisted foot would be covered by the hem of her skirts, but Yeva found her eyes going there anyway. Her sister walked with difficulty and great pain, but managed everything else with such ease that most people tended to forget the malady she was born with. At the leech's office she was admired for her compassion, and for the long hours she spent limping along the beds, fetching down tinctures and salves without a word of complaint.

Yeva's fists clenched around handfuls of her skirt, fury replacing the uneasy roiling in her stomach. Why should it always be *beauty*? Why could her sister not be sought after for her kindness, her empathy, her strength? Why could she not be loved for that, instead of passed over because of one misfortune of birth that supposedly marred her?

Anger prompted her to rise, mouth opening to burst out with the truth, the injustice of it. Her sisters looked up at her, mouths forming identical Os of surprise. But before she could speak, the sound of the door opening in the hall interrupted her.

"Father's home!" cried Lena. "Yeva, how do you always know?" She helped Asenka to her feet, and the two sisters made their way to the hall. Someone outside the family might speak of the cruelty of naming a baby with a twisted foot after grace. But in everything but her step, Asenka was the most graceful girl Yeva had ever seen. Gentle of smile, long-fingered, slender and lovely. Her voice was always soft, her laugh never too loud in a quiet room. Even as she leaned on Lena, the way she walked was careful and smooth with deliberation.

Yeva stood clenching her jaw, tongue pressed against her teeth to still it. Let them believe she had leaped to her feet to greet their father. How could she break Asenka's heart with the truth?

"I was thinking of spending next summer in the city," her father was saying as he mopped up the last of the gravy on his plate with some of the fresh bread.

Yeva lifted her head, torn from the thoughts swirling around Solmir and Asenka. Her father had taken Yeva and her sisters with him to the city on business once years ago, and while they had lit up at the flood of new sights and experiences, Yeva had found it overwhelming. The streets stank and every face was strange, and she could not follow any paths or trails through the churned-up streets or across the uneven cobbles. She had spent every moment clinging to her father's hand.

Now, his glance passed between his older daughters before coming to rest on his youngest. "I have some business with the cartographers there, and it'll take some time to get my affairs settled. So I'll be required to take a house in the area for a few months. It'll be quiet there all by myself, so I was thinking of bringing you three to live with me."

The older girls exploded with glee, chattering and laughing, celebrating their good fortune. While none of the sisters was solely fixated upon fashions and society and standing the way the baronessa was, the prospect of being surrounded by so much of it for three months of the summer was a delight.

Yeva alone was quiet, watching her father. She knew how much it cost him to move away from the wilderness; it cost her the same. But she knew why her father wanted to go. None of the men here had spoken for Asenka. Perhaps somewhere new, her loveliness would catch a man's eye the way it hadn't here. Her father raised eyebrows peppered with gray, watching Yeva in return. She took a deep breath and summoned a smile. He nodded and leaned back in his chair.

"Of course," he said, speaking now primarily to his older girls, "you'll be required to bring along any husbands or fiancés you may have acquired in the meantime." This pronouncement brought on further shouting and laughing, and even Yeva's smile grew less stiff in the face of her sisters' glee.

"Pechta!" called her father, summoning the cook into the doorway. "I believe the girls would like some sweets to celebrate." The cook bobbed a curtsy and vanished back into the kitchen.

The dogs had crept in during the merriment, as if hoping they wouldn't be noticed. Lena, as lady of the household, objected to them in the rooms where people ate and slept, but for right now even she could not be distracted. Pelei stood watch beside her father's chair, and Doe-Eyes slunk over to Yeva, nose nudging up under her elbow and into her lap. Doe-Eyes had been purchased during that trip to the city all those years ago. Yeva sat stroking her absently, watching her sisters' excitement.

Outside, the wind had picked up, beginning to beat against the sturdy frame of the house. The servants had shuttered the windows already to prepare for the storm, but Yeva felt a flicker of the uneasiness she'd experienced at the baronessa's, a restlessness she could not name.

Suddenly, over the howl of the rising storm, a heavy pounding against the front door broke through the sounds of chatter and laughter. The sisters exchanged glances as their father leaned to the side to look around the edge of his chair toward the hall.

"Is it Radak?" wondered Asenka, glancing at her younger sister. It was unlike Lena's fiancé to come calling without first having made an appointment with their father.

"He is away on business. Maybe it's Solmir," whispered Lena before dissolving into quiet laughter again at the blush that crept over Asenka's face.

Yeva volunteered no guesses. She could hear the howling of the wind, and could imagine no one who would venture out in such weather except due to some terrible emergency.

The pounding came again, this time so urgently that the

smiles faded from the older girls' faces. Albe had finally arrived at the door and was nearly thrown back as he opened it by the force of the wind on the other side. Yeva couldn't recognize the man who stumbled through it, covered head to toe in winter gear. Only the tip of his nose was visible over his muffler, red and shiny from cold. He pawed at his face to free his mouth, gasping their father's name.

"Tvertko," he said, choking in the sudden heat of the house as Albe struggled to close the door again. "I need to see Tvertko. Where is he, I must see him immediately."

Albe gaped at him, stammering his usual greeting. The man glanced past him to see Yeva's father in his chair and shoved his way into the room.

"Tvertko," he said, throwing himself forward. "It's gone. It's all gone."

Her father's face became very still, brows lowered. "What's gone, Pietr? Speak clearly, man."

"All of it," the man moaned again, dropping to his knees. He was exhausted, that much was clear. And he was not a local, or Yeva would have recognized him the moment he pulled the muffler from his face. And yet, her father knew him. One of his contacts in the city, perhaps?

Her father was silent, watching the man gasping for breath and dripping melted snow onto Lena's immaculate floorboards. Then he lifted his head, addressing his daughters. "Girls, please go upstairs. Take the dogs. And please tell Pechta to boil some tea."

"But Father—" Yeva began, startled. He had never excluded them from his business discussions before.

"Go, Yeva." His voice was no louder than it had been, but so firm that it brooked no opposition.

Her sisters were on their feet, Lena clinging to Asenka as much as the other way around. Yeva leaned down to lay a hand on each of the dogs, murmuring to them to go upstairs. Sensing her urgency, they obeyed, slinking up the stairs with their tails low. As Lena guided Asenka to the first step, Yeva ducked into the kitchen.

She found all four of the servants there, wide-eyed and midgossip. Albe was still in disarray from having opened the door to the storm, his hair standing up roughly in every direction. "Tea," said Yeva. "For my father and his guest." She was not usually so abrupt, but something cold had seized her belly and she couldn't find it in her to soften the order. Pechta merely nodded, forgetting to curtsy, and hurried to the fireplace and the kettle.

Yeva took the long way back around to the stairs, passing through the hallway instead of the living room where her father still sat, listening to his visitor. Halfway up she paused; some acoustical anomaly in the building of the house conspired to throw their voices so clearly she could hear what they were saying.

". . . and every man of them dead," the visitor was saying, his voice rough with exhaustion. "Barbarian swords in their guts, heads piled in the wagons and burned. All the goods stolen or destroyed."

"No one was left alive?" Her father's voice was full of quiet grief. Yeva could imagine his head bowed, eyes closed as he listened. "Not even the boys?"

"No one," repeated the visitor. "Are you hearing me, Tvertko? It's all gone. You're ruined."

Ruined. Yeva's ears rang with the word in the ensuing silence.

"Yeva!" a voice hissed. Yeva blinked, finding her eyes watering in the stillness, and looked up. Lena was at the top of the stairs, beckoning to her. "Come."

Yeva joined her sisters, not wishing to hear any more than she already had. They all piled into Asenka's bed, the three of them and the dogs too, and for once Lena didn't push them away. Doe-Eyes lay with her head trembling in Yeva's lap, keeping as still as possible in the hope that no one would notice her and make her leave. Pelei kept licking and licking at the hem of Yeva's skirt, scenting the nervousness in the air and trying to make sense of it.

They waited, none of them talking, although Asenka moved now and then to shift her weight and ease her twisted foot. It wasn't until they heard the front door open again, a brief gust of air howling through the house and tossing their hair back, that Yeva lifted her head. The door slammed again, leaving them in utter silence.

Lena spoke first. "Should we——?"

Yeva drew in a breath, trying to still the shaking in her legs as she slipped out from underneath Doe-Eyes's head. "I'll go." Both of her sisters relaxed a fraction—they had been waiting for her to offer. She was their father's favorite, though it was no source of angst or friction among them. It was part of her family duty to be her father's daughter.

She told the dogs to stay, although Doe-Eyes scrambled off the bed and followed her as far as the doorway of the room. Bare feet tingling against the chill of the floorboards, Yeva made her way back down the stairs.

She found her father still sitting in his chair, though he was leaning forward, feet braced against the ground. He looked somehow smaller, elbows propped on his knees, forehead resting on his balled fists. The firelight granted false color to what she could see of his pale face, the lines etched there throwing ghastly shadows. Yeva had never realized that her father's face was wrinkled.

Yeva swallowed and crept forward. Her father gave no sign that he was aware of her presence, but when she reached out and touched his shoulder with the tips of her fingers, he didn't jump or cry out.

He merely sighed, the breath leaving his body in a low groan. "Oh, Beauty," he said, without lifting his head. He raised one of his hands to grasp at hers, fingers wrapping around her hand with the strength of a drowning man. Saying nothing else, he only sat there clasping her hand against his shoulder, head pressed against his fist.

"Oh, Beauty."

BEAST

We are uncertain how many years it has been, or how many centuries. To half of us the passage of time is tiny and measured, and with no measuring devices it is impossible to track. To the other it is infinite, immeasurable, a stream in which all things drown in the end. We are at odds because of this and so many things, and when the sun fades and the dark returns we mark it only as a change in the light.

The storm that comes tonight is not the change we felt coming. But in the howl of the night wind and the blinding violet of the snow, there is nothing else to be sensed. And so we retreat, to pace inside our den, to remember sleep, to wait for another change in the light.

TWO

YEVA'S FATHER ASKED FOR the night to think of a plan, so Yeva did not share with her sisters what she had overheard, nor participate in their whispered speculation after they had blown out the candle in the room they shared. She lay awake after her sisters had drifted off to sleep, watching the ceiling and listening to the wind beyond the window.

At dawn she rose sandy-eyed and stiff and crept down to the kitchen, carrying her shoes so as not to wake her sisters. The kitchen was cold and empty—Pechta had declined to make an appearance yet, unsurprising after the previous evening's excitement. Yeva stirred the fire back up, checked on the bread rising in its nook in the hearth, and put the kettle on over the flames. Then she slipped her icy feet into her shoes, shivering and standing with her back to the kitchen fire.

After a time the household drifted to life again, the servants waking and accepting mugs of tea, her sisters joining them once the sunlight reached the edge of the window. The wind had tossed around the snow but the storm had not brought much more of it, leaving the world newly coated in a thin layer of white, with dark patches of frozen slush all up and down the sides of the buildings and the windowpanes. The ice shattered the light as it entered the house, sending it in knives and sunbursts across the rugs and floorboards.

No one spoke of the previous night, neither the sisters nor the servants. And yet there was an air of uneasy expectance, as if everyone were waiting, but too fearful to ask what they were waiting for.

Eventually Yeva's father appeared in the entryway to the kitchen. His eyes were red-rimmed and tired, his face drooping and mouth tight. He looked as if he'd gotten no more sleep than Yeva had.

"Girls," he said, the sharp-cut sunlight outlining his form in the doorway. "Staff. Would you all please come join me in the parlor?"

Yeva poured a mug of tea, then followed the rest of the assemblage out into the living room. Her father had relit the fire there, but only moments before. The room was still freezing, and she pressed the mug of tea into her father's hand before huddling close to her sisters by the fireplace.

He stood next to his chair and gazed at the floor near Yeva's feet for a time. He lifted his head. "A month ago," he began, "I sent out a caravan headed for Constantinople. If the venture were successful, it would mean a new trade route, which would bring you girls—and the town, and all the surrounding cities—countless luxuries. And perhaps the return of the priests and of books, education, maps, life from beyond our borders. The Mongols prevent us from making outside contacts, but I thought—" He shook his head, as if at the folly of such a dream.

"It was a foolish risk. A gamble I should not have taken."

Yeva wanted to look at her sisters to see if they had figured it out yet, if they were beginning to understand the meaning of the visitor in the night. But she could not take her eyes off her father's weary face.

"Our entire fortune was tied up in the caravan, along with investments from merchants and noblemen, vouchsafed by me. It is all gone."

The breath went out of the room. Yeva felt Lena go stiff, and from across the room she heard one of the maidservants stifle a gasp.

"I have thought all night on what to do, and spent some time adding up what I owe to the investors. Our only option is to sell the house and most of our possessions. For you, the staff, I will find positions with the neighboring households. You will all have outstanding references. I still own my hunting cabin in the north wood. The girls and I will move there, and I will take up hunting again, and attempt to earn enough to pay back our debts."

Silence followed this announcement, as though everyone in the room were waiting for him to continue. He stepped to the side and sank down into his chair, doubled over with his elbows resting on his knees, mug dangling between them from his fingertips.

Pechta began to wail, turning to one of the maidservants and burying her face in her shoulder. It seemed this was the cue for the entire household to break down—the two maidservants started to sob, as Albe stood gawking in shocked silence and Yeva's sisters put their arms around each other. Yeva stood alone, watching her father. Amid the chaos, he lifted his head to meet her eye.

Yeva had always longed for nothing more than to live at her father's hunting cabin, where she had spent so many happy days with him as a child on their expeditions. This—this meant she was free of trips to see the baronessa, free of figuring out how to deal with Solmir, how to tell her sisters where his interest truly lay. But at what cost? Would Radak still want to wed Lena if she had no wealth and connections to offer? And the hunting cabin was leagues from the nearest town. There were no eligible young men in the wilderness to speak for her and her sister, only the trees and the wind and the beasts.

She had seen the spirit die in her father's eyes. He sat doubled over, looking up at her like a man of eighty. How long could he continue to hunt? He had not had to provide for himself, much less a family, solely by hunting in nearly twenty years.

A chunk of ice detached itself from the roof and slid off, scraping loudly across the sniffles and sobs punctuating the quiet. Winter was coming fast.

Yeva's sisters watched their possessions and their futures being auctioned off to the highest bidders with no tears and with no outward signs of sorrow. Though in private Lena's face was often drawn with worry—for her fiancé, Radak, was away on business and would not hear of what had befallen them until after they had gone—to the outside world, she and Asenka were as sunny as ever. They cheerfully explained to prospective buyers why this mirror was their favorite, that dress the most stylish, this mother-of-pearl box the most beautiful. If Yeva had inherited her father's skill at hunting, they had inherited his ability to negotiate a deal. They earned more from their possessions than their father had calculated, but it still was not near enough to pay back the investors he owed.

In his youth, Yeva's father had been widely considered the best hunter in the land. Though there were many hunters who took advantage of the rich wilderness in the black wood, he was the only one who ventured into its heart. Yeva's father had told her stories when she was little of the things he claimed to have seen: the life-sucking *kudlak*, the great bears to the north who could change their fur to match the ice, the *stuhac*, who would steal the ligaments from a man's legs to make bindings for his own feet in the snow. Soaring above them all was the story of the Firebird—Yeva's favorite for as long as she could remember. Despite the darkness and danger of the black wood, the Firebird at its heart was a burning beacon. No hunter could catch it— the only one who had ever come close was nothing more than a legend of a hundred years or more. And he had only caught a single feather from its tail.

Yeva used to dream of being the one to catch the Firebird— she dreamed of it long after she stopped believing in the other tales her father spun for her. But even without the kudlak, without the monsters of the fairy tales she loved as a child, the depths of the wood were dangerous, far more deadly than the more commonly hunted perimeters of the wilderness.

Her father had once fearlessly ventured into the deepest reaches of the wood, but how could he return to such a life now? He had given up the danger of the hunt for love of Yeva's mother, who could not bear to see him disappear into the black wood day after day.

And what of his heart? He'd huddled in front of the fire that night like a broken man. He was proud, as proud of his mercantile empire as he'd been of his hunting abilities as a younger man. He could not hope to earn enough simply from pelts and meat of deer and rabbit; he would have to venture deep to bring back the heads and skins of trophy game. How could he hope to be so bold and so strong now, with this humiliation and ruin weighing on him like twenty extra years?

So Yeva's sisters tried to earn as much as they could from their treasures, parting with them readily. Yeva lacked their skill with people and was more than happy to leave the sale of her own possessions to them. She kept aside only a few of her plainest dresses to bring with her to the cabin.

There was talk of selling the dogs as well, for they were purebred and Yeva's father could still hunt without them. Yeva's heart nearly broke at the idea, but she recalled her sisters cheerfully handing over their cherished books and trinkets, and she agreed to meet a man who had asked about purchasing them. Pelei was cautiously interested in the prospective buyer, sniffing at his hand with great determination, but Doe-Eyes— the gentlest dog Yeva had ever encountered—flung her ears right back and growled when he approached, the fur standing up along her back in a ridge.

Yeva's father had shrugged after the buyer had left, and said only, "I suppose we will have to build them a kennel to sleep in at the cabin."

With the dogs safe, Yeva turned her mind to packing the family's few remaining belongings. At her father's instruction she had placed three of their four servants with new families—only Albe remained. He came to them one morning and dropped to the floor, knees striking wood with a loud thud.

"Please let me come, master, mistresses," he begged, taking hold of Tvertko's hand. "You know I'm no good, I'll only be thrown out of another house. I break things and I forget. But for you I'll be better. I can do a bit of cooking and cleaning and whatever you need, I'll make it worth keeping me, I will."

"But we can't pay you," Yeva said gently, as her father patted Albe's hand and tried to get him to stand back up.

"Don't care, miss," he protested. "Where else would I go? Been here since me mother died, been with you since I was seven. Where else would I go?"

From then on Albe oversaw the packing, and would relieve Yeva of anything she tried to carry out to the wagon. He generally made a nuisance of himself, always underfoot and performing his tasks with such enthusiasm that he nearly knocked the sisters over. But his antics caused them to smile more often than shout at him, and so when the family finally departed the house, their spirits were not quite as low as they might have been otherwise.

With the men walking and the dogs trotting alongside, and the wagon pulled by the plow horse they'd borrowed from a neighbor in exchange for a rug, they set off on the road north.

It was a three-day journey from their house in town to their father's hunting cabin. They stayed in inns along the way, an expense Yeva protested each night. But her father refused to allow his girls to spend the night in a barn, or worse, wrapped in their cloaks on the ground beside the road—they had not sunk that low, he said, in a too-calm voice that Yeva knew better than to question. On the third day the weather took a turn for the worse, the skies lowering and gathering gray until the air turned white with snow in the late afternoon.

As the day faded toward twilight Doe-Eyes began to stumble, her long legs shaking in the snow. Yeva hopped down in order to help lift the dog up into the back of the wagon, and joined her there. Doe-Eyes was built for speed, bred in a land far to the west, with a slim body and shorter fur; a summer dog, not bred for the winter hardships she'd face at the edge of the black wood.

Yeva rubbed and rubbed at the dog's body and legs until the

tremble left them. Doe-Eyes licked her wrist and curled herself into a nest Yeva made of her remaining few dresses. They'd be covered in hair and smell like dog, but what did Yeva care? Out here there would be no baronessa to notice. Yeva left the dog slumbering in her nest and rejoined her sisters atop the broad wagon.

Beside her she felt Lena tremble, and she glanced aside. Her sister's face was turned resolutely out toward the passing trees, but Yeva saw her hands, folded so tightly in her lap that the knuckles shone white. They had sent word of their misfortunes to Lena's fiancé, but they'd had no time to wait for a reply, especially since there was no guarantee the message would even find him. Radak would mostly likely return from his business trip to find Lena gone, and all reason for marrying her too. There was no good now to be had from an alliance with the family—to marry one of them would be to marry their debts, which could well cripple a young entrepreneur.

Yeva folded her hands over her sister's. They were nearly as cold as hers were, but they relaxed under her touch and after a time, both Yeva's hands and Lena's warmed to the company.

The weather worsened as they turned from the high road onto a smaller path into the woods, and they had to break their own trail through the snow, for no one had come this way since the storm had begun. Albe called out, suggesting they turn back and make for the inn several leagues behind. Yeva's father said something in reply that she could not hear, but Albe quieted, tugging his coat more closely about his shoulders. She jumped down from the wagon, landing calf-deep in snow, and shouted over the wind, "Take my seat awhile, Albe."

He protested, face flushing beet red, but she shook her head. "Please—I'd like to speak to my father in private."

Reluctantly Albe let her give him a leg up onto the wagon as it groaned along through the snow. Yeva stepped over to her father and linked her arm through his, for warmth as much as companionship.

"That was kindly done," he said, patting her hand.

"Right now, Albe is our only friend in the world."

Her father's hand stilled against hers, head bowing against the biting cold. For a time there was only the jingle of the horse's harness and the groaning of the wagon, the dull thud of hoof on snow, the occasional distant thump as a branch gave way and dropped its heavy burden to the forest floor.

"I was a fool." Her father's voice was a whisper, but the quiet of the snow did little to hide it. "Such a fool."

Yeva had never had to comfort her father before. Her heart squeezed with the kind of fear she never felt outside of nightmares, the kind of fear that made her blood pound. "It isn't your fault," she said finally, searching for any words that might ease the tension in the arm linked through hers.

Her father exhaled a grunt of a laugh, the mist of it hanging in front of his lips like a ghost. "We had enough. More than enough. That caravan—I was a fool to put everything we had into such a fragile venture. But I wanted more for you, for my girls—I wanted—"

His voice cracked, and with it Yeva's heart. For decades their town, along with a vast stretch of the country, had been cut off from other parts of the world by marauders who intercepted travelers and convoys alike. The books her father owned all came from a time before the Mongols; the priests who had blessed Yeva at her naming ceremony were some of the last to make it through on their pilgrimages.

"You wanted the world for us," Yeva whispered, hugging

her father's arm close against her body. "There's no shame in that." Still, her heart stirred uneasily. Had she not been berating herself the same way for wanting more than the life a husband like Solmir could offer her?

"I had the world," her father replied, his pace faltering for a few steps until Yeva stopped too. Her father's red-rimmed eyes met hers, the snow melting on his cheeks and trickling into his beard. "I was just too blind to see it."

Yeva swallowed hard. "You have us," she said softly. "We have you. That's all we need. Come, Father—you'll get stiff if you stop moving."

As they continued, Yeva found movement warmed her, and that walking was much more preferable to riding on the wagon— but she had not been walking for three days through ankle-deep snow. After just half an hour she found that little-used muscles had begun to ache and protest the exercise.

As dusk fell the cabin came into view, the same white and black with snow and wood as the forest. The huddled occupants on the wagon leaped down, Albe unhitching the horse as soon as the wagon pulled into the lee of the house. Exhaustion made them all slow and stupid, even those who had ridden on the wagon, for the cold and the swaying, jouncing movement were nearly as wearying as walking. Asenka could barely move, her bad leg was so stiff, and Lena helped her through the snow with some difficulty. Yeva collected Doe-Eyes from her sleepy warm nest and whistled for Pelei, who had roamed too far, dancing around the trees, sniffing and shivering with excitement at their new surroundings. Albe put the horse in a dilapidated shed to be tended later, and everyone made their way to the house. It had lain unoccupied for the better part of a decade, and with a long breath their father shoved the door open for the first time since

Yeva had been a child.

It was covered in dust and dirt, half the window shutters broken, drifts of fallen leaves and snow filling the corners. Something rustled in the back, its nest disturbed by the human arrivals. The only light came from behind the broken shutters and from a hole in the roof, plugged mostly with snow, allowing only for the cold blue glow of twilight through the ice. Flakes drifted down from the hole, glinting in the shaft of light.

This was not the cozy home Yeva had remembered from her childhood. She found herself wishing her father had listened to Albe back on the road—if he had, they would be warm and fed in an inn by now. But then, her father's too-thin purse would be several coins leaner.

They all stood inside the doorway, dripping snow and ice onto the floor, surveying the dank interior of the cabin in silence. Asenka spoke first, taking a limping step forward. "Albe," she said softly, "if you will be so good as to use the shovel there at the hearth and remove the snow from inside, I will lay a fire."

Lena, as if shaking herself from a dream, stumbled forward to take her older sister's arm and help her to the hearth. The two set to clearing leaves from the fireplace as Albe took the ash shovel and began hauling the snow out the windows. Yeva knelt and whispered to Pelei, one hand on his quivering shoulder, "Go on, I know you smell them. Remind them that this is our house." When she straightened and pulled her hand away, Pelei was off to the far corner of the cabin like a bolt from a crossbow, sending frantic rustles throughout the leaves there as the house's previous occupants fled before him. Yeva located the broad, sturdy table amid the debris and, with Albe's assistance, set it on its legs and then smoothed her hands over its top to wipe off the worst of the dust.

Yeva's father remained in the doorway, unmoving, watching his family get to work. When Yeva turned toward him he inhaled sharply through his nose, passing his hand over his face. "My girls," he said hoarsely, pressing his lips together. After a silence he shook himself and cocked his head toward Yeva with a smile. "I will go excavate the tea." And he left to begin bringing things in from the wagon.

Over the next few days the cabin slowly became habitable. Albe was put to work felling a few nearby trees and hewing rough timber to repair the worst holes and shore up the loft space to make it safe. There was one bedroom at the back of the house and two pallets in the loft. Tvertko and Albe took the beds in the loft, for Asenka could not manage the ladder—she and Lena took the bed at the back of the house, the one that had been their father's when he still used this as a hunting cabin.

Yeva herself made a pallet by the hearth. In the evenings it was warm from the day's fire, and as night grew thicker, the dogs curled up on either side, and she was as cozy as any in the house. Her father protested the arrangement, and her sisters too, but when Lena offered to take it in turns with her sleeping on the floor, Yeva turned her down.

"They are my dogs," she pointed out with a smile, "and you'll only complain in the mornings of their smell." Yeva was usually the first in the family to wake anyway, and so it became her habit to stir the fire at dawn so that the water was just beginning to boil for tea when Albe came down the ladder rubbing his eyes.

Yeva's father began making forays into the surrounding forest, learning the woods again. He'd taught Yeva that the key to being a good hunter was not to track a creature through the forest but to know the forest so well it was like tracking your prey through your own home. He rarely came back with much those early days, but he made imminent plans for trips deeper into the woods.

Yeva begged him to let her come along.

"You're not a child anymore," said her father with a sigh. "When I've paid my debts we'll move back to town. By that time, I fear, you'll have gone so wild that the confines of civilization will break your heart."

"Please," was all Yeva could think of to say. She had no argument against it—even years after the last time they had been hunting together, she still longed for the dark, cold cathedral of the wood.

He shook his head. "I won't be persuaded on this, Yeva." She still flinched to hear the use of her proper name from her father. "Besides, if you come with me, Doe-Eyes will try to follow, and you know she can't weather this cold."

And so he left her behind, traveling deeper and deeper into the forest each time with Pelei at his side. Sometimes he was gone two or three days, leaving Yeva and her sisters, and Albe, alone in the house. Yeva kept to her bed by the fireplace. Doe-Eyes would have whined and cried all night, unable to climb the ladder to the loft, had Yeva taken over her father's room in his absence.

It was during one of her father's excursions that they received their first visitor to the cabin, on an afternoon full of pale, cold sunlight. Yeva and Lena were blocking up the gaps in the timbers of the floor and the walls with clay, while Asenka sat by the hearth, mending one of their father's shirts. Doe-Eyes was executing a circuit around the house, as she did every hour or so, alert for Pelei's return. But instead of the perk of her ears and frantic lash of her tail that heralded his arrival, she went rigid, nose pointed toward the door and tail unmoving.

Yeva paused, her eyes on the dog. "Albe, is someone outside?"

The servant's head peeked out from the edge of the loft, where he was tidying. "I don't hear anyone, miss."

Yeva put a hand on Doe-Eyes's shoulder and found the muscles there solid as rock. "Could you please check?"

Albe slid down the ladder to land with a solid thunk on the floor. He opened the door a crack, peering out across the gleaming snow. "There is someone coming, miss," he said, surprised.

Lena dropped her bowl of mud, sloshing some of it on the floor. "Radak," she whispered, glancing first at Yeva and then over at Asenka, who had stopped mending and was staring back at her sister. "It has to be. Oh, what if he's come to break our engagement?"

"He hasn't," said Yeva firmly. "He wouldn't. And if that was his intention, he would hardly travel three days for it, he would just never come at all."

"It isn't your young man, miss," said Albe. Yeva regretted having spoken—now each day that Radak didn't come, Lena would be more convinced he never would.

Albe stepped into the gap of the door, straightening his shoulders. "Welcome, sir. May I help you?" He spoke to someone Yeva couldn't see, his form silhouetted by the blinding light off the snow behind him.

"Is this Tvertko's new house?" asked the visitor. "I've come to see him—and his daughter."

Albe stepped back, allowing the man inside. As soon as the door closed behind him and shut out the daylight, his features became clear. It was a young man, perhaps five or six years Yeva's senior, with dark hair and an easy smile. He had friendly hazel eyes that cast over the room, going first to Asenka at the fireplace and then to Lena by the wall, and then to Yeva. And there his eyes stayed. There was a gasp from the hearth, and Yeva turned to see that Asenka had gone white, staring at the man in the doorway.

It was Solmir.

BEAST

Something comes.

A man and a beast, moving slowly, scanning the ground. We watch from only a few feet away—we know how to disguise our scent from the canine. The man is surefooted and strong, if old for his kind, and we watch with interest. Something about him is familiar; we have encountered him before.

Yes, we know him. He would not have been the first hunter we turned to our purposes but he was the most promising. We were so certain he would be our salvation, until one day he vanished and never returned to the wood. It was years ago—or weeks? Perhaps generations. His hair has changed and his face has grown lines, but he walks with the same knowledge of the lifeblood of the wood.

We growl, the sound blending with the wind and the groaning of the trees under their weight of snow. We are patient. We still remember our plan.

As the man makes his way through the forest, the dog blowing steam at his side, we move on silent paws to follow.

THREE

YEVA STOOD ROOTED TO the spot, staring at Asenka as she stared at Solmir. Yeva was closest to the door, and knew she ought to greet him properly, but she felt that if she looked at him everything would unravel.

Finally Lena stepped forward, smoothing down her skirts as if they were made from fine silk, and not mud-spattered wool. "Welcome, sir!" she said, brushing past Yeva and holding her arms out for Solmir's heavy cloak. "Please forgive us, you're the first visitor we've had since we moved."

Solmir let her remove his cloak with a murmur of thanks, glancing at her briefly before shifting his gaze back to Yeva. "I apologize for not sending word, but by the time a messenger arrived and returned, it would be a week gone at least. I have a room at the inn some leagues back—I can return another time if I'm inconveniencing you."

"Of course not," said Lena. "You must be cold. Please, sit

here by the fire." She pulled one of the chairs from the table over
to the hearth, placing it nearer to Asenka's than was necessary.
Asenka, whose white face had gone red as she twisted her hands
together in her lap, flashed Yeva a look of alarm.

Solmir shifted his weight from one foot to the other.
"Actually, I don't have much time. Your father is not at home?"

Lena shook her head. "He is hunting," she explained, one
hand still on the back of the chair, as if hoping to usher him
there by willpower alone.

His face fell a little. "Well, I will have to come back another
time to speak with him—but that wasn't my sole purpose."
Solmir had dropped his gaze to the floor, as if he might find his
next words written there.

"Yes?" said Lena expectantly, the hand on the back of the
chair creeping over to rest on Asenka's shoulder.

"I—had hoped to be able to speak with Yeva." His eyes
flicked up, meeting Yeva's before she looked away, startled.
"Alone."

Heart straining against her rib cage, Yeva could not help but
look at her sisters. Lena's face was blank, confused . . . but Asenka
understood. Her lips parted, but no sound emerged; the flush of
nervous excitement warming her face fled; her hands went still
in her lap. She caught Yeva's eye, and after a long, heavy second,
the corners of her mouth turned up in a smile.

Unable to stand it any longer, Yeva darted forward, fumbling
for the latch of the door. "As you can see," she said harshly, "we
have only the one room aside from the bedrooms. I will speak
with you outside, if you please."

She stumbled out into the snow without waiting to see if
Solmir would follow. *Why*, she thought furiously, *could it not have
been Radak?* In her haste she'd left her cloak behind. For now, hot

humiliation and distress coursed through her, immunizing her against the cold.

Solmir's horse stood obediently by the snow-covered trail, snorting steam into the air. Well trained, that it required no hobbling or tying. A voice cut through her thoughts. "Yeva?" Solmir was closing the door behind him, having grabbed his cloak back from the hook on which Lena had placed it.

"What are you doing here?" Yeva turned abruptly enough to send up a spray of snow.

Solmir's mouth opened in surprise, his brows furrowed. "I— why are you so angry?"

Yeva had not known her emotions were so obvious. She closed her eyes, sucking in a frigid breath of air that burned the insides of her nose. "I am sorry, you came at an awkward time. Please, sir—why have you come?"

"Solmir," he corrected her. "I hate it when people call me *sir*. I came—" He paused, brows lowering further as he peered at her in the winter sunlight. "You really don't know?"

The fury ebbed, leaving her with only confusion and dread creeping through her as quickly and surely as the cold. "No." She shivered.

"Here." Solmir stepped forward and draped his cloak over her shoulders before she could protest. Taking a step back, restoring a respectful distance between them, he leveled his scrutiny at her again. His eyes were friendly, warm—it was unsurprising that they were what Yeva remembered most about him from the dinners they spent together.

"I apologize. I thought you had understood." Though he spoke softly, he spoke with confidence. "I know we haven't spent much time together but of everyone at those dinners, you were the only one I wished to speak to. The other ladies spoke of weather and fashion, and of the baronessa's silver. You explained the proper way to skin a leopard so as not to mar its fur."

Yeva felt the bottom falling out of her stomach. "I—never—"

"Not to me," he said, with a smile. "To one of the huntsmen in the baron's service. I overheard you. I tried in vain to talk about hunting with you but I think the baronessa had you too well trained. Never before have I so envied a mere huntsman."

Now that he spoke, Yeva remembered more clearly the evenings they had both attended dinner. He had always sat at her elbow, always spoke of the huntsmen and asked if she knew any of them. She had thought he was engaging in some form of gossip, and had deflected the questions as best she could. Yeva closed her eyes again. How had she been so blind?

"Please," said Solmir. Yeva heard a soft footfall, knew he had taken a step toward her. "When I got the news of your father's caravan, your family was already gone and I had missed my chance. And now I've come all this way, instead. I will have to come back and speak with your father but everyone knows how he loves you. If you want something, he won't refuse you. Please, Yeva. Consider my offer. I would like to take you back with me—as my wife." He had run out of breath, forced to gulp down another before his last words.

Yeva felt as though the weight of his cloak on her shoulders might drive her to her knees. She forced herself to meet his eyes and immediately wished she hadn't. He was too earnest, gazing at her with such feeling. How had she never noticed?

"I can't marry you," she mumbled, shivering again despite the warmth of his cloak. "I'm sorry."

"Why not?" He looked merely puzzled, not comprehending what she was saying.

"I can't marry anyone." As the words came out, Yeva realized how much truth they held. Of all the men in the world who might ask for her hand, she could not hope to find someone more suited for her than this one—and yet the thought of marriage made her want to startle like a wood thrush and fly away into the forest. "I'm not—I'm not a wife. You should marry my sister, Asenka, she's kind and good and—"

Solmir shook his head, moving forward and reaching for her hands. Yeva, too dumbfounded to protest, stared as he enclosed them in his. "It's not your sister I want, Yeva."

She looked up, caught by the longing in his voice. The depth of it left her speechless.

He met her eyes and the corners of his mouth drew up in the tiniest of smiles. "Yeva," he repeated softly.

"I can't." She pulled away, dragging the cloak from her shoulders and presenting it to him at arm's length. "I'd offer you refreshment but we've only just moved and we aren't ready to receive company. Please, go." If she weren't so thrown, she'd be shocked at her own behavior. She was being unforgivably rude.

But Solmir only gathered up his cloak, hugging it to his chest. He kept hold of her outstretched arm with one hand, his fingers encircling her wrist. He was watching her as though wishing it was she, and not the cloak, pressed against him, but he made no attempt to draw her nearer. "I must come back to speak with your father. A fortnight, perhaps. That will give him time to return. Please, only think about it until I come again. We can hunt together, travel together, until the baron names me his heir. Then you will be my baronessa, and no one will dare tell us what we should do."

Yeva could say nothing, breath stuck in her throat, heart thrashing against her rib cage.

Solmir bowed over her captive arm, and Yeva expected him to kiss her hand the way a gentleman would kiss a lady's. But then fingers as dexterous as a weaver's turned her wrist over, and he bent her hand back gently so that her fingers opened like a flower. Then he placed a kiss in her palm. Yeva shivered again—and this time not from the cold.

"Please give my regards to your sisters," he said, releasing her hand. "And tell them I'm sorry I can't stay longer to speak with them." Then, pulling his cloak over his shoulders, he made his way back to his horse and mounted with practiced ease. He sat like someone born to the saddle, which was plain and unadorned—worn with use and care. Solmir saw her looking and smiled.

Yeva dropped her gaze to the snow, but felt his eyes on her for long moments before he turned his horse and disappeared back into the forest.

She longed to remain where she was, neither returning to the house nor going after Solmir, but cold inevitably drove her indoors. She opened the door as quietly as she could, slipping inside, but stealth was useless. They were all waiting for her.

Her eyes went immediately to the figure standing in the house's center, one hand steadying herself on the table. Asenka smiled, and Yeva could see no hint of anything but pleasure in her sister's face.

"I'm so happy for you, Beauty," said Asenka, raising her arms. Yeva went to her, ducking her head against her shoulder, and felt her sister's arms wrap tightly around her. "He's a good man."

Late that night, as Doe-Eyes dreamed of fat rabbits and twitched at her side, Yeva heard a sound from the back bedroom. Whispers, barely audible over the wind and leaves—and then a sob, low and quickly muffled. Just once, a single cry in the quiet.

Yeva spent the rest of the night awake, arms wrapped around Doe-Eyes, the palm of her hand burning in the darkness.

Yeva rose before dawn, dressing in the dark and wrapping herself up well against the chill. She took a slice of day-old bread and slipped it into her pocket, then made for the door. Doe-Eyes scrambled up from her nest by the fire and trotted after her, toenails clicking on the wood, but Yeva held out a hand and the dog dropped to her haunches. "Mind the house, Doe-Eyes," she whispered. Doe-Eyes cocked her head, trembling with the desire to accompany her mistress, but when Yeva slipped out, the dog remained obediently still.

The sky was beginning to lighten in the east as she crossed the snow-covered yard toward the run-down shed that butted up against the edge of the property. Albe had taken the borrowed horse back to town, but the wagon was theirs, and some of what they had brought had yet to be unpacked. Yeva hoisted herself up into the back of the wagon and threw aside the heavy canvas that covered its contents, tossing up wayward snow as she did so.

There—a long wooden chest, one of the few things of value that her father had not parted with. It was carven with intricate depictions of ash and oak, rowan and hickory. Amid the tangle of leaves and branches there were eyes peeking out, a flash of a tail there, a glimpse of a paw. Yeva ran a hand along the box and then opened it.

Her father had taken his heavy bow with him and his ax, but the lighter bow was there, unstrung, and a quiver of fine goose-feathered arrows. These were hers, had been since she was young. Her father's bow had always been much too heavy for Yeva to draw, and anyway, she'd never needed the power the strong bow offered. He was a large-game hunter, while Yeva was quick and resourceful, with good aim and well-hidden traps.

Yeva pulled out the bow, testing the wood with her thumb. She had neglected it these past years. When was the last time she had oiled the wood? And yet it was smooth to the touch, and when she bent it across her shin it curved gracefully. Someone had been caring for the bow. And who other than her father would know what it needed?

She strung the bow with some difficulty, bracing the wood against her leg and discovering that the muscles she'd had when she was twelve had atrophied over the years. Her arms shook as she slipped the string into its groove at the bow's tip. After retrieving her knife and her spool of wire from the bottom of the chest and tucking them into the band of her skirt, she hopped down from the wagon. She slung the bow and the quiver of arrows over her shoulder and slipped back out of the shed, shutting the door behind her.

Yeva glanced to the east, where the rosy violet sky over the trees had grown several shades lighter. Albe would be rising soon, and he would find the hearth cold and the kettle empty. But if Albe woke to find her there, she would be drawn into the daily life of the cabin, and she could not bear to face her sisters, not yet.

And her father had not forbidden her to hunt—only to accompany him.

She set off through the silent, snowy forest, blood coursing past her ears. Though she'd slept little, energy flowed through her and drove her onward. She stopped now and then to set a wire snare in the snow. Her fingers fumbled with the task at first, but they soon remembered the trick of it, growing more sure as she went. Her skirt hampered her more than she'd expected; she would have to make herself a pair of trousers out of one of her dresses, if she was to do this regularly. And now that she'd tasted again the fresh air, felt the snow-covered world enclose her, smelled the crisp brightness of the ice underlain with spicy fir, she knew she would do it every day she could.

She saw little sign of anything nearby in the forest, coming across only old tracks: deer and fox, and occasionally the strange hopping troughs in the snow that told of rabbits. The day passed quickly, the morning turning to noon almost without her noticing. Just after noon she stopped to rest, wishing she'd been thinking clearly enough to bring food for lunch.

She would have to turn back soon, retracing her route to see if any of her snares had borne fruit. And at the end of her trail: the house, with Albe and Lena—and Asenka.

Yeva breathed deep, despite the way the cold air stung her nose and lungs. She thought of Asenka, the tiny sting of a smile on her face when Yeva had reentered the cabin after Solmir left. Her voice, without recrimination, as she congratulated her little sister on a match well made. That same voice, lost in a single sob in the darkness.

Yeva would have to turn back—but not yet. She stalked off, deeper into the forest, heels kicking up snow as she moved. This was not a hunter's gait, but she was too angry, too unsettled, to care.

How could Solmir have come, with no warning and no announcement, to ask Yeva such a thing? And when she had scarcely ever spoken three words together to him. And yet, he'd been watching her. Listening to her chat so easily with the lowly huntsmen. *Envying* them—because they were the ones to whom she chose to speak.

And wasn't Yeva always criticizing the townsfolk for their skittish indecisiveness? Hadn't she wished for them to be more certain about their decisions, to act quickly and with strength and confidence?

She stopped, placing a hand against the tree trunk at her side. *Speaking of wishes,* whispered her thoughts, *who wished for a man who would love her for her skill?*

Marriage. To Solmir.

It would mean that she, her father, her sisters—all would be taken care of, no matter what might come. She would be baronessa, and her family secure on the baron's estates. They would be safe. Happy. Solmir would take her hunting, would love her for her abilities. It was what she wanted. More than anything she'd dared to hope for.

So why did it feel as though a hollowness was crouched inside her? Why did she feel as though the bindings of a cage were closing in around her?

She tore the bow from her shoulder, nocking an arrow to its string with ease. She'd had no opportunity to test the bow that morning, but found that her body still remembered the motion. Her shoulders would ache later, but she could still draw it. She sighted along the arrow's shaft, wrist straight and strong, elbow level.

A cascade of sound exploded from the right, and she nearly sent the arrow whistling off into the forest in shock. She managed to lower the bow instead, instinct preventing her from loosing an arrow she could not afford to lose. She whirled to face the sound, only to see something burst out of the brush toward her.

"Doe-Eyes!" exclaimed Yeva, knees weakening. The dog collided with her leg and ricocheted off, shaking snow from her short fur and beaming at her with a wide, gap-jawed smile, tongue lolling out to one side.

Adrenaline drenched Yeva's thoughts, narrowing them into

one furious torrent. It could have been a boar, a wolf, a bear; she had been paying so little attention. "Go home!" she ordered the dog, her voice cracking.

Doe-Eyes stared at her, tongue going still. She cocked her head in confusion.

"Bad dog!" Yeva shouted, waving the arrow at the creature. "Go back home, *now!*"

The dog backed up a step and then lay down tentatively in the snow, dropping first her front paws and chin and then her hindquarters. Eyes rolled upward, she gazed desperately at Yeva, tail thumping once in pathetic appeal.

Yeva passed a hand over her face, the rush of fear fading and with it, her anger. She dropped to her knees; recognizing forgiveness, Doe-Eyes leaped up to throw herself at her mistress. Yeva ran a hand down the dog's spine as a cold nose thrust itself against her neck.

"You shouldn't be out here," Yeva whispered, pressing her hand flat against the dog's body. Doe-Eyes was trembling, but whether from cold or from eagerness and delight, Yeva could not tell. "What possessed you to burst out of the wood like that?"

As if the dog could understand her, Doe-Eyes wriggled from her grasp and went dashing back into the bushes. Yeva could hear her thrashing, and was about to step closer when something small and brown came shooting out of the undergrowth, cutting back across the path Yeva had trampled.

Before she had time to think about it, Yeva had an arrow nocked to her bow and drawn back. When Doe-Eyes flushed out a second rabbit, she let the arrow fly.

The rabbit's scream sent a thrill of satisfaction down Yeva's spine. Elation coursed through her as she lowered the bow and slung it over her shoulder. The thrill faded as she approached and saw that the rabbit was still thrashing—not a clean kill. Her aim was not what it used to be, and she'd drawn a sharp, piercing arrow—a deer-hunting arrow. She'd have to relearn her own fletching codes to tell by feel which were the blunter-tipped arrows for small game.

She quickly reached out and wrung the creature's neck, putting an end to its suffering, then lifted her head. No sign of Doe-Eyes, although she could hear a faint rustle in the distance.

Retrieving her arrow, she wiped it off, staining the snow bright crimson in the dappled afternoon sunlight. She ran a loop of her wire around the rabbit's hind legs and hung it from her belt. *Stew,* she thought happily, *or roasted on potato mash.* It would be the first fresh meat they'd had since moving to the cabin. She began to retrace her trail, humming a marching song her father had given her to sing while she ran to keep time with his steps.

Doe-Eyes caught up to her a few moments later, shivering her delight and licking her chops. The first rabbit had clearly fared no better than its fellow, and Yeva would not have to feed Doe-Eyes scraps of bread and dried meat tonight.

She made her way back home, all thoughts of Solmir banished the second her arrow found its mark.

"Beauty, you didn't." Lena held the skinned, cleaned rabbit at arm's length, although there was an undeniable eagerness in her voice at the prospect of fresh meat. "Father said you were not to go hunting."

Yeva had stowed her bow once more in her father's chest outside, and removed any trace of the day's work. Her snares had turned up empty, but she would check them again at first light tomorrow. "I laid a few traps," she said. It was not a lie—the traps were laid, after all.

Lena sighed. "And the checking of the traps is what kept you out most of the day?"

Asenka had not risen from her chair by the fire, but had smiled at Yeva when she came. It was like nothing had changed between them, despite the chasm Yeva felt stretched there. She saw that Asenka no longer sat with her skirt covering her feet, but had her twisted leg stretched out to the warmth of the fire.

No need any longer to hide her flaws.

Yeva closed her eyes. "I will go check my snares again," she blurted, turning to make for the door.

"Yeva," said Asenka. Her voice was soft, but it was enough to stop Yeva dead in her tracks. "Will you wind my wool for me?"

Yeva wanted nothing less. Except, perhaps, to upset her sister. So she went, sinking down onto the floor at Asenka's side as Lena began to dismember the rabbit for stew. She picked up the loose skein of wool from the basket at Asenka's feet and wound loops of the yarn around her hands, holding it so that it would feed easily as Asenka knit.

Asenka began to hum a tune their mother had favored. Yeva remembered it more from her sister, for she had been too young when their mother died for clear memories of her to take root. Yeva sighed and turned her head to the side, laying it against her sister's knee. She felt the slight movements of Asenka's body as she wound the wool around a needle, dipped it through the fabric, wound again.

After a time, under the sounds of Lena cooking dinner, Asenka whispered, "If you are happy, Beauty, then so am I." She bent and pressed her lips to the crown of Yeva's head.

Yeva said nothing, eyes burning and blurring as she stared resolutely at the uneven floor. If only she were as selfless.

Yeva took to spending her days in the forest, under the tall
straight pines in the snow and the silence. Her skill at the bow
returned quickly, muscles remembering what the rest of her did
not. Her fitness was slower to return, forcing her to stop for rest
far more often than she would have liked. She came to know the
forest again, finding it as familiar and as comfortable as an old
friend.

Doe-Eyes accompanied her on days when the sun was high,
the temperatures otherwise too harsh for her slight build. Though
Asenka promised to lavish her with affection on the days Yeva
left her behind, the sight of the dog with her head slung low,
haunting the doorway, often made Yeva relent at the last minute
and allow the dog to come. She was grateful for the company,
and for Doe-Eyes's ability to flush prey out of brush and thicket
that Yeva might never have discovered on her own.

She never came back to the house empty-handed, and often
with more than they needed for the day's meal. Albe constructed
a rudimentary smokehouse by the shed, and they began to
supplement their stores of food rather than deplete them. The
prey Yeva took was too small and unremarkable for saleable pelts,
but she cleaned and scraped each hide anyway in the evenings, to
save for their own uses in the burgeoning winter. They could not
afford to waste anything.

She made a point of rising early enough to avoid her sisters,
but once she woke to find Asenka kneeling at her side, stirring
the fire. Yeva started to rise, but her sister set the poker down and
laid a hand on her arm.

"Yeva," she whispered, her eyes anxious. "Stay. You don't
need to go out every day. We have food. Stay with us today."

Yeva's eyes blurred, and she blinked hard. "I can't," she
whispered back.

Asenka's hand shifted to touch Yeva's cheek, then brushed some of her sleep-tangled hair out of her eyes. "What is it you're looking for out there?"

Yeva blinked again, about to reply that she wasn't looking for anything, just game for their survival—but her throat closed. How was it her sisters knew her so well, better even than she knew herself? She drew a shaking breath. "I don't know," she breathed. "Something more."

After a week had passed, their father returned. He arrived in the evening, knocking his feet against the doorframe to dislodge the snow on his boots, a thick, wild growth of stubble half masking his face. Pelei came barreling in so that he and Doe-Eyes could turn circles around each other, sniffing and sniffing and remembering.

Yeva's father threw himself into his chair by the fire while Lena made tea. "It knows I'm here," he said, stabbing a finger at the arm of the chair. "It is driving the other animals from me. Tracking me. I've seen not even a single rabbit all week."

Yeva exchanged glances with her sisters. Not one of them mentioned the gradually increasing store of dried meats in their larder. Yeva took her father's chilly hand in hers, as much to keep him from harming himself in his frustration as to comfort him. "Perhaps you are still learning the forest again," she said carefully, "and that's why you haven't come across any game."

"No," grunted her father, sinking back into his chair and watching the fire, pulling his hand free of Yeva's in order to rub at his bristly face. "No. There is something out there. Something cunning."

"Father, surely there can't be—"

"I have seen it before."

Yeva glanced up to find Asenka watching them, her expression bathed in concern. Yeva tried again to touch her father's hand, but he would not be calmed.

"What did you see before?" she asked softly.

But her father only shook his head, and shook his head again.

Eventually Albe and her sisters ambled off to bed and it was only Yeva and her father by the fire. And after a time, because she was tired from her day's hunt, Yeva too drifted off to sleep. She had no memory of her father leaving the chair for his own bed.

He could not be convinced to stay, planning to depart again with Pelei at his side when the morning dawned clear and cold. He took food from the stores, not noticing that they had grown since he was last home. The single-mindedness with which he planned his return to the forest chilled Yeva. Always, he had confided in her. She had seen hints of this passion in him when she was very young, when he would tell her stories of the things he had seen in the heart of the wood. Things he'd hunted—things he'd killed. Things that had escaped.

The creatures he used to tell her about—the monsters and the wonders hidden deep within the forest, where the other hunters refused to go—they were stories. Fantasies invented to teach children good manners, to fascinate them on cold winter days when they could not play outside. Her father had always spoken of them as if they were real, but that was to delight Yeva, to let her believe, when she was still too small to know better. The way he was acting now, muttering about the thing tracking him, pacing as he recounted the old stories to himself, still acting as though they were true—it no longer delighted her. She was frightened.

"Father!" she shouted finally, on the morning of his planned

departure. "Father, you must stay. Something is wrong. Please—
let Lena make you some tea."

"I don't need tea," he said, strapping his crossbow to his
back and stamping his feet into his boots. He rubbed at his arm,
which had been stiff and sore all morning.

"Then bring me with you," she said, moving forward to take
his hand. "If there is some creature out there with intelligence
then two sets of eyes, two minds, will be better than you alone."

"Too dangerous," Tvertko grunted, jerking his hand away.

"You don't know that," she argued.

He stopped, looking up from his pack to meet her gaze,
though he seemed to be staring through her at a distant memory.
"It is a Beast," he said. "A monster unlike anything in any story.
It was there twenty years ago. When your mother asked me to
give up hunting, it was the one thing I had not, could not catch.
And it is there still. When I kill it, its head will bring such a price
that we will be able to return home."

Yeva heard one of her sisters, she could not tell which, stifle
a gasp behind her. There was madness in her father's face, and
Yeva fought for control of her voice. "Let us just live here," she
begged. "Leave the Beast to the forest. We will hunt for food and
sell pelts when the snow leaves in spring, and we will be happy.
This is a fine home." She wanted to tell him of Solmir's offer,
but the words stuck in her throat.

Her father only shook his head and moved to leave, calling
Pelei to his side.

Yeva darted around him, putting her body between him and
the door. "Daddy," she whispered. "Please."

"Step aside," he ordered, the harshness of his face nothing
like the smiling one she knew best. Pelei's tail was tucked firmly
between his legs, his head low as he watched.

"No."

Her father barely gave her time to react, brushing her aside with an easy sweep of his arm. His physical strength had more than returned—but the wildness of his gaze frightened Yeva far more than the effortless way he knocked her to the ground. Pelei tried to lick her face, but her father gave a piercing whistle and the dog dragged himself away, slinking with his belly low to the ground in unhappiness.

Lena rushed forward to help her up, but by the time Yeva struggled to her feet again, their father was gone.

BEAST

We should not have let him see us.

He is mad with memory now, crashing through the forest loudly enough to frighten away the slowest and most dim-witted of creatures. He leans on his dog, who nudges him upright in the snow when he stumbles. We watch from some distance behind him as he forces his way through the forest. There is no beast in him left, no predator—there is only man. A madman.

He is useless now. When he was young he saw us and lived to dream about us. He could see the edges of the other world, the one that binds us. But now age has turned him, and we cannot use him for our purpose. We want to howl our rage and frustration, want to tear him limb from limb for making us hope, even the tiniest flicker, after all these long years. We want to destroy every part of him.

We follow him on silent paws.

FOUR

A COLD DREAD SETTLED in Yeva's belly after her father left. Her sisters looked to her when it came to their father, for she knew him better than anyone. Yeva could not afford to let them see how frightened she was, or else they too would live with the same heavy tension at every moment, the feeling of the ax overhead, of waiting for it to fall. And so when she was at home, she smiled and asked her sisters about the inconsequential events of the day, and saved her fears and worry for the hunt.

Yeva saw his face as she moved through the forest, the distant gaze that had looked right past her, the negligent sweep of his arm as he shoved her from the doorway. She feared for whether he would come home—and she feared for what he might be when he did.

Despite her dread, the hours she spent in the wood were like light in the darkness. There was no Asenka, with her broken heart, no Lena to scold Yeva about muddying the floors. The weight of pretending all was well, that everything was normal and as it should be—it fell away. She knew she should be with her sisters, should be grateful they were all well and together and safe. Running to the quiet of the forest was selfish. But that shard of guilt, that tiny flicker of shame, fell silent when she stepped outside each sharp-frosted morning.

She felt herself growing stronger each day, moving more quickly, more quietly. Her breath no longer puffed loudly in the air when she paused, and the soles of her feet no longer ached when she returned home in the evenings. Albe and her sisters ate rabbit, fox, brush-hen, and deer. They cured the hides, and Asenka put her skill with the needle, learned from the leech, to work on leather instead of wounded flesh. She fashioned Yeva trousers, and the freedom they offered made her faster still.

Yeva was forced to leave Doe-Eyes at home more and more often as winter took hold of the forest. She kept her own trails clear, walking them each day there was new snow to tamp them down, but elsewhere in the forest the snow deepened. If the slim dog, bred for far warmer climates, tried to wade shoulder-high all day long, she'd risk frostbite or worse.

Yeva was striding down one of her trails one afternoon on her way back to the cabin, a trio of rabbits hanging from her belt, when the hairs on the back of her neck lifted in warning. She kept moving, but her senses went on alert, one hand shifting toward her bow. Her father's words came back to her as if he were standing at her elbow.

There is something out there, he'd said. *Something cunning.*

Then, the words had sounded like madness. But here, in the silence of the forest, with her instincts speaking far more loudly than her good sense, his warnings were fresh in her mind. Here it seemed possible that every tale he'd told her as a child could be true.

Yeva disguised her movements by striding faster, letting the bow slip down off her shoulder and swatting at it as though it inconvenienced her. She always carried an arrow free of the quiver, in order to shoot quickly should a rabbit dart in front of her. Now, her fingers wrapped around it.

Behind her and to her right came a dull thud as a clump of snow slid from a pine bough. The image flashed in her mind of a shadow behind the tree she'd just passed, its thick branches weighted heavy with snow. Four steps behind her, maybe five.

Her right hand tightened around the bow's grip as she stepped over the snow-covered shape of a branch along her path. Two steps farther, and the branch cracked behind her.

She whirled, nocking the arrow and drawing it back in one movement, sighting down it at the figure in front of her before she registered what it was.

"Yeva!" it cried, throwing itself backward onto the ground.

Yeva was following it down with the point of her arrow by the time the voice registered. "Solmir!" Her hands tried to let go of bow and arrow both, in surprise and relief. She managed to throw the bow aside instead, sending the arrow to thump harmlessly into the ground.

"What are you doing?" she cried, heaving a breath into lungs that were fighting to work properly.

"Looking for you," gasped Solmir, still sprawled on his back in the snow, staring up at her. "What are *you* doing?" Wild-eyed, hair in disarray from his tumble, he looked more like a boy of twelve than a man of twenty-five.

Yeva lifted her hand to brush it, shaking, across her forehead. "I thought you were—something else."

He picked himself off the ground, brushing the snow from his cloak. "Something else? What, a bear tiptoes over your path to catch up with you?"

She shook her head, adrenaline leaving her angry, but not without relief. "Why are you here?"

Solmir's expression was blank for a few long seconds. "It has been a fortnight," he said. "I came as I promised. Your sisters said you were out gathering barks and winter herbs for remedies. The trails are not hard to follow." His eye fell on her bow, chin lifting to point at the rabbits dangling from her belt. "I see your medicine chest will be full indeed."

Yeva fought against the flush rising to her cheeks. "Why did you sneak up on me?"

"I had thought to surprise you," Solmir said. "Foolish. Don't worry, I don't intend to try it again. At least not unless I am certain you are unarmed."

She began to bristle, but he held up his hands, palms outward. A gesture of peace. "Please, I didn't come to argue. I know that Yeva comes armed. I would not have her any other way."

Have her. The blush won, and Yeva cast her glance away to focus on the snow trampled by his body when he fell. "My father is out again. You have missed him by more than a week."

"I know, your sisters told me." Solmir paused, the hesitation betraying that he was choosing his words carefully. "Did you speak to him? About what I asked two weeks ago?"

"It—did not come up." Yeva could not quite bring herself to look at him.

"Oh. I see." The silence stretched between them, only the distant sound of snow falling from another branch to lessen it.

"He was only here for a short time," Yeva burst out, the silence drawing the words before she could stop them. "I am sorry. It wasn't because—because I intended to refuse."

"But you do intend to refuse?"

Yeva lifted her eyes at the catch in his voice to find him looking at her, gaze full of that same mute appeal it had held when he first made his offer. "I know I should not." Her voice was a whisper.

Perhaps Solmir saw something in her face to give him hope, for he strode forward to bridge the gap between them. "I am not asking you to love me," he said, his voice ringing in the quiet winter air. "Only that you let me love you. As I do."

Yeva wished she could remove her cloak—the cloying warmth of it stifled her thoughts. "You don't even *know* me," she protested.

"I know enough," said Solmir. "You and I are the same."

"That is not reason for marriage!"

"It *is!*" he countered.

"I am not gentle and wifely, I am coarse and—and impossible! *This* is impossible."

"But you will *learn* those things, Yeva! There is time for you to learn gentleness after we've had our adventures, after I become baron. When there are children you will—"

"Children!" she exclaimed. Suddenly the forest seemed to close in around her like the woven bonds of a cage.

"Yes! Children. You act as though I'm trying to hold you captive. If you would only cool your temper and listen to me, I am trying to offer you a life beyond *this!*"

"I don't *want* a life beyond this!" She paused, breath steaming on the frigid air as she panted. Even as she spoke them, she knew the words were not entirely true. There was a yearning in her, something that had lodged deep in her heart since the first time her father had told her of the wonders that lived in the forest's heart. But what she wanted, Solmir could not offer. She drew another breath, slower this time. "I'm not what you want."

"I'm not trying to fight you," he said quietly, breath misting in the air between them. "You must know how hard it will be to survive this winter here. I would wait, and bide my time, and let you come around, but neither of us has that time. Every week that passes could bring a storm that makes travel impossible. If someone in your family should become unwell, what would you do?"

Suddenly it was not Solmir's face that Yeva saw, but the wild, unnatural focus of her father's stare before he left, determined to catch the thing that he imagined was tracking him. Yeva closed her eyes. Her heart fluttered against her rib cage like a bird trying to beat its way free.

"Please," said Solmir. "Let me help your family. Let me help you."

Yeva remained silent for some time before opening her eyes. Solmir's face was inches from hers. Only her breath steamed the air, as he held his and waited.

"I cannot accept your offer," she began in a whisper. His face went wooden, and she hurried to continue. "Not without making clear my situation. My family's situation."

"There's nothing that would change my mind." His voice was tense with cautious anticipation.

"M-my father is unwell." Her voice broke, to her horror. Yeva found her throat closing, the anxiety that had hunted her the past week bubbling up without warning. She had discussed it with no one, not even her sisters, but now the need to speak overtook her. "I fear—I fear he is going mad."

Solmir stepped forward, his hands going to her shoulders. He gently pulled her close. "Then we will find him help. Together."

Yeva wanted to pull away, but the fear lodged inside her since her father shoved her down fought its way out. And Solmir was warm, and as his hand pressed at the small of her back, pulling her closer still, she found that part of her didn't mind his touch at all. She knew she could not reasonably spend her life wandering these forest trails in search of something she could not even name—not when Solmir's proposal offered answers to every misfortune her family had suffered.

"Then I accept," she whispered, mumbling the words into the leather of his tunic.

His arms tightened, robbing her of breath, and then released her again. "Come. Let us get your barks and herbs into the stewpot, and tell your sisters the happy news."

Solmir visited almost daily after that, joining Yeva at her tasks. She stuck to her snares in his company, bringing her bow along only for defense. Her daylong hunting expeditions turned into pleasant strolls, Solmir at her side, discussing horses, and hunting, and how to skin leopards. Though she longed for the solitude to which she'd grown accustomed, she found herself growing fond of Solmir nonetheless, with his boyish enthusiasm for all things hunting. At first Yeva feared he might take advantage of the quiet, empty forest to embrace her again, but he remained a respectful distance from her, only offering her his hand now and then to help her over a log or across a frozen stream.

The relief that he was willing to help her father was dampened, however, by the uneasiness still haunting her. She could not quite place it—true, she did not love Solmir, but that was hardly reason not to marry him. She was fond of him, and growing fonder every day. The life he'd spoken of was a far better and richer one than Yeva ever could have hoped for, and yet there was a shadow over her heart, a tight emptiness she could feel every time she took a deep breath. She told herself it was fear for her father. She told herself it would pass once her father returned. She told herself she would be happy, then.

Solmir left in the afternoons to return to the inn where he was staying, giving Yeva a few precious hours before dusk in which to do some real work, checking her traps a final time and using her bow on any stragglers heading back to their dens for the night. She was not as productive as she had been before he began accompanying her, but she still brought home enough food for her sisters and Albe.

The days stretched on into weeks, and there was still no sign of Yeva's father. She watched for marks of him in the forest, but the trail of his passage from the house had long since been erased by snowfall, and she could not tell in which direction he had traveled.

Her dread grew. It woke her at night with a pounding heart, distracted her during the day when she ought to be listening to Solmir. Her sisters said nothing, and she offered nothing in return, but the tense silences in the evenings were eloquent nonetheless. She felt stretched as taut as the wires of one of her snares, waiting for the tiniest shift to send her springing into action.

So when a commotion outside interrupted the quiet just before dawn, Yeva was up off her pallet by the fire and halfway to the door before Doe-Eyes had even lifted her head.

Yeva threw open the door, but before she could scan the area for signs of her father, a shape launched at her out of the inky blackness. Behind her Doe-Eyes yelped recognition. Someone lit a lamp, and as its illumination fell upon the doorway, Yeva recognized what had thrown itself at her.

"Pelei," she whispered, dropping to her knees and not

bothering to reprimand the dog when he began mopping her face with his tongue. She was too busy staring through the night beyond him, searching for her father's form, waiting for him to emerge out of the darkness.

The dog was whining insistently, shoving his nose against Yeva's neck and sniffing anxiously. Yeva dropped her eyes. "Where's Father?" she whispered, her heart constricting. The dog began to wriggle away but she gripped his front legs, holding him still. "Pelei? Where's Father?"

She could say nothing else, repeating the words over and over until she felt hands at her shoulders drawing her back. "Yeva! He cannot answer, Father isn't here!" It was Lena, her voice choked with fear.

"No!" Yeva tore her arm from Lena's grip. "Pelei, why did you leave him? Father!" she called, into the night, knowing at any moment she would hear his voice call back to her.

"He's not here," whispered Lena. "Yeva—he's not here."

Yeva turned to see a trio of pale faces in the lamplight, all staring at her. "He has to be," she whispered back. "Pelei would not have left him. Pelei *never* would have left him. Something has happened."

She rose to her feet and began to dress in silence, not even bothering to warn Albe—he whirled around, turning his back as she traded her night shift for her trousers. Lena tied the dogs by the bedroom as Asenka tried to speak to Yeva, her voice shaking.

"What are you doing?"

"Go back to sleep," Yeva said calmly. She was putting things into a leather bag Asenka had made from rabbit skins. A water flask, flint and tinder, dried meat and some tubers wrapped in an extra cloak. Lengths of wire, goose feathers, a pot of glue for arrow fletching in the field. Needle and thread. Bandages.

Medicines for pain, bleeding, frostbite, broken bones, every eventuality she could think of.

"Yeva, you don't know where he is."

"I will find him."

"It's dark—please, calm down—wait until morning."

"No time. His trail may be lost by then."

Asenka grasped at Yeva's arm with uncharacteristic strength. "Yeva, *stop*. We need you here. You can't go tearing off into the woods. I am as worried about Father as you are, but *we* need you too."

Yeva hesitated, arm flexing under Asenka's grip. Her sister was right—if something had happened to their father, then she was the only one who could ensure her family would not starve this winter.

But if something had happened to their father . . . Yeva's heart shriveled, and her instincts took over. She shook her sister's hand off, then closed up the satchel and swung it onto her back. "You have enough food for several weeks. I'll be back before then, I promise."

"Yev—"

"*I promise.*"

She took one last look at the house: Lena with her arms around the dogs, holding them back; Asenka, white-faced and leaning against their father's chair by the cold hearth; Albe in the corner, hands clenched together and hair sticking straight up. All of them still, round-eyed and frightened as they watched her.

A sharpness stung her heart in the brief, heavy silence while she stood in the doorway. She could not leave them—and yet she had to find her father. If he was alive she would bring him home. Solmir would help her find a doctor for him, and together they would take him away from the wood that had driven him mad.

And she and her family would have peace. *If* he was alive . . .

If he was not—then she would find him anyway. She stepped out into the predawn gloom and let the door close on the lamplight behind her.

Pelei's tracks through the snow were obvious despite the darkness. The dog had been moving quickly, bounding across deep snow and leaving a trough created by his body. Yeva followed the trail, grateful for the dog's large size, and that he had forged such a path for her. She fell into the rhythm of her stride, mind reverberating with each step and each breath that steamed away behind her.

Keep moving. Keep running.

The sun rose behind a heavy curtain of clouds, leaving the forest in a false twilight that threatened to play tricks on her eyes. She kept her head down and kept moving, ignoring the burning in her legs that began just after noon. If her father was injured or trapped somewhere, she would not have much time to find him. This cold could kill someone within hours if they were not properly prepared—and even her father, master of these woods, could falter.

Pelei's tracks grew fainter as the day wore on, hidden under a light dusting of snow that had begun to fall. By the time twilight crept in again she was forced to stop and make camp, as much to rest her burning legs as to wait for daylight to show her the way onward. She slept little, fear shrieking at her to keep moving despite logic telling her she must rest. She passed the time mending holes in her cloak with the needle she'd brought with her.

As soon as the sky lightened, she packed up the camp and doused the fire. She sucked on some of the dried meat until she was able to chew it as she moved out. She had not gotten more than ten steps, however, when a voice cried her name. She stopped, the sound ringing in ears that had grown used to hearing only the quiet evenness of her own breath.

She stopped long enough to let Solmir catch up with her, his breath coming in great ragged gasps. "Wait," he panted. "Wait. Wait."

"I can't," she said tightly. She could not afford to dwell on her fear, or else she felt she might be paralyzed by it. "He could be hurt."

"I've been following you all night," he gasped, hands on his knees as he struggled for breath. "Please. Your sisters explained. Let me help."

"How?" Yeva shook her head. "I'll move more quickly on my own."

"Two sets of eyes," he managed, lungs still heaving.

Yeva felt the hairs on the back of her neck prickle. Had she not used the same justification to try and convince her father to let her come with him? She closed her eyes. "I am sorry, Solmir," she said quietly. "I have to go on alone. I can run farther than you—you're in no shape to continue on. And I must."

He coughed breathlessly, but could manage no more words, merely lifting his gaze enough to watch her with silent appeal.

Yeva's lungs constricted and she clenched her hands into fists, trying to fight the urge to give in. "If you would help me," she murmured, "then—would you look after my sisters while I'm gone?"

"But—"

"Please," she said simply. "Please, Solmir."

"But what about Albe?"

Yeva's lips twitched—the first hint of a smile she'd felt since Pelei had returned. "Yes," she agreed. "You will need to look after Albe too."

"That's not what I meant." He was regaining his breath somewhat, but his face still burned with the flush of exertion, and his voice was still ragged.

"I know. But he is more brother than servant, and he doesn't know these woods. He can't provide for them. You can." She stepped forward to clasp his hands in hers. She had never voluntarily reached out for him before, and he seemed almost as surprised by the gesture as she was herself. "This is what I'm asking you to do."

Solmir was silent for a time, breathing hard through his nose. "When you return—"

Yeva nodded. "When I return I will marry you. And we will see my father settled, and go out hunting as often as you like, and sit at the baron's table together. But for now I have to find my father. And I need your help—at home."

Solmir freed one hand from Yeva's grasp and lifted it to take hold of her chin in his fingers. He leaned forward and brushed his lips against hers, the briefest of touches before he pulled away again. "For luck."

She knew she ought to feel changed by his kiss, that her lips ought to tingle or her heart swell—but her lips felt only numb with cold, and her heart pounded only with urgency and exertion.

Yeva let go of him and staggered back so she could retrieve her pack and her bow. "Thank you," she whispered, and then turned and stumbled off again.

She put as much distance as she could between her and Solmir, praying he didn't change his mind. If he kept his word— and she had no reason to think he wouldn't—then it would buy her some time. If she could not return in the next few days, then at least her sisters would be taken care of, and Solmir would not come blundering after her through the woods.

She had no time to think of Solmir. She knew, now, what she was searching for in these woods.

By the end of the day her vision was blurring with exhaustion. She knew she needed sleep, but after so long moving she found it hard for her limbs to settle. She put her head down on her pack, wrapping herself in the extra cloak by her meager fire. Her tired eyes sought patterns in the flames, saw wings of fire stretching skyward, and she fell asleep hearing her father's voice telling her stories of the Firebird deep in the heart of the wood.

In her dreams a serpent glided toward her, red-gold eyes capturing and holding her as if she were a rabbit facing its death. Unable to run or cry out, she could only watch as it slithered across her chest. Its skin was ice cold and smooth as it reached her face, sliding over her lips and cheeks like a frigid kiss. It hissed as its head brushed her ear, jerking her out of her daze.

She sat bolt upright, gasping for air and clawing at her face, trying to throw the serpent away only to find her fingers closing around half-melted snow. The fire was nearly dead, its last embers hissing desperately under the onslaught of a new storm. Yeva blinked and looked up to find heavy snowfall drowning the camp, covering the whole lower half of her body.

"No," she gasped, numb lips struggling to form the word. "No, no—Pelei—"

She scrabbled under the snow for her bow and her pack, then stumbled over onto her hands and knees. Dawn was breaking, pale light cast diffusely across the wood. Pelei's trail was only visible as a faint series of hollows in the snow, almost indistinguishable from other features, obscured by the new snow—and filling fast.

Yeva scrambled to her feet and bolted down the trail, still shaking off the remnants of her nightmare, mind barely functioning. But Pelei's trail was nearly gone, and without it she would only be one person in a vast, uncharted wood, with no way of ever finding her father. She could not afford to waste half a second collecting herself.

The snow fell more and more thickly, the wind picking up to toss it against her face and blind her at every turn. Pelei's trail had also become more twisted, reflecting some confusion in the dog's original path. Twice she had to stop and go back, retracing her steps to the point where she had mistaken a dip in the terrain for the trail.

She lost all track of time in the storm, the clouds and the falling snow too heavy for her to see any sign of the sun. The trees were growing together more thickly here, allowing little of the snow through. It meant there was less snow to cover Pelei's trail, but that there had also been less snow to preserve it in the first place.

Eventually she stumbled over a hidden log, falling hard onto her stomach. Her breath stopped, leaving her groaning and trying to force her lungs to suck in new air. She rolled onto her back and lay there until she could fill her lungs normally, head spinning. She sat up, casting about for Pelei's trail—and could see nothing. There was only the uneven expanse of snow in every direction, and her own scattered trail leading back the way she'd come.

Yeva dragged herself to her feet, shivering now that she'd stopped moving and the perspiration from exertion settled on her skin. Though the denseness of the trees prevented the snow from being too blindingly thick, she could no longer see any distinct path to follow. She stood there, eyes straining through the gloom, heart pounding and breath steaming the air.

As she turned in a slow circle, something stung at the insides of her nose, distinct from the icy burn of falling snow. Tracking by scent was usually impossible in such cold—everything was wiped clean by the frozen air. But Yeva could smell a faint, metallic tang that made the hairs rise on her arms.

Blood.

BEAST

Blood everywhere. It burns us, horrifies us, sets us ablaze. We hunger. We roar. We want to revel in it, and we want to run. We pace across the blood-soaked snow, our heart thrumming in our ears.

But something comes. We pull back and hide our scent, waiting. Another hunter—so like the first, but younger, smaller. We slink closer through the thick trees to look.

It is female. We stop abruptly, sniffing again. Her scent is unmistakable. A mate? No. She is young and he was old.

Offspring.

Perhaps our plan is not lost. We watch her from our hidden place, breathing her smell and listening to the silence of her steps. She moves like an animal in a woman's body.

She moves like beauty.

FIVE

YEVA DROPPED INTO A hunter's stance. Where there was blood there would be scavengers—and wolves fed as a pack. And while wolves would ordinarily flee a human's presence, if they felt their kill was being threatened, they might try to defend it. With her every sense tuned, she crept forward, feet feeling for any hollows or obstacles that might trip her up.

Whatever had been killed here was much larger than a rabbit or a fox. Blood splashed the area, painting the trees and the snow red in the half-light. The falling snow had covered large portions of it—she estimated that the blood had been spilled only hours before.

Had her father been here? Had he encountered the Beast of his stories, and killed it? Yeva dropped to one knee to touch a finger to the ground. The blood was frozen. Perhaps it had been longer than she'd guessed. A shadowy irregularity caught her eye a few steps away, and she reached down and cleared the snow from the object.

It was her father's ax.

Yeva stared at the weapon, her mind refusing to process what it was seeing. A sense of wrongness built up in her gut. Why would he have abandoned it? Its handle was specially-carved, shiny-smooth from use, and fitted to his hand. Had he dropped it after killing the Beast?

And then Yeva saw what the sense of wrongness was trying to tell her.

The blade of the ax was clean, unbloodied. It had not shed the blood staining the ground.

Some distance beyond, a familiar shape dragged her forward—she uncovered his bow, then a few feet farther she found his pack, the leather torn and the contents strewn about beneath the snow.

With shaking hands she knelt over the next snow-covered hump, brushing the snow aside. She glimpsed something like raw meat, the white of bone glinting in the dim light.

A moan tore itself from her throat as she hurled herself away from the thing, which was too small to be a whole body. She fell onto her hands and knees, gasping for breath, staring blindly at the red snow before her eyes. There was only the rushing in her ears and the agony in her chest as her lungs fought for air.

She realized she was clutching his bow, its string pressed against her cheek, its long curves digging into her chest. Her numb arms refused to let it go. Her body shook, nausea clawing its way up from her belly.

A smell made its way into her awareness and her mind seized on it, grasping for anything with which to distract itself. This scent wasn't blood, but something wilder, richer. Musky, but not unpleasant. Yeva opened her eyes, staring through the gloom of the forest. Her blood surged through her, a wild flood of fury.

The bow was still in her hand. She gripped it hard enough for her knuckles to shine white as bone.

All at once an immense shadow moved, and Yeva was stunned into momentary inaction. She had been searching for a creature the size of a wolf, but it was as though an entire section of the forest had suddenly thrown itself backward through the clearing.

Without further pause she swung her father's bow around and drew it in one smooth movement. The arrow flew straight and true. There was a bone-shaking roar of fury and pain that threw her to the ground with its intensity, and then the shadowy giant bounded off through the wood.

She lay there stunned, brain trying to understand what it had seen. No natural animal could have made that sound or loomed so huge. It wasn't until the smell of her father's blood reminded her of where she was that she shook her head to clear it.

Yeva strapped her father's ax to her back, then lurched to her feet and took off after the Beast. She left her own bow behind, gripping her father's bow white knuckled, no space left for rational thought. There was only the hunt, the need to kill, to spray the creature's blood across the snow. The blizzard had stopped, and the sun was setting behind its concealing layer of clouds. The forest grew darker by the second, but she didn't care. The Beast who had slain her father was here. And she was going to destroy it.

Just there—a spatter of fresh blood some distance from where she stood. Too fresh to have belonged to her father. Droplets led from the spot, and a trough in the snow told of something large moving away.

She broke into a long, smooth run, her eyes on the ground, intent on the trail. Even if the tracks of its great body dragging through the snow weren't a clear path, she would have been able to track its scent. Its blood was a black, wild tang of metal in the back of her throat. Were it a smaller creature she would've guessed it to be an arterial hit, but she had seen the size of the Beast as it loomed up, before she pulled the trigger. For an animal so huge, the quantities of blood spattering the ground would not be fatal. If she was lucky, she'd punctured a lung, and the Beast would be slowly suffocating. If she could track it far enough, she'd be able to kill it.

Her father had taught her this stride, steady and low to the ground, covering distances smoothly and quickly and quietly. She raced along behind the Beast. The smell of it grew stronger with each step as she closed the gap between them.

All was silent save for the occasional dull thud of snow sliding from the pine boughs. With the storm now passed, the forest was still and dry and aching with the weight of winter. There were no other animals, only the Beast and, closing on its heels, its hunter.

The dusk leached the color from the world, and the spots of blood on the snow were a rich gray. Not long now.

Up ahead she heard a sound. Something coughed. Wet, labored breathing rippled through the air. Yeva's pulse beat fiercely in her temples. Her father's bow held at the ready in her right hand, she reached up with her left to finger the handle of her father's ax. The weight of it was a comfort.

A clearing opened up ahead of her. The gloom of the forest lightened to a treacherous twilight, revealing the massive shadow slumped in its center. The rise and fall of it was uneven. It heaved labored, rattling breaths that caught and gasped on the exhale. Great clouds of condensation rose, catching the mix of moonrise and sunset.

She crept forward, searching under the snow with the tip

of her boot until she found a stick. She stepped on it smartly, sending a sharp crack into the air, no quieter for its muffling white blanket.

The lump of shadow twitched, its breath wheezing. It extended a forepaw and tried to rise, only to collapse to the snow again, where it lay still but for its heaving breath and quivering fur.

Yeva could wait for it to die, for the air and the blood to run out. But she could not bear to wait, and that was too gentle a death—a gradual slowing of the body that ended in sleep. That death was too kind for this monster. The lust was rising in her, the wild hiss of revenge bubbling up to replace the hunter's cold reason.

She wanted to feel the crunch of its skull through the handle of the ax, see its life spill onto the snow in a steaming torrent. She wanted to see the face of the Beast that killed her father in the moment it understood it had lost. She wanted to watch it die.

Slinging her father's bow over her shoulder, she reached up to free her ax from its strap, gaze intent, every step pillow-soft in the powder. As she drew nearer she saw that it was not a monstrous bear, as she had thought, but something different and strange. She decided she would sever its spinal cord and take its head, which had the delicate elegance of a wolf's with the bone-crushing jaw muscles of a wolverine's. This trophy she would not sell. This one was hers.

She shifted her grip on her ax, careful to stay back out of range of its claws, which now dug into the snow, grasping for salvation.

Closer still, and she could see its eyes in the gloom. It rolled them at her, baleful, pleading, animal. The bloodlust swelled.

How had her father ever given up this life? In her mind's

eye a tapestry unfurled, the life she could have led as her father's daughter, side by side with him. If only he had brought her on his final hunt. If only he had then not found this Beast on his own. If only.

The Beast growled and the tapestry vanished like the ghost of its breath in the air. The growl turned to a whine, and she guessed her earlier shot had indeed punctured its lung. It tried once more to rise, but buckled again with a thump, its fur dusted white with snow. Its eyes rolled shut, mouth hanging open as it gasped and bled.

She was close enough now that the force of its breath stirred the fur lining her hood. The air smelled of blood and damp, and wild musk. She inhaled, nostrils flaring.

"For you, Daddy," she whispered, lifting her ax.

Her only warning was the glitter of its eyes as they opened. Too late she saw that the Beast's hind legs were crouched beneath its bulk, muscles tense and ready. Too late she saw the corpses of several rabbits, decapitated and cooling in the fresh blood that led her to the clearing. Too late she realized how close to the Beast she was standing.

The Beast lunged at her, knocking her ax aside with a blow that numbed her from the shoulder down, arm falling uselessly to her side. The sound of its roar was the sound of the forest, the vibrations shaking snow from every branch and flinging it to the ground in a perverse echo of the winter storm that had brought it. The impact of the Beast's body hitting hers sent her head snapping forward out of its concealing hood, as it lifted her from her feet.

Her last thought, strangely rational as their bodies sailed through the air, was: *This is no Beast, to lay such a trap for me. This is a hunter.*

And then its body crushed hers into the ground and it was to the dull snap of her bones breaking that she lost consciousness.

Yeva woke in utter darkness. The air was heavy with the sense of earth pressing in on her. She blinked several times, convincing herself that her eyes were working—there was no difference between having them open or closed.

She was lying on her back, spread-eagled on stone. Staving off the panic that she'd gone blind, she attempted to sit up. Shooting pain pierced through her right side, causing her to gasp aloud. She tried to clap her hands to the spot, but only her right arm moved. The left twitched with the clanking sound of metal, a frigid cuff cutting into her wrist.

Yeva slowly took inventory of the rest of her body. With careful fingertips she found not one but three ribs that made her eyes water when touched. She could move her legs, bend her spine—with great pain in her side—and her neck. Her head ached, and when she moved it she felt an agonizing tender spot at its back. Whoever had put her here had dropped her without care. She must have hit her head on the stone floor. She could smell blood in the air, and wondered if it was hers.

I am chained underground with broken ribs and no light, she told herself, closing her eyes and letting the fear wash through her. Her father had always told her that no matter the predicament, a hunter should never lie to himself. Only by understanding the problem can one see past it. Her father—Yeva clamped her lips together, eyes prickling behind closed lids. She could not afford to think of him now.

The last thing she remembered was the roar of triumph before the Beast had flung itself at her. She swallowed, neck prickling. *It should have torn out my throat.* By comparison, captivity and broken ribs seemed trivial.

Had someone saved her before the Beast could finish killing her? But why save her only to chain her in a cave?

Before she could think of an explanation there came a grating rasp of metal and stone. She inhaled sharply, feeling the stab of the breath in her broken ribs, and lifted her head but could see nothing in that direction. Something clattered to the floor and then scraped across it, as if it was being shoved toward her. Yeva strained and blinked in the blackness. Before her eyes could discern anything except the faint outline of a rectangle, the grating shriek of hinges came again, followed by the sound of something slamming closed.

Forcing herself to take shallow breaths, Yeva tried to calm herself. Not a cave, then, if there was a door—although the sensation of being underground remained. She tried to think if she had seen a figure in the doorway, but the darkness had been too complete.

She tried to sit up again, gritting her teeth against the pain, and managed to lift herself up on an elbow. Reaching out with one leg, she hooked her heel over the edge of the object that had been placed in her cell, and dragged it toward her. She was barefoot—someone had removed her boots. And her cloak and pack too, she realized.

And her weapons.

She got the object close enough to reach it with her fingertips, and then drew it the rest of the way to her. It was a tray, she discovered, exploring its contents with her fingers in the dark. She recognized the texture of dried meat, as well as uncooked tubers and a skin of water. They were from her own supplies.

There were also two strips of something rough and semistiff under her fingers. She picked one up, holding it to her nose and then brushing it with her lips, which were far more sensitive to touch than her fingers. Tree bark.

Her heart surged with confusion as she touched the strip to her tongue. Willow bark. For pain. She broke a bit off with her teeth and chewed, the bitterness so strong she had to fight the urge to spit it out again immediately. *Chew, don't swallow.* She sucked at the bark, head aching with the foul taste of it—but the pain began to ease, both in her head and her side. She spat out the pulpy mass and reached for the water skin to wash away the taste.

Why would someone lock her here and then bring her food and medicine for pain? She ate the rations, some part of her mind asserting itself and reminding her that if she hoped to escape, she'd need her strength. With difficulty she followed the manacle chaining her left hand back to the wall and tried to prop herself up against it—but the pain in her ribs was still too great, despite the dulling effects of the willow bark.

The food and the medication had arrived only seconds after she'd awakened. Could someone have heard her gasp?

"Hello?" she called to the darkness, her voice rasping like the scrape of a knife cleaning leather. The sound of it was small, dull and without echo. The room she was in couldn't be large. She swallowed and tried again, her voice a little stronger. "Hello? Thank you to whoever gave me the bark."

Perhaps it was a servant of whoever held her, feeling sorry for her. "Please, I need light. I'm injured, but I can't tell how badly without being able to see."

There was no answer. She let her head fall back against the wall to which she was chained. The blackness spun around her, though she could not tell if it was from fear or pain or an overdose of the willow bark. She closed her eyes, and fell into a doze.

Her sleep was fitful at best, haunted by monstrous images

and flashes of light. She dreamed she was blind, able only to see red streaks as though trying to see behind closed eyelids.

The streaks became a pair of eyes, the serpent's eyes from her dream in the forest, but also the Beast's—they stalked her and she found she was paralyzed as well as blind. The Beast moved closer, and when she tried to scream her voice had fled, and she jerked upright and felt the sting of fangs in her lungs and cried out, eyes flying open.

Yeva stared, gasping, at the ceiling as the dream fell away. Her side ached where her sudden movement had jarred her injured ribs. She blinked at the gray stone ceiling for long moments before her mind caught up with her.

The gray stone ceiling? She could *see*.

She rolled over onto her side with difficulty, her chain scraping the stone below her. A few feet away, sitting on the floor by the door, was a tiny oil lamp.

Someone had brought her light.

Yeva reached out and dragged the light closer, unable to take her eyes from it despite the way they burned and watered after so long in darkness. "Thank you," she whispered to her invisible ally. "Thank you."

She eased herself down again onto her back, unlacing her tunic so that she could raise her undershirt. Angry red and blue bruises spread across her side, tinged with the yellow of a stormy sky. She explored their edges with her fingertips and shuddered against a stab of pain. Broken, as she had feared. She slowly eased her shirt back into place and looked around.

The light allowed her to see that her cell was roughly square in shape, a bit longer than she was tall. There were no windows, only a solid timber door bound with iron and a thick lock. In the corner adjacent to the one where she was chained was a wooden hatch, no more than half a foot square. Though she could smell nothing, Yeva assumed she was meant to relieve herself there. The room was otherwise empty but for Yeva, her light, and the tray of uneaten, raw tubers.

She considered trying to roast the tubers over the oil lamp, but after a few halfhearted attempts decided that the flame was not hot enough. Whoever had left her food had merely taken the supplies from her pack and deposited them on the tray, with no thought for whether they were actually edible uncooked.

The lamp gave off a tiny amount of heat, and so she drew it in close to her body, trying to ignore the monstrous shadows she cast on the four walls of her tiny cell. The shadows reminded her far too much of the creature in the clearing before it had struck.

Yeva took in a deep breath, stirring the air enough to make the flame flicker across the walls. "I know you can hear me," she said, voice sounding much more certain than she felt. "I don't know who you are, or why you're helping me. But I need medicines from the pack I brought with me. The willow bark was good but it is not enough."

She waited, but there was only silence.

Yeva glanced her fingers over her ribs again, wincing at the pain but unable to leave it alone. "I need the salve from the small red pot. It will help me heal. Please." She strained to listen, ears ringing with the quiet. There came a light scrape as of fabric or leather on stone, so faint she would have dismissed the sound, if it hadn't been followed by a voice.

"You will have to put out your light."

The voice was a rumbling bass, heavy and musical and rich. Yeva shivered in spite of herself—if anything she had expected a meek, gentle voice. Someone sympathetic enough to help but too weak to actually set her free. Everything about this voice spoke of strength, and very little of compassion.

"But it is the only light I have," she replied, her free hand moving instinctively to the lamp. "I have no way of lighting it again."

"I will leave you flint and tinder," said the voice. The swish of leather or skin or cloth on stone came again, as though someone was shifting, unseen in the small cell. "But you must put it out."

"Why?"

"No questions."

Yeva shivered. The thought of being left alone in the dark again was enough to make her eyes sting, but she had no reason to distrust her benefactor. He would not leave her a light only to take it from her again.

"Very well," she whispered, and turned the wick down, the light shrinking and quivering. Yeva almost didn't see it go out, afterimages dancing before her eyes and blinding her.

The door squealed open, the noise of rusty hinges shredding the quiet. Yeva clapped a hand over her ears, grimacing. Then came that tiny sound, a footfall. The person, whoever it was, was wearing the softest of shoes. Or else they were barefoot, like she was.

"Are you a captive too?" she asked the darkness.

The voice didn't answer right away. There came a quiet clatter as something was placed down on the tray of food. "Yes," said the voice then, the word emerging like a sigh.

"And yet you are free to move around and see other prisoners?"

"I said *no questions*."

There was a growl to the voice, a hint of anger that made Yeva want to scramble backward. She held her ground, calling on hours spent waiting outside rabbit dens to aid her in keeping still. "Thank you for helping me," she said softly. She could not afford to alienate the one person who could give her aid.

"I wish you to get well." Though the words were kind, the voice was not.

Yeva swallowed. "These roots. They must be cooked before I can eat them."

"I care not," said the voice. The door slammed shut with a screech of angry hinges, leaving her, once again, in silence.

Yeva's breath left her in a gasp, her heart pounding. She crawled toward the tray, ignoring the pain in her side, and retrieved the salve. Then she felt around the tray's surface until her fingers found what they were looking for: a pair of flints and a braided strip of wool for tinder. Yeva tightened her hand around them, not caring how the stones dug into her palm. At least she would not be left in the dark.

BEAST

We had no intention of hurting the female, but the bodies of humans are fragile. Even broken, she will serve. We will keep her alive until a hunter comes to retrieve her, and then we will take him to serve our purpose.

We stand often outside her door, listening to her breathe and learning the scent of her. This way if she tries to run we will be able to hunt her down. The light in the room is no more than a sliver along the bottom of the door. Very rarely it flickers as she passes between it and the door, a shadow of movement.

"Thank you," she whispers when we leave her things.

We do not understand this gratitude—we

are her captor. We will be her death. We are beast and she is as fragile as the other one was. We should show her our face and let her scream until she breaks. They will come for her whether she has her mind or not.

We do not do this. We ask her to put out the light when we open the door so she will not see our face.

Why?

SIX

HER RIBS HEALED SLOWLY, in large part due to her inability to sit still. Yeva tested the confines of her cell, able to reach the hatch in the corner only by stretching as far as the chain would let her go. She could barely touch the edge of the door, fingertips grazing the iron bindings. When her meals arrived she never heard the sound of a lock turning. The chain kept her here—the door itself was unlocked. Which explained how it was that her ally could come and go.

Yeva asked questions of the darkness, hoping for the voice's return. Though its tone had offered nothing of kindness or sympathy, the invisible ally had brought food, medicine, light. It didn't speak again, but now and then Yeva's requests were granted. She was given bandages for her wrist, which had gone raw and bloody within its manacle. The fuel in her lamp was replaced. The hinges on the door were oiled and no longer shrieked. And after one particularly cold and fitful stretch of sleep, she woke to find that a blanket had been deposited at her side.

But the voice never spoke.

She understood that if she wished her requests to be granted, she had to turn out her light and wait. The darkness then was so heavy, so stifling, she'd speak to fill the empty blackness.

Yeva had always preferred silence to the chatter of others, daydreaming of the forest quiet while the baronessa's ladies laughed and gossiped. Her thoughts came to life in the stillness of the wood, nurtured by the air and the scent and the vividness of it. But as the days crept by in her cell, she discovered that she had never known silence—not true silence. In the forest the air was alive with smells of wood and wet, the sounds of her steps echoing in the vastness. Always there was the possibility of movement and life, a rabbit flashing out of a burrow or the briefest glimpse of a fox's tail as it disappeared from sight.

The silence of her cell was small and stagnant. Heavy air pressed in on all sides, and any sounds she made were swallowed up by the weight of the earth overhead. She longed to hear the sound of a human voice, even if it was her own.

She took to speaking of anything and everything that came to mind, to fill the hungry silence. She described her featureless cell: the way the gray stone fitted together so seamlessly she could not see the mortar, the aching chill of the rock beneath her, the musical clatter of the tray, the frigid brush of her fingertips against the iron bindings on the door. She spoke of her lamp, gazing at its flame for hours, breathing in the faint burning scent and making it flicker with the breath of her words.

She imagined that the owner of that deep, rumbling voice was listening to her, and that when she spoke she was in some small way offering an exchange. His help, for her words.

When she ran out of things to describe she spoke instead of her family. Though she could not bring herself to remember her father, she talked about her sisters. She described Asenka's twisted foot and explained how five minutes with her smile and her laugh made anyone forget her disability. She recalled Lena's silly moodiness with a smile, though there was no one to see it. She even spoke of Albe and his clumsiness, and how his desire to please more than made up for his bumbling attempts to help.

"I left them," she confessed to the shadows. "They begged me to stay, and I promised I'd return. I *promised*." Her eyes burned. If only she had listened. She had not been able to help their father, and now . . . now it seemed likely she would never see any of them again. *What is it you're looking for out there?* Asenka had asked her. Yeva's throat closed.

Not this.

When she could no longer talk about her family without crying, her mind wandered to the stories her father used to tell her of the creatures that lived in the heart of the black wood. At first the stories were disjointed. It had been so long since she'd heard them, and the silence edging in on her was a distraction. Her cell was always cold, and the chill had weakened her, a gradual decay of strength that she had no way of preventing.

She told of the poor working boy who made the princess laugh and stole her heart, and of the girl who was polite enough to Father Winter to be rewarded with a chest of treasures. She told of Vasilisa the Beautiful, and how in one tale she bested her wicked stepsisters with Baba Yaga's magic light; and in another, how she fooled a king who wanted to marry her into believing she was a boy by riding and hunting better than any man.

It was one of her favorite stories. Her voice had a tendency to go hoarse after she'd been speaking into the darkness for more than a few hours. She was half whispering by the time she neared the end of this last story, with her lamp turned low to conserve the oil. She sat leaning against the wall, eyes closed.

"And so finally the king commanded that the 'young man' take a bath with him," she whispered. "But Vasilisa—" Her voice caught in her throat and turned into a cough, and she reached for the water skin to soothe it.

From the corridor beyond the door came a sound that she'd come to recognize: that lightest of scrapes signifying the step of bare feet or soft leather. Yeva froze, listening over the sound of her pounding heart. The invisible ally was outside.

The silence stretched until, so quietly Yeva felt it in the stones more than heard it, the voice said, "Go on."

A smile tugged at the corners of Yeva's mouth. She swallowed a mouthful of water and then whispered, "But Vasilisa was too quick for him. She changed and bathed and left before the king had finished taking off all his finery. She left a note for him, saying that for all his wealth and power he was not as quick or as smart as she, for she was not Vasili but Vasilisa, and he'd been fooled by a girl."

Again there was silence, and then a melancholy sigh from beyond the door.

Yeva swallowed, crawling forward until she was as close to the door as her chain would allow. "Will you not help me escape?" she pleaded, voice cracking again into a whisper. "I don't even know where I am, or who has captured me, or for what purpose."

She heard him shifting his weight on the other side of the door. "I cannot."

"Why risk helping me then?"

Silence. Then: "Why has no one come for you?"

"For me?"

"To rescue you. A brother or a mate. There is a trail to find you if they look."

Yeva swallowed. "I don't think they know I'm caught. They believe I'm looking for my father." Her throat tightened at the mention of him.

"That is not how it should be." The hint of a growl was back in his voice, the sound of barely controlled anger. "Someone should have come."

Yeva stretched her hand toward the door, her fingertips touching the iron. "No one will come for me. You are all I have. Please, help me?"

There was no answer but the sound of footsteps fading down the corridor again.

The next time Yeva woke from her troubled dreams, she found by her head a plate full of tubers, roasted in their skins with oil and salt. They were still hot, steaming gently in the lantern light.

Her lungs and throat worsened over the next few days until speaking prompted a rattling cough that forced her to brace herself against the stone wall. The unrelenting chill of her cell had settled into her bones, and not even the blanket was enough to shield her from it. Her ally provided her with more of the willow bark from her supplies, but before long the store of medicine gave out, and no more bark turned up on her tray.

She knew she was showing signs of fever, but there was little she could do. She stopped telling stories, for they required more energy than she had, and she could not speak without coughing. Her head throbbed when she put it down to sleep, and ached when she sat up again.

"I am sick," she whispered, stubbornly sticking to her father's advice to be honest with herself about her predicament. It had been several days since she'd heard from the voice, and only the fact that food still appeared in her cell told her he was even

there anymore. She strained to hear the sound of his footsteps
in the corridor beyond, but heard only silence punctuated by the
throbbing of her head.

She sipped at the water skin until the rawness of her throat
triggered more coughing, and then put her head down. The lamp
burned at her eyes even closed, so she put out the light, bathing
her eyelids in blessed darkness. Yeva rolled onto her back, lungs
rattling with the effort of breathing.

"Can you walk?"

She had not heard the door open. Since her ally had oiled
the hinges the door was quieter, but not silent; it was the labored
sound of her own breathing that had masked it. Her eyes flew
open, struggling to peer through the gloom. She could see
nothing in the complete blackness, but she could sense him there
nonetheless, no more than a few feet away.

"I think so," she whispered.

Something soft fell against her ribs where she lay. "Put this
on." The voice held no emotion, though it was far from flat—
full of richness and depth. There was no disobeying it.

Yeva sat up with difficulty, reaching for the object to discover
that it was a strip of cloth, finer than any she'd felt in months.
Silk, folded many times over. Her fingers closed around it.

"Over your eyes," the voice clarified, impatience emerging in
the barest hint of a snarl.

She hurried to comply, fingers shaking. Was he going to take
her out of the cell? Was the blindfold so that she could not see
him, and implicate him later if she were to be caught again?

The manacle around her wrist clanked open, and for the
first time in weeks Yeva was able to press her naked arm against
her body without the chafe of iron. She felt like collapsing with
relief. But the voice commanded her to rise, and she did so by

holding on to the wall and standing on quavering legs. How had she lost so much strength so quickly? And after she'd fought so hard to win it back again. Behind the blindfold she shut her eyes more tightly.

"Follow me," ordered the voice, before the sound of his footsteps whispered against the stone.

"Wait." Yeva turned her head this way and that in the doubled darkness of cell and blindfold. "How can I follow if I cannot see?"

"Can you not track by sound and smell?" There was a brief silence, and then his footsteps again. "Put your hand against my shoulder and I will lead you."

Yeva stretched out a trembling hand until her fingertips found fur. What she wouldn't give for her rich fur cloak, now gracing the shoulders of an opportunistic buyer's wife. She dug her cold fingers deep into her invisible ally's coat and moved away from the wall.

He led her out of the cell and turned left, down what Yeva guessed was a corridor. They turned again, and again, until she lost all sense of direction. She tried to count their steps, but her head spun from fever and cold, and she gave up tracking their route.

From fever and cold—and from the scent. She smelled something musky and wild, something familiar that she could not place. *His fur coat,* she thought, but as soon as she thought it she knew it was not true. This was no dead pelt. *Perhaps my captor owns dogs.* But that could not explain it either, for Yeva knew the smell of dogs well enough to know this was not the same. The hairs rose along her arms, and she was grateful for the solid warmth under her hand, the slow movement of his body beneath his coat.

Her escort came to a halt, forcing her to stop as well. There came a faint whoosh of air, as of a door sliding open, and then a wall of heat struck her. She gasped, lifting her hand from the coat and reaching without thinking for her blindfold.

"*Don't.*" It was more growl than word, spoken so close to her ear that the force of his breath stirred her hair.

Her hand froze, and she fought the burning need to flee blindly back down the corridor. *He is my ally,* she reminded herself, face turning to the unseen heat. *He is my ally. He is not to be feared.*

"Come."

She found his shoulder again, and he led her forward into the room she could not see. Behind her the door slid closed again with a scrape and a click. The cold stone under her bare feet gave way to lush carpet, sending a wave of unexpected pleasure through her. How long since she'd felt such riches? Not for the first time, she wondered where she could possibly be.

Her ally led her forward and then bade her sit. Yeva relinquished her hold on his shoulder with reluctance. The fur had been warm and soft, and she'd found herself enjoying the feel of another person under her hand. She felt around with her feet and discovered a pile of cushions, and sank down onto them. To her left was the crackle and hiss of a fire, heat hammering at her skin.

"You may stay in this room as long as is necessary for you to recover your health," said the voice. Yeva's heart surged. "On one condition."

"What condition?"

"That you never remove the blindfold for any reason. If you do, you will die. Do you understand?"

Yeva swallowed. She would rather die warm and comfortable than cold and ill. But better not to die at all. "Yes. I will not remove it. You have my word."

* * *

"Tell me about your father."

Yeva paused midmeal, swallowing her mouthful of roasted pheasant. "My father," she echoed.

"You speak of your sisters, your servant, your mother. But never your father. Do you hate him so much?"

She blinked behind her blindfold, trying to read the hazy shapes beyond it. Some light made it through the silk, but she could not track anything unless it stood between her and the light. "No. I loved him."

"Then, do you not speak of him because he is dead?"

Yeva's throat closed again, despite having recovered over the past three days from the chill from the cell. Her cough remained, but mostly when she slept. Now, her throat constricted with grief instead.

"How do you know he's dead?" she whispered.

"You said you loved him." The voice emphasized the word *loved*, the past tense sounding final and heavy.

Yeva fell silent, listening to the fire, meal forgotten. Her ally had managed to source more food for her since her reprieve from the cell, the richest of game cooked to perfection. Perhaps he, too, was a hunter. Perhaps he'd understand.

"Before my father met my mother he was the greatest hunter in all of Rus. Maybe the world. He stopped to please her, for it was dangerous work, but in his heart he loved the forest. He was the only one who could venture into its heart, hunt the wildest and strangest of creatures who lived there."

"You have only mentioned sisters. Had he no sons?"

Yeva shook her head. "Only my sisters and me, the youngest." She hesitated. But what did it matter what her ally thought of her? He would not risk the anger of her captor to help her and then turn away because of scandal. She took a slow breath. "When I was young he treated me as he would a son, teaching me what he knew. I hunted at his side. I was happiest there."

"He trained you to hunt? Hunt as he did? With the same skills?" For the first time something colored the heavy voice—surprise, perhaps. Or dismay. Yeva found it difficult to read the emotion.

She lifted her chin. "You disapprove," she commented. "Because I'm a girl?"

"No." The voice paused. "Females are often the best hunters. They must provide for the young and survive when the males are too busy posturing to do so. But this is not the way with humans."

"Humans?" Yeva's thoughts ground to a halt. How could he speak as if he weren't one?

Another pause. "I apologize. I spend all my time here in the forest, and find myself more at home here among the beasts than among men. By now I am more beast than man myself."

This time Yeva had no difficulty reading the emotion there. Bitterness, thick and black and bringing the color to her cheeks. "I don't think that's true," she found herself saying.

"No?"

"No," she replied firmly. "You've helped me when you didn't have to. When whoever put me in that cell could return and punish you for letting me leave."

The air stirred, and Yeva saw a shadow move beyond the blindfold. The shape was huge—her ally must have been closer than she had thought.

"You know nothing," snarled the voice. His steps moving away were heavy on the carpet. The door opened and closed, and Yeva was left in silence again.

BEAST

We pace, more at home right now in our den of earth and cold than within four walls of stone and fire. Over our head the earth trembles with our steps, showering our fur with dirt.

He trained her to hunt as he did. She has his skills. We have been waiting for someone with the skills to rescue her, the skills to serve us, when she has been within our grasp all along. And we nearly let her rot to death in the cell.

Our breath comes in short, angry growls. We must show her what we are, force her to do our will now. We must not waste any more time. And yet . . .

And yet she tells us stories. And it has been

so long since we have heard a voice that was not screaming.

She put her hand on us and did not pull away.

She told us we were not a beast.

We growl, coming to a halt. Even our den smells of her now, and part of us thrills to it, sensing prey. Our mouth fills with saliva and we flee to the world above, to find something on which to feed.

We are always the beast.

SEVEN

"AND SO TO REWARD him for his love and faithfulness, the ghost gave Ivan the chestnut horse. With it he was able to leap higher than any other rider in the kingdom and win the heart of the princess. She knew him by his kiss."

The crackle of the fire at her back was the only applause Yeva received for finishing the tale, but she had grown accustomed to silences from her ally—her friend, as she was coming to think of him. She still had not dared ask his name, for it was clear he wished to remain anonymous. She had long since grown well again, but neither of them had suggested a return to her cell, and so she spent her days by the hearth, relishing its warmth.

The presence at her side shifted, shadows moving across her blindfold. Again she caught the faint tang of wildness, making her heart constrict. She missed the forest, for all she could not complain about her treatment here.

"This Ivan," rumbled the voice, its heavy bass tone weighted still more by deliberate thoughtfulness. "You have mentioned him several times."

To pass the time, she had asked for, and been granted, her arrow-making supplies. The small knife for trimming the wood and feathers was not enough for her to fight her way free, even if she wished to harm her friend. She'd learned to work by touch and feel, and just now she was fitting the fletching at the arrow's end. "He is the hero in many stories," she replied, running the edge of her finger along a strip of fletching, judging its straightness. "Sometimes it is Vasilisa who is the heroine."

"Vasilisa the Beautiful," echoed her friend, the uplift of his voice turning it to a question.

"Yes."

"What is your name?"

The question came suddenly, and Yeva's fingers froze at their work, feathers falling to her lap. "Beauty." Perhaps it was the task she was performing. The word came without thinking. Her father's name for her.

"Beauty?"

"No—no. My name is Yeva. The other is only a nickname. Yeva is my given name."

The voice was silent for a while, and then moved again. This time Yeva felt the brush of fur at her arm and shivered. Why did he continue to wear his coat despite the roaring blaze behind them?

"I shall call you Beauty," he said finally.

Yeva opened her mouth to protest, sure that the sound of her other name would stab deeply into the still-raw wound of her father's death. But in her friend's warm voice it merely felt true, and right, and she exhaled without speaking instead. "What is yours?" she whispered.

"I do not remember."

Yeva longed to pull her blindfold away, read the expression on his face. "How can you not remember your own name?"

"I said I have been here, alone, for many years. When you do not use a thing it withers and becomes dust."

"What does your master call you? The one who captured me?"

Silence.

Yeva swallowed. "I must call you something," she protested gently. "Shall I call you Ivan then?"

His exhale was almost a growl, although the sound no longer frightened Yeva—the thrill had changed from fear to something else entirely. "I am not a hero."

The heat of the fire rose to Yeva's face. She could feel it radiating against her blindfold at the curve of her cheeks. Forcing her voice to remain even, she said softly, "You are to me."

The presence at her side moved abruptly, the sound of footsteps leading away. Yeva clenched her jaw, arrow lying half made in her lap. But just as his footsteps would have reached the door they stopped and came close again, bringing with him that spicy wildness on the warm air.

"Tell me more of this Ivan."

Yeva fought to keep the relief from her tone. "He's in many of the old stories. He's often the youngest of several brothers— and often foolish. But he usually has a kind heart. The most famous story of Ivan is probably the tale of him, the Firebird, and the gray wolf."

The pacing stopped, air going still. Yeva suddenly felt tension snap into place in the room, the hairs on her arms standing up in response. She could not even hear her friend breathe. "Shall I tell that one?" she whispered.

"Yes."

Yeva closed her eyes behind her blindfold as her ally sat down again, fur coat brushing her arm. She began as her father had often started the story, and found she remembered it as clearly as if she'd read it yesterday.

There was once a king who had the most magnificent garden in the world. At the center of the garden was an enchanted tree that bore golden apples. But every time an apple would ripen, the Firebird would come in the night and steal it away.

Furious, the king called his two older sons and told them that whoever caught the Firebird would gain half of his kingdom and become his heir. His youngest son, Ivan, begged to help, but the king saw him as weak and foolish while his brothers were strong, and he refused. So the older brothers set out to catch the bird, and drank and caroused all night in celebration of their impending rewards. But they passed out in the early hours of the morning and when they woke, the apples were gone again.

So the king allowed Ivan to try. True, Ivan was not as strong as his brothers, but he was clever and resourceful. He stayed awake all night and did not touch a drop of wine, and so when the Firebird came he was ready. The bird was quicker than he, however, and so Ivan was only able to catch a single feather from the bird's tail.

The king sent his sons out into the world to catch the Firebird, and again Ivan had to beg to go. When his father finally relented, Ivan set out alone and came to a crossroads with a sign. Whoever took one path would learn hunger and cold, whoever took the second would survive but his horse would die, and whoever took the third would die, but his horse would live. Ivan chose the second path, and soon a huge gray wolf came out of the forest and ate his horse, forcing Ivan to walk. But Ivan was determined, and walked until he fell over with exhaustion.

The wolf took pity on him and offered to carry him on his back, and together they found the kingdom where the Firebird lived in a golden cage.

The wolf warned him not to take the cage, but Ivan was greedy and took both, setting off alarm bells throughout the castle. The ruler of that kingdom caught Ivan and, after hearing his story, said that he could have the Firebird if he would bring him the horse with the golden mane.

And so the gray wolf carried him farther still until they came to the next kingdom, where the horse with the golden mane lived, wearing a beautiful golden bridle. Again the wolf warned him to take the horse without the golden bridle, but Ivan did not listen, and again he was captured. This ruler listened to his story and said that he would let Ivan have the horse if he would agree to capture Yelena the Beautiful, a princess in yet another kingdom, and bring her back to him.

And so the gray wolf brought him to the next kingdom, and warned him not to fall in love with Yelena when he carried her off. Again Ivan did not listen, and when they returned to the second kingdom, Ivan begged the wolf to help him. The wolf agreed to take the form of Yelena to be given to the king, and so Ivan took the horse and kept the woman he loved. The wolf escaped the king and accompanied Ivan, Yelena, and the horse back to the first kingdom, where Ivan again persuaded the wolf to change shapes. Ivan pulled the same trick exchanging the wolf in the horse's form for the Firebird, and again the wolf escaped and met up with him later.

And so Ivan returned to his kingdom with Yelena, the horse, and the Firebird. He and the wolf parted ways, but when he lay down to sleep, his brothers found him. They had been confounded by the very first crossroads and so had done nothing. Jealous of their youngest brother's success, they killed Ivan in his sleep and cut his body into pieces. They agreed that one would marry Yelena, and the other would exchange the Firebird for half their father's kingdom.

But again the wolf felt sorry for Ivan, and so with the help of the water of life, he restored Ivan's body. Ivan awoke in time to ride once more on the wolf's back to stop the wedding and regain his share of the kingdom, while the wolf ate his treacherous brothers whole.

After the last words of the story, Yeva fingered the newly shaven shaft of the half-made arrow, listening for signs of life from her companion. He was even quieter than usual; Yeva thought he must be able to hear her heart pounding.

"So it is a happy ending for Ivan?"

Yeva nodded. "He kept the horse and Yelena and the Firebird, and inherited his father's kingdom as well."

"Why did you not tell me this story in the beginning?"

Yeva's fingers closed around the arrow shaft. "It is the most popular, but it's one of my least favorites," she admitted. "It doesn't end right."

"Why?"

She hesitated, trying to think of a way to explain. "Fairy tales are about lessons. Those who are virtuous and true are rewarded, while those who are wicked and greedy are punished. Ivan is said to be clever and resourceful but in this story he seems only greedy and careless. The wolf warns him over and over and Ivan never listens. And yet, Ivan never gets punished. The wolf helps him every time, and neither he nor the wolf have to pay for what they've done. In the end Ivan gets everything he wants and lives happily ever after."

Silence from her companion, though Yeva could hear the soft, rich sound of his breathing not far from her elbow. "You may call me Ivan," he said finally, surprising her.

"Because of that story?"

"Because your Ivan is not a hero."

Yeva turned toward the sound of the voice, arrow craft forgotten. She reached out toward where she guessed his hand or arm might be, fingers closing around fur.

"What are you doing?" The fur pulled away from her abruptly.

Her heart pounded against her barely healed ribs. "I was going to take your hand."

"No." The snarl had returned, but it no longer made her want to scramble back in fear.

"I would never betray you. I want only to see your face."

"You promised," came the voice, low and dangerous. "You gave me your word."

Yeva reached up for the blindfold anyway, only to have her arm knocked back so forcefully that it tingled, numb at her side. "I don't care," she said. "I've come to care for you, Ivan, or whoever you may be. I want to see your face."

She reached up again and this time something huge flung itself at her, knocking her back onto the ground. Her head struck hard enough to stun her, despite the carpet to cushion it. The knotted silk gave way under the blow.

"You gave your word," snarled the voice, his breath hot against her cheek. His weight, fur coat warmed by the fire, pinned her underneath him.

Her heart pounded with fear and longing both, knowing that Ivan's face was only a hand's breadth from hers. Yeva turned her head, the knot loosening yet more—and the silk slipped down from her eyes.

Inches from her face was a nightmarish visage, snarling fangs and red-gold eyes. She screamed, every muscle going rigid as she tried to struggle free, but claws dug into her skin on all sides, giving her no room to move. She stretched out with one arm anyway, ignoring the tearing pain of it, fingers brushing the hilt of her fletching knife.

"YOU GAVE US YOUR WORD." The voice was almost unrecognizable, the roar tangible against her face as the teeth flashed in the firelight. The claws tightened, piercing her skin all

over and causing her to cry out in pain and terror.

Yeva's hand closed around the knife, and with a scream she brought her arm up in an arc, sinking the knife to its hilt in the Beast's shoulder. Its roar of rage and pain overtook hers, and she let her arm fall again as the room spun into blackness.

Yeva woke once more in darkness, body cold and stiff. She dragged herself to her knees, her aching body prompting recognition—she was back in the cell. Her fingers found multiple puncture marks across her shoulders and chest and legs. The blindfold was gone, but she was in darkness again. She explored the confines of the cell by feel and found nothing, no manacle and chain, no blanket, and no tray—and no lamp. This time, the door was locked.

No fire, no blanket, no lamp; she had little heat to conserve, but little was better than none. She sank onto the floor and drew her knees up to her body, ignoring the way the movement sent aches screaming down her limbs. She dropped her head, clenching her teeth together.

I am locked in a cell, she said to herself, mind stuttering and unfocused as she tried to follow her father's advice, *with no food and no light and no hope of escape. And the one friend I had is the monster that killed my father.*

Her eyes burned, but when she lifted her head they were dry. Carefully she stretched out her legs one at a time, biting her lips when the movements tugged at sore muscles and punctured skin alike. Then her arms, then her back, then her neck. She had no weapons and no plan but she was quick, and maybe—just maybe—if the Beast thought she was wounded it would give her a chance to run.

She was doing her best to clean the dried blood from her skin when the door swung open, a huge blackness filling the space.

She had never seen the massive shadow before, but then, she had not been looking for it. She had been looking for a shape the size of a man.

"Get up," said the Beast.

Every muscle was rigid. The voice was still the one she knew, the musical bass with hints of wildness. But she recognized its ferocity now—and the voice no longer warmed her. Her bones were like ice.

"No."

"Get up or we kill you now."

Yeva clenched her jaw so tightly it ached. She dragged herself to her feet, playing up the soreness of her muscles and acting more stiffly than she felt.

"Come." The shadow threw the blindfold at her and then moved from the doorway.

Now was her chance. Its back was turned, and she could try to run. Yeva glanced at the lighter area of shadow that told of the empty corridor. *I am the captive of the monster who killed my father,* she thought with sudden crystal clarity.

She hadn't left her sisters behind for nothing. She hadn't tracked her father and discovered him dead, only to die herself the captive of a Beast.

She knew now why she was here. She would see the monster dead.

Yeva fell into step behind it, following it by smell and sound down the corridor. From the sound of its steps it was limping. Her knife had wounded it. She felt a surge of satisfaction so strong her ears rang with the triumph.

"Where are you taking me?" she whispered, lifting the blindfold into place and securing it behind her head.

Into the quiet came its despicable voice once more. "Training."

BEAST

We were wrong. There is no animal in her. The way she speaks to us now, so full of fury, is more human than anything we have experienced in many long years. Animals don't hate. That is the rightful domain of humanity.

It is better this way, that she see us for what we are. We are pleased. She is strong still, despite her illness, and skilled. She will do what we require of her, and it will be done. We will be free.

There is no more subterfuge, no more pretending at humanity. We do not have to provide her assistance or hide in the shadows.

We do not have to listen to her voice or her stories, we do not have to suffer her giving us a name as though we are a man. We do not have to feign feeling.

It is better this way. She has seen us and that, too, is freedom. It will go quickly now. We know this.

It is better.

It is better.

It is better.

EIGHT

YEVA FOLLOWED THE BEAST as it led her through a maze of corridors. She stumbled more than once, but the Beast did not offer its shoulder to guide her, and she did not ask. She thought there was a slight upward slant to their path, but she could not be sure until cold, clear light burst upon her, bright enough to see even through the blindfold.

The sensation of the heavy underground fell away, the air coming alive again with movement, smells, and distant sounds of life. The sun, pale and cold in the winter sky, was tangible on her skin.

For the briefest of moments Yeva forgot her fury, stumbling along through the snow and breathing the sharp freshness of the air as someone who'd been suffocating to death. But her relief faded with each step, as she struggled blindly in shin-deep snow. She focused on each breath, the stabbing of air in her lungs, trying to memorize how far they were going, what turns they made.

"Remove your blindfold."

Yeva halted, reality slamming back into her and jarring loose her half-formed mental image of where they were. She forced her hands to steady as they pulled the blindfold from her eyes. She stood, blinking, half blinded. The sky was overcast but the snow was brilliant enough that she could barely see.

At her feet she made out a familiar shape. Her father's bow, and next to it her quiver.

"That is your target." The Beast sat on its haunches like a huge wolf some distance from her, its immense body in no way diminished now that it was outside instead of in the confines of the corridors. Its thick, shaggy tail wrapped neatly around its body like a cat's.

"You will shoot the target, and if you succeed we will try at a farther distance."

Yeva reached down for the bow, not bothering to shift her gaze from the creature long enough to see what target it was indicating. She ought to have felt relief and triumph that it had provided her with a weapon—but she felt only ice. She fitted the grip to her palm, and though she turned her eyes toward the target, she saw nothing but a red mist descend over her vision.

"Shoot when you are ready."

Yeva drew in a deep breath as she nocked an arrow, mind calculating the arc between the target she was meant to hit and the Beast to the side. Not far. She blinked the haze from her eyes, the bloodlust rising in anticipation. Releasing the breath she was holding, she drew and twisted to the side to aim at the Beast, then released the arrow in one smooth motion.

The Beast barely moved. It lifted one paw and flicked the arrow aside in midair, where it buried itself in a tree.

Yeva stood staring and panting, the hands holding the bow

suddenly nerveless. It was impossible. Nothing could move that fast, animal or man. The Beast stared back at her, the red-gold of its eyes unperturbed.

"Again," it said, with no sign of the fury it had displayed when she'd pulled the blindfold away by the hearth.

For all its power, the bow would not help her. She let her arms fall and dropped the weapon into the snow at her feet.

"No."

The tip of the Beast's tail flicked. Irritation. "You will try it again, or die."

"Kill me, then." Yeva knew she ought to be afraid, but there was only room inside her for anger.

With careful deliberation the Beast rose to its feet, the size of it once again robbing Yeva of breath. It came toward her, each paw landing so softly that it made no sound in the snow. Yeva stood her ground, even when the Beast halted only inches from her face.

"You will do it again," it said in its low, dangerous growl, "or we will kill your family."

Yeva froze.

The Beast sat back down, the musky-sweet smell of its fur nearly overpowering in the frigid cold. "Ah," it said, bitter satisfaction coloring its otherwise emotionless voice. "Yes. You will do as we order from now on, or we will kill them all."

She had told him about each of them, about Lena's scolding and Asenka's twisted foot, Albe's clumsiness and well-intentioned gestures. She had described the trees around the cabin, how it nestled at the fork of a stream that ran to either side of it. She had *described the house.*

"Pick up the weapon." The Beast's eyes bored into hers.

Yeva's began to water from strain and cold, burning in the

freezing air. She stooped, not taking her gaze off the monster as she retrieved the bow. She pulled another arrow from the quiver at her feet, fingers closing around its shaft like she was clinging to her last hope of survival in a howling blizzard.

The Beast rose and turned its back, moving toward where it had been sitting when she removed her blindfold. Yeva lifted her arm to stab the arrow down into its spine.

"If you try to kill us again," said the Beast without turning around, "make certain you succeed."

Yeva froze again, her arm suddenly heavy as lead.

"For if you try and fail, your sisters will pay the price. You we will keep alive long enough to watch."

"Again."

The Beast's voice had become so familiar that Yeva's ears almost didn't register it. She felt it like a vibration deep in her chest, a stirring of the fury still surging through her veins. He brought her outside day after day to shoot at the same target, an old, gnarled tree with a blackened spot of rot the size of her fist. First he made her shoot at thirty paces, then forty, fifty. Her accuracy with her father's stiffer bow was not what it had been with her own, but she'd abandoned her lighter bow when she took up her father's weapons to pursue the Beast that killed him. As her strength improved, though, so did her aim with the old, heavy bow. Each day she was made to practice, and each night she was returned to the frigid, dark cell to eat cold rations and sleep. At first she stayed wakeful and restless, pacing, thoughts thrashing against the confines of this prison, seeking a way out—but as the days passed she could not help but fall into exhausted, dreamless sleep.

Instead of loosing the arrow she'd drawn in numb response

to the command, she lowered her bow and closed her eyes.

"I said *again*." The Beast's voice rose, and though there was no anger in it, Yeva could sense the quickening, the intensity of it. "Your aim today is worse."

"I cannot," Yeva said, dropping both bow and arrow into the well-trodden slurry of ice and snow at her feet. "My shoulders ache—I've had no rest, no time for my muscles to repair themselves."

The Beast—sitting, as it always did, just far enough away that she could not lunge for it—rose up from its haunches and narrowed its red-gold eyes. "The need for rest is a human weakness."

"And I'm human," Yeva snapped, exhaustion robbing her of good sense. For the moment, she couldn't bring herself to care if she angered her captor. For the moment, she forgot about the cabin nestled at the fork of the river, her sisters and her friend, her dogs, the lives she had to protect. For this moment she could only think of the bone-deep ache in her body and the certainty that she could not aim even one more arrow.

"An illusion," the Beast snarled. "You only imagine you need rest."

"Is it an illusion that my arrows cannot strike their target today?" Yeva braced her feet against the ground, determined not to give in to their desire to buckle beneath her and send her sprawling in the slush. "Is it imagination that yesterday I missed the tree entirely and lost one of my arrows?"

The Beast was silent, continuing only to stare at Yeva with that unnerving, unblinking animal gaze. She stood her ground, willing herself not to shiver. Days, maybe weeks, had passed and she still could not reconcile the animal eyes with the fact that its fanged mouth formed speech, that its lips could purse and flatten and curl around words like a man's.

Yeva drew her cloak around herself, stepping back from the bow. "You tell me I am training, but you do not tell me what I'm meant to be training for."

"Because you do not need to know yet."

Yeva clenched her jaw. "You insist I shoot at a dead tree, but unless it is some archery competition in some distant kingdom, this training is worthless. No target stands there, waiting to be shot at again and again."

The Beast didn't answer immediately, and if it were a man, Yeva would think him hesitant. But it only looked at her. Unblinking. Unmoved. Then, ponderously, it replied, "We have need of a hunter."

Yeva's skin prickled, and she suppressed the surge of anticipation threatening to show itself in her features. It was the first hint of an answer she'd ever received from the creature. "Why?"

"There is a certain quarry we require captured." The Beast's bass rumble of a voice was as unruffled as ever.

Yeva scanned the Beast's face for some time before realizing she was searching for some hint of its thoughts in its expression—some *human* hint. But this was no human. She swallowed hard on the white-hot anger that had sustained her since she learned the identity of her captor. "Capture your quarry yourself. You lay traps as efficiently as any hunter."

"We cannot." The Beast's face rippled for the space of a heartbeat. In the lupine features, the glint of teeth, the red-gold eyes—for the tiniest instant, Yeva recognized it. Frustration. Anger.

Helplessness.

"Why not?" Yeva whispered.

"Because we—" The Beast's words halted as suddenly as if its lungs had no air. Its brows drew in, brows Yeva hadn't noticed before. It shook its head, the movement traveling down the creature's body like a shiver until it hunkered low, belly nearly resting in the snow.

Perhaps, if she had not spent so much time in the cell telling stories, bringing to the surface the tales she'd heard as a child, or if she had not spent these last weeks the captive of a creature that could only exist in such tales, Yeva would not have had the thought that came next: *He cannot tell me, for he is under a spell.*

In every fairy tale there were rules. Even the monsters could not break them.

And where, except in fairy tales, did there exist talking beasts?

BEAST

We thought hatred would make it easier. That if she continued to believe we were her father's death, her fear and her fury would free us from our human side. We thought she would become no more than a tool, a weapon to be wielded, an arrow to be loosed from a bow.

We thought . . .

We thought too much.

Because while hatred is a fire only man feels, he does not hate the beast that comes in the night. Mankind fears it, fights it, drives it off, but he does not hate it. No one hates the bear, the wolf. They don't hate the wind or the snow. They don't hate death.

They hate each other.

NINE

YEVA HUDDLED IN THE corner of her cell, cloak drawn tightly about her as she sank into a half doze. The cold seeped from the stones into her body like poison, making her curl more against herself, despite the protests of her muscles. The strain of drawing her father's heavy bow day after day was tearing at the joints in her shoulders, ripping at a knot of tension between her shoulder blades that re-formed tighter and tighter each night she spent in the cold.

She knew she ought to stand, ought to pace the room and stretch and remain as limber as she could. And at first, she had done so each night. But she couldn't bring herself to move anymore. Perhaps if she tore a muscle so she could not draw the bow at all, the Beast would let her rest.

Her mind, as it often did during these dark, silent hours, tried to turn toward thoughts of her family. Of her sisters, and how they would worry; of Solmir, and how long he would continue to care for them; of how long it would take them all to believe she was dead. But she could not afford to think of them, for she could not imagine her home without her father there too, and remembering him was a stab of pain as real as her broken ribs, her aching muscles. She refused to think of them, of any of them. There would be time for grief later, once she had killed the Beast.

A sound beyond the door of her cell brought her sharply back to the present. It was nothing more than the barest whisper, but it was a sound she knew well, from days, weeks, maybe months ago. A sound that meant it was time to resume the story she'd been telling to her invisible ally, waiting in silence just beyond the door.

Her invisible ally. Yeva could have laughed at her blindness. Ally? He was always her captor.

Yeva shivered so violently a sound escaped her lips, a tiny moan snatched up by the hungry stones of the empty room.

"You said you required rest." The Beast's voice was quieter, and for a moment there were two faces in Yeva's mind: the one she'd imagined belonging to her friend, and the one she had seen snarling and roaring in front of her eyes when her blindfold fell away.

She didn't answer.

The Beast's footfalls came again, the soft scrape of his footpads against the stone. He was pacing in front of her door. "You require rest, and we require—" The pacing halted for a heartbeat, then resumed. "*I* require . . . I require talk."

It was the first time since she'd learned what he was that he hadn't referred to himself as "we." Yeva had always imagined there must be others in this place, servants or perhaps other creatures out of the old stories. Someone had cooked the potatoes she'd eaten. Someone had opened her pack and sorted through the medicine bundle, prepared trays for her, lit an oil lamp. The Beast could not have done it, not with the great velvety paws now pacing back and forth before the door.

But the two faces flashed again before Yeva's eyes, and suddenly she wasn't so sure. She swallowed, her throat dry. "Talk?"

"Yes."

Yeva's head spun, and she slipped one hand free of her cloak to press her cold fingertips to her temple. "You want me to *talk* to you? In exchange for rest?"

The footfalls ceased, and silence spread through the stones like the cold. Then the Beast's ferocity returned in the form of the reverberating growl that made some primitive part of Yeva's mind recoil and send urgent commands through her body to flee, hide, defend herself.

"Never mind," he snarled.

And the footsteps retreated, back into the silence and the dark, and Yeva was left alone.

"You may begin."

They were the same words the Beast used every day to signal that Yeva could remove her blindfold for the day's target practice. He always led her to the same spot, far enough from the building that held her cell that she could not see it, could see nothing but trees.

But when she pulled the silk down around her neck this time, it was different. The old, gnarled tree she'd used as a target was nowhere in sight, and the forest around her was new. She hadn't noticed how familiar the other clearing had become. She could see her tracks leading off through the snow, and the Beast's beside hers, the snow indistinct around his paw prints where his fur and his tail had swept it aside.

Her bow and quiver were at her feet as usual, but there was

no clear target. She hesitated, turning toward the Beast, who sat watching her as he always did. "I don't understand," she said slowly.

"You were correct." Only the tip of the Beast's tail moved, flicking side to side where it curled around his haunches. "Real prey does not stand still, waiting to be shot. Today you will hunt."

A spark jumped in Yeva's heart. She stooped to retrieve her father's bow from the snow without taking her eyes from the Beast. "What am I hunting?"

"Whatever you wish."

Yeva's fingers curled around the bow grip, feeling where the carving was suited to larger hands, hands that would never draw it again. "And what's to stop me from running?"

"I will be watching you."

Yeva straightened, feeling a frown crease her forehead. "You'll drive away the game," she protested. "They'll smell you, hear you. They'll know there's a predator after them."

The Beast's tail stirred again, the only outward sign of any impatience. "They will not know I am there."

"It happened when my father was hunting," Yeva argued, hand tightening still more around the bow. The fingers of her drawing hand itched to reach for an arrow—the instinct could not be reasoned with, or convinced of the futility of trying to fire upon the creature.

"No." The Beast's reply was curt, the red-gold eyes the only color besides his fur in the snow-covered wood. But as he stared back at her, he seemed to soften, something about the pupils changing, the roundness of the eyes elongating into features more like a man's. He blinked, then dropped his gaze from hers. "He drove the game away himself."

Yeva opened her mouth to protest, but a flash of memory prevented her from speaking. She saw her father bursting into the house after weeks in the forest, shedding snow as he stomped here and there, wild-eyed and impatient. The same madness that had him shoving her to the ground could have swallowed his skill and stealth as well.

Then a thought stirred, falling into place. "You were watching him," she whispered. "In the wood, before he died."

"Yes."

"You have need of a hunter."

"Yes."

A surge of anger so hot she could not swallow it down flooded Yeva's mouth with the bitter taste of metal, and her hand shook where it gripped her father's bow. "He was the best hunter in this country, perhaps in any country. You were following him, you could see his skill—why kill him? Why tear him to pieces and leave him for scavengers to pick over?"

The Beast's head snapped back up, eyes fixing on Yeva as they narrowed. He didn't answer, but instead went still. Even his flicking tail stopped moving, leaving him so statue-frozen that the snowflakes caught in his fur, quivering with each beat of his heart.

"Why?" gasped Yeva, her voice cracking, passion making her vision blur and body shake. *"Answer me!"*

The Beast abruptly rose from his haunches and stalked a few paces, tail sweeping long troughs in the snow behind him. By the time he turned, Yeva felt she must have imagined that she'd seen something other than his bestial nature—his wolflike head hung low, gap-jawed, as a predator might scent prey on the wind. "Why we do anything is no concern of yours," the Beast snarled, the words distorted as though speaking around his fangs had suddenly become difficult. "You may begin."

Time seemed to slow, as if caught by the roar of Yeva's blood rushing past her ears, held back by the tension singing through every muscle. Her body stirred before her thoughts did, as if the hand reaching for an arrow from the quiver were giving the commands, and not her heart. She'd fitted the arrow to the string and stepped back on her left foot and drawn the bow before the impulse traveled deep enough to reach her thoughts, and by that time all she could think was *I will kill him, kill him, kill him.*

And by the time she turned toward the Beast, he was gone.

Yeva stood panting, bow still drawn, shoulders shaking with effort and breath steaming the air. The spot where he'd been was trampled, its outer edge more distinct with paw prints, the center only flattened snow and mud. There were no tracks leading away. And as she stood there, even his smell, that strange, ferocious musk, faded into the frost until all that was left was the sting of winter in Yeva's nose while she struggled to catch her breath.

She lowered the bow slowly, the tip of the arrow inscribing an arc through the snow as she moved. *If you try to kill us again,* the Beast had told her, *make certain you succeed.* He'd vanished before she could make that attempt and test the threat behind those words.

Woodenly, jerkily, Yeva slung the bow over her shoulder and slipped the arrow back into the quiver, gathering herself to move. She didn't know whether the Beast's disappearance was magic or skill, whether he could will himself invisible or if he was simply so in tune with the forest that he could use it to mask even his scent. It didn't matter. Either way his ability was greater than hers, and she had no choice but to do as he'd ordered.

So she would hunt.

Yeva looked up at the sky, what she could see of it through the spindly black arms of the trees. The sun's position was concealed by a thick gray blanket of clouds, but she thought one spot of the sky seemed brighter than the rest. She'd been unconscious when the Beast brought her to the cell, and she'd been blindfolded each time she was led away, so she could not know where in the forest she was. But her father's hunting cabin was north through the wood from the town where they'd once lived, and Yeva knew the Beast's lair had to be farther into the dark heart of the forest than the cabin. So she chose the direction she thought might be south—and struck out.

Despite the weeks of captivity, she fell into her old habits like she'd fall into a comfortable bed—the long-legged strides that ate up the ground without overtaxing her, the tuning of her ears to register each new sound and file it away as part of the background canvas. Compared to the silence of her cell the forest was alive with color and sound—the shading of the snow beneath an old gnarled tree, ranging from palest ice blue to deeper lilac, told of a hollow there, and a burrow beneath. The stirring out of the corner of her eye of a branch, far above her, betrayed the path of a squirrel leaping treetop to treetop. The harsh cry of a distant jay warned his fellows of an intruder, and told Yeva to move more carefully, more quietly.

And all around, crossing this way and that like trails on a map of the invisible roads of the forest, were animal tracks. Some were fresh, like the long hopping troughs left by rabbits, or the delicate holes of dainty-pawed foxes trotting circles around their territories. Others were older, half filled with snow blown across them, more difficult to read.

Yeva's nose caught a faint, quick breath of a musky scent and her heart jumped, thoughts immediately conjuring an image of the Beast—but this scent was different, duller and more familiar. A few moments of searching uncovered a tree with long rents in its bark and tufts of brown-black fur caught in the splinters. Somewhere nearby a bear was hibernating with her young. Yeva could read that signpost as clearly as if it were spelled out with letters, and she gave the area a wide berth.

Time passed, impossible to track without a clear view of the sun—an hour, maybe two, and the back of Yeva's mind began to prickle, summoning thoughts that more and more she couldn't ignore. *Where is the Beast? It's been hours since I saw or smelled even a hint of him.*

And then, *Perhaps I can run. . . .*

He'd promised that he could disguise his presence from the animals whose senses were so much sharper than Yeva's, and it was true that the only creatures startled from burrow and den were driven out by Yeva's steps, not some unseen predator's. But did that mean he was telling the truth? Or did it mean that he was no longer following her?

There is something out there, her father had whispered, as he stared mad-eyed and wild at the fire in the hearth. *Something cunning. Tracking me.*

Yeva, alone in the forest, shivered because she knew she wasn't alone.

Despite the hairs lifting on the back of her neck, her heart seemed to lift too, surrounded by the world she knew, the world she loved. Though she was still a captive, for these few hours she was free, and freer than she'd ever been on her hunting forays from her father's cabin. Something about this world, the Beast's valley, made her life at home seem like a far-distant memory. Her steps came easier, and the ache in her ribs seemed to ease as she breathed the fresh winter air. The tiniest tendril of a feeling flickered in her heart, licking out like flames to warm her freezing toes and aching fingers. She felt . . . at *home.*

She came across the fresh tracks of a solitary deer almost by accident, her thoughts preoccupied. She had rarely hunted deer on her own before—her bow was not heavy enough to consistently puncture a deer's thicker hide. But her father's bow was. She pointed her boots in the direction of the deer's tracks and set off.

Without knowing when the last snow had fallen, or whether there had been recent wind to disturb the top layer of snowfall, it was impossible to know how long ago the deer had passed this way. It could have been an hour, or days. But she had no other choice than to follow where the tracks led, and hope it would bring her some success. By whatever measure the Beast was using.

She'd been following the trail for an hour or two when a sound, distinct from the background tapestry of noises she'd cataloged, interrupted her. She paused midstep, one hand reaching for the bow over her shoulder, and listened.

Something was coming toward her, and coming fast. Too large for fox or rabbit, but too small for bear or boar. The cracking, crashing noise of underbrush told of a creature with great, leaping strides, and as the seconds stretched, she heard labored breath coming in great renting gasps.

A wolf?

Yeva grabbed for the bow, pulling it off her shoulder and nocking an arrow to the string in a second. She braced herself, facing the sound of the oncoming animal, eyes searching the frozen wood.

There. A torrent of motion, a furrow of flying snow and twigs. She caught a brief flash of fur amid the underbrush, not the shaggy gray she'd expected, but a pale gold. A wheezy yelp split the air, and Yeva froze, confusion washing through where certainty and had been moments before. *That's no wolf, that's . . .*

The creature burst out of the bushes and flung itself at Yeva, knocking her backward into the snow. All was fur and yelps and whines and a tongue bathing her face, and freezing-cold paw pads stabbing at her gut, her thighs, a tail beating at her knees, her face, as the creature turned and turned and barked and panted hot breath on her skin.

"Doe-Eyes!" Yeva cried, her voice tearing, grief and love and relief and fear tangling in her throat. How long must her dog have been searching for her? And in the kind of snow and cold she was not bred to withstand. "Oh, Doe-Eyes—you bad dog, you wonderful, terrible thing—"

Then Doe-Eyes stomped on her chest in her enthusiasm to get as close to her mistress as possible, and Yeva's ribs, still only partially healed, seared white-hot. Yeva let out a shriek of pain before she could stop herself.

And then the Beast was there.

He came from nowhere, snarling rage and fury, fangs bared and fur bristling with readiness. He leaped toward Yeva, turning her yelp of pain to a scream of genuine terror, and she pulled herself in tightly to shield herself from the blow she knew was coming—

And then she opened her eyes to find the Beast standing over her, growling and shaking himself, staring down Doe-Eyes, who was now only a pace or two from her, all four legs planted in the snow, her own teeth bared.

She felt the Beast gathering himself to attack, felt it like she could feel her own intentions, and she threw herself forward, grabbing for his shoulder, too suddenly fearful to realize it was the first time she'd touched him since the blindfold fell away and she saw who—what—he was. Too fearful to process what she'd seen—that he was protecting her.

"No!" she cried, and felt his muscles bunch and halt under her hand. "No! She's my friend—don't—"

The Beast paused, the lupine head turning so he could fix his eyes on Yeva once more. The pupils, dilated with the rush of the hunt, suddenly contracted in the snowy glare as the fight left his gaze.

"I—" he said, and then Doe-Eyes leaped.

She was a fraction of his size, and built for speed, not for fight—her long slender limbs let her vault as high as his shoulder, her teeth sinking into the flesh there and gripping. Her eyes were frantic, wild, full of fury toward the Beast she thought was attacking her mistress.

The Beast gave a little roar, no more than a sluggish ripple of annoyance, and gave his great body a shake that dislodged the dog and sent her flying. Yeva's heart shriveled, then snapped as Doe-Eyes collided with a tree and dropped into a heap in the snow, unmoving.

BEAST

I moved without thought.

Instinct. Animal. Nothing more. The actions of a predator defending its kill, its territory, its property.

And yet we did not decide to act, I did. Alone. I heard her voice, her stories, her softness as she spoke of her family, and her iron as she spoke of me—I heard her scream, and I moved without thought.

We need her skills. That is all. Only she can free us from this torment, and that is what we were protecting. Our freedom. Our lives. Our hope.

And yet . . .

TEN

"NO!" YEVA SCRAMBLED FROM beneath the Beast, who was still standing over her. Ignoring him, she lurched to her feet and sprinted to the spot where Doe-Eyes had fallen.

Her dog lifted her head, and Yeva gasped for a breath as her heart started once more. Doe-Eyes whined at her, tail thumping once in pathetic appeal. She tried to stand, fumbling in the snow and yelping in pain.

"No—stay." Yeva pressed her hand against the dog's head, firm and warm. "Lie down, don't move." That she was hurt somewhere was obvious, but Yeva could not see where. If she was bleeding, it was internal.

She felt the Beast move up behind her, but could not find any spare feeling for him—her attention was on Doe-Eyes.

The Beast rumbled once, an echo of the growling roar he gave when he reappeared. "She will die," he said, voice as still and calm and emotionless as it ever had been.

Yeva whirled, the movement kicking up snow. "No! She will *not*."

The Beast dropped onto his haunches, staring at her with those disconcerting eyes, wrapping his tail around himself and tilting his head like a great cat, unconcerned. "Why should it matter?"

"Because I love her," Yeva snapped back. "She's mine. She came here searching for me. She's my responsibility. Do you not understand loyalty? Love? Do you have no concept of anything other than the hunt?"

The Beast did not answer, continuing to stare, continuing to sit, continuing to exist in that hateful way, as though everything Yeva said was of no consequence. As though everything she thought or felt or did was a minor irritation to him, an annoyance to be borne and dismissed.

Yeva spat a wordless cry at him and turned back to Doe-Eyes, reaching out to run a light hand down her dog's body, watching her and trying to see if any spot caused her pain.

The Beast's voice came again after a moment. "Her leg is broken."

Yeva glanced over her shoulder. "How can you know that?"

The Beast blinked. "How can you not?"

Yeva ran her hand down first one foreleg, then the other— then jumped as Doe-Eyes yelped, her tongue lolling out immediately after, as if apologizing for having felt the pain at Yeva's touch. "That's the only injury?" she asked, eyes still on her dog.

"Yes," said the Beast.

"You said she would die," Yeva protested, stroking her dog's head, doing her best to keep her still.

"She will. In this cold, unable to walk or feed herself, she will die of starvation or exposure. It is . . . it is merciful to end her suffering." The Beast paused, his gaze troubled again, that same look as before, like a man would furrow his brow. "I will do it if you wish."

Yeva's hands trembled, and she kept one on Doe-Eyes as she stared at the Beast. One part of her longed to scream at him for his callous dismissal of life, to rail against the cold heartlessness of his offer to kill her beloved Doe-Eyes, her only friend in this bleak wood. But there was another part of her, the same corner of her heart that could read the scratches in a tree and tell the difference between the rustle of a rabbit and that of a squirrel. And that part of her heart ached with sudden understanding.

In the wild, in *this* wild, it would be merciful to kill a wounded animal. And more merciful still not to make her be the one to deliver the killing blow to her own companion.

But what could a Beast know of mercy?

Yeva drew in a shaking breath. "How far are we from—from your home? I will carry her."

The Beast paused, either calculating the distance or hesitating to share the information, Yeva did not know. "You cannot carry her if you are blindfolded."

"No," agreed Yeva, gazing back at him.

The Beast's tail twitched, darting one way, then the other. "It is not far," he said finally. "Follow me."

Doe-Eyes was not a small dog, and though the weeks of drawing her father's bow had strengthened her shoulders, Yeva still staggered under her dog's weight after the first hour. The Beast did not offer any help, and Yeva did not expect him to—if she ever drew too near him, Doe-Eyes would stiffen in her arms, legs flailing about as her instincts told her to get her feet on the ground in order to defend herself and her mistress.

After casting a few glances her way, the Beast stalked on ahead of them, as if he were frustrated by Yeva's slow pace. But as he moved, his bulk trampled the snow ahead of Yeva's steps, making her journey considerably easier. Though he clearly had some way of traveling through the forest without leaving a sign, now he walked like any common beast, forging a path ahead.

Now and then Yeva set Doe-Eyes down in order to rest her back, and the dog would hobble a short distance on three legs. Though Yeva knew she must be in considerable pain, Doe-Eyes kept gazing up at her with that gap-jawed smile of hers, tongue lolling out, eyes seeking assurance.

The Beast led them up a long slope, a slope Yeva did not remember descending while blindfolded. She assumed he must have led her away by some other route, and was now taking a more direct path. Up ahead the trees thinned, telling Yeva that they were approaching a ridgeline overlooking one of the many valleys in the forest. She set Doe-Eyes down again in anticipation of pausing at the top of the ridge, and was unable to prevent the groan that escaped her lips. The bones in her spine popped in protest as she straightened, and she pressed her hands into the small of her back to stretch the muscles.

When she opened her eyes again the Beast had stopped. He was watching her. That unblinking stare was still unnerving, but the rush of terror that ran through Yeva every time the massive creature looked her way had dwindled to a trickle. He was still frightening, alien, unpredictable—but she found she could return his stare now without shivering.

As if sensing her thoughts, the Beast broke his eyes away first and looked toward the thinning trees. "My home is in the . . . valley," he said haltingly, as though he had to pause to remember the right words. "You will not ask me questions."

Yeva knit her brows and took a step toward the ridge. "What do you mean? Why would I—"

"Did I not just tell you there were to be no questions?" The Beast's voice quickened with irritation.

"You did. But I didn't agree to your terms."

The Beast drew himself up on his haunches. "There is no negotiation. I gave you an order."

"How nice for you." Yeva clicked her tongue at Doe-Eyes, who was sniffing furiously at a patch of yellow snow left by a passing fox. The dog left the spot reluctantly, falling into hobbling step beside her mistress as Yeva set off for the ridge.

She felt the Beast's consternation, heard it in the wordless rumble of protest as she passed him. She regretted moving ahead instantly—it had been some time since she'd had to break her own trail through the snow, and she'd grown used to the trampled path left in the Beast's wake. But she wouldn't let the creature see her struggle. She fought her way through the snow, keeping her eyes down.

It wasn't until a flicker of light caught her eye that she looked up and found a valley opening below her. The overcast sky was clearing in spots, letting trickles of sunlight out to wash the vista ahead. A river ran through the valley, only a narrow ribbon of treeless white expanse in the frozen winter. The trees thinned off to one side of the valley, suggesting a meadow or marsh beneath its blanket of snow, and on the far side stood a ridge of small mountains, barely high enough for their peaks to clear the tree line and stand stark white in the patches of sun.

But none of this was what held Yeva's gaze. Because in the

bottom of the valley, straddling the river nestled in the foothills, was a castle.

Yeva stood stunned, dimly aware of Doe-Eyes leaning against her legs. The castle sat dark and gray, as much a part of the landscape as the trees or the distant mountains. Its peaked roofs were coated with snow, and from this distance it hardly seemed real—like a picture of a castle that, as soon as Yeva moved, would betray itself as fake.

The Beast waded past her, his great body low to the ground and churning up the snow like a plow in the fields. He did not pause to admire the sight, or to take in Yeva's shock, but rather began making his way down into the valley. Yeva stood until Doe-Eyes gave the tiniest of whines, and jerked her out of her confusion. She swallowed hard, stooped to pick up the dog, and moved to follow the Beast.

BEAST

We will not break the terms of our sentence. We cannot explain, or we risk remaining trapped together for the rest of eternity. But the girl's face, when we turn to look at her, carries a thousand questions, and she is clever. We must tread with care.

Do you not understand loyalty, she asked us, or love?

We wanted to answer: no. They are human concerns, and we have not been human for centuries. We are, we have always been, beast.

But the question hangs on the air like the smell of a coming storm, and we fear the change the storm brings.

ELEVEN

AS THEY NEARED THE castle, Yeva saw that it was in terrible disrepair. Crumbling stone, cracked by centuries of freezing and thawing, was covered in frozen lichen, and many of the great carved gargoyles lining the eaves were broken or missing altogether. The windows were dark and cold, and many of them shattered, leaving only carved stone frames around the blackness beyond.

The palace looked like it had been abandoned for centuries.

Most of the building lay on the other side of the river, with a gatehouse on the near side, connected to the rest by a bridge. Though Yeva hesitated at the idea of crossing such an ancient, crumbling structure, the Beast continued on ahead without pausing.

If it can hold his weight, Yeva thought dubiously, *it must be able to hold mine.* But then, the Beast seemed able to make himself as light as air when he chose, to leave no prints in the snow and make no sound as he moved.

Yeva walked very, very carefully.

On the other side of the bridge, a section of the palisade lining the walk had crumbled away, and Yeva saw a well-trodden path leading down toward the river. Churned mud and snow led to a hole in the rock foundation supporting the castle, some dank hollow or cave. A home befitting a Beast. Yeva half expected the Beast to turn and lead her down the slope, but instead he set his shoulder to one of the great doors at the far end of the courtyard and shoved until the rotting wood groaned open wide enough for them to slip through.

The only light inside came from a row of grime-coated windows high above, centuries of cobwebs and dust turning the pale winter sunlight the color of dusk. The Beast kept moving without pause, able to see in the dark with those animal eyes, but Yeva stumbled when her feet encountered a broken stone in the floor. She gasped and nearly dropped Doe-Eyes, who yelped as Yeva's grip shifted and she jostled the injured leg.

Yeva heard the Beast stop, no more than a change in the way the air moved. She couldn't see him, only a shift in the shadows ahead. "Wait here," he said, and before Yeva could answer, he was gone.

Yeva dropped to her knees on the cold stone floor, uncertain what the Beast meant her to wait for, but grateful for the rest. Doe-Eyes settled beside her and laid her head in her lap, and though it was too dark, Yeva saw in her mind the look the dog was giving her: eyes rolled up, seeking Yeva's face, tail thumping in the dust. She stroked Doe-Eyes's ears, and stared up toward the thin gray light trickling down from the windows high above.

The castle was not large—or rather, it was far larger than any building Yeva had ever seen, including the baron's estate, but it was far smaller than the castles Yeva had seen depicted in paintings and tapestries. The castles of old stories were vast and sprawling, with fantastical turrets and buttresses that stretched toward the sky. This one was more compact, lacking the ornamentation and fancy of the ones in pictures. *This was the sort of castle that could have been defended in a siege,* she thought.

The Beast was gone so long that Yeva considered lying down right there on the stones to sleep. But just as she started to lean over, the shadows ahead of her moved abruptly. A flame sprang to life—a lantern, unshielded. Yeva could not quite see how the Beast managed it without fingers, and yet there he stood, sitting on his haunches, the lantern hanging from one massive paw.

"Here," he said, blank-faced.

Yeva pulled herself up, getting to her feet with some difficulty, as her abused muscles had stiffened. She reached out for the lantern, willing her arm to steady despite its desire to tremble, so close to the Beast's claws.

The Beast turned again without speaking, and led Yeva across what must have once been a grand foyer. The lantern only cast enough light for Yeva to see the floor beneath her feet and the barest hint of the room around her, but she spied a great stone staircase off to the right, so wide she could have lain down across each step many times over. She got the impression of vast tapestries against the wall, and she veered off in that direction a little, keeping one eye on the Beast as she lifted the lantern higher.

She saw only faded cloth and dust, too old and too dirty to reveal any images underneath, and a twinge of disappointment took the place of her curiosity.

"This way," said the Beast, voice quickening in that way it did when he was annoyed.

Yeva saw that he was standing before a smaller door that

stood ajar, opening onto a narrow staircase leading down. Yeva
knew what lay in the dark under-places of castles. She drew back,
and Doe-Eyes, hobbling at her side, dropped to her haunches.

The Beast halted when she did, and Yeva saw the gleam of his
eyes catching the lamplight.

"Don't make me go back to that cell," Yeva blurted, before
she had even fully resolved to speak. "You bring me out, you
make me hunt for you, but you keep me locked away where I
cannot see the sky, cannot tell what weather has come and gone
in the night—how can I know how old a set of tracks is if I
don't know when the last snow fell, or whether the wind has been
strong enough to stir snow from the tree branches? How can I
learn the forest well enough to track its creatures if I never know
where I am, or where I'm going?"

The words came out in a rush, her voice rising with the
strength of her plea. She could not live out the rest of this
existence, however long it took before the Beast was done with
her, in a locked room of stone.

"I'll die in there—the part of me that hunts will die,
anyway—and I'll be useless to you. And Doe-Eyes—she wasn't
built for cold. Her leg will ache in there, with no warmth, and
she'll never heal properly if I can't see her to treat her and make
her well. I—"

"The dungeons," said the Beast calmly, interrupting her, "are
through the door on the other side of the hall."

The rest of Yeva's breath fell out in a stuttering gasp,
punctuated by the wavering light of the lamp dangling from her
hand.

"My home," the Beast went on, "when I choose to live there,
is down here."

Yeva swallowed. *Here*, where the Beast had been leading her.

She shifted her weight, her tired muscles trembling and making the flame dance and shiver. "All right, then."

The narrow stairway curled around and around, and as they descended farther into the depths beneath the castle, the air grew colder and heavier. Yeva began to shiver in earnest—not from exhaustion or fear, but from a cold more penetrating than the bitter wind outside. This cold crept in from everywhere, chilling all of her, even her bones, despite her cloak and thick wool undergarments. Doe-Eyes managed the stairs with great difficulty, but it was too narrow for Yeva to carry her, and even if she could, she needed her hands to keep from slipping. The steps were worn low in their centers, bowing inward by centuries of feet carving smooth hollows in the stone that threatened to send Yeva's boots sliding.

The staircase ended in a narrow hallway with doors on either side. Yeva guessed that this area must have once housed the castle's servants, and she wondered again how the Beast came to live here; whether the castle was in ruins when he found it, or whether—and this made her shiver all the more—he was the reason the castle had been abandoned.

The Beast halted in front of a door a few down from the staircase, and lifted one paw for the latch. Yeva raised the lantern, determined this time to see the trick of it, how he mastered human tasks with nothing but his claws—but despite the light on him and the door latch, her eyes couldn't quite grasp what they were seeing. Her gaze kept trying to slide from what was happening. However he managed it, he opened the latch as easily as she would have done, and pushed the door open.

Beyond, the room was dim and cold. But as Yeva stepped forward, her boots hit carpet. She paused. Below her feet was a lush red rug, and as she looked around, she realized it was the room the Beast had brought her to when she was ill. It was furnished with dilapidated, mismatched furniture, obviously from various rooms of the castle. Some of it seemed in better care, if faded, while other items, like a crooked, battered table that stood on three legs and a stack of moldering books in place of its fourth leg, wouldn't have been fit for a hovel. The floor was covered by overlapping rugs of clashing colors. Along one wall was a fireplace, and though it held only ashes and blackened charcoal, next to its hearth was a stack of feathers and hafts—Yeva's arrow-making supplies. And there, some distance from them, was her fletching knife. Its blade was stained rusty brown, and with a jolt, Yeva remembered stabbing it down into the Beast's shoulder as he railed at her for removing her blindfold.

You gave us your word, he'd roared. At the time, she'd been too terrified to think. But now, as the Beast stood aside while she explored the room, she wondered at the depth of his fury. He scarcely seemed to notice her stabbing him, but the betrayal, the breaking of her word, sent him into such a fury that the memory of it made Yeva's body grow colder still.

Yeva halted in the center of the room, trying not to think of the faded blue divan a few paces away, and how easy and lovely it'd be to drop onto its moldering cushions and close her eyes. But the Beast was still there, and as exhausted as she was, that primitive part of her brain would never be able to dismiss the presence of a predator in the room with her.

"You may remain here," the Beast said coolly, "as long as you give your word that you will not try to escape, and that you will not try again to kill us. Remember that we know where your family lives, that we have watched them, that we could kill them at any time."

Yeva swallowed hard, this time forcing her hand to still.

"I give you my word," she said slowly, "that I will not run away."

"You lied to us once," the Beast said softly.

"Perhaps I regret doing so." Yeva's own voice quieted. For it was true. Maybe, if she had not let curiosity get the better of her, she would never have learned the identity of her captor, and she could have gone on in ignorance, telling stories to her friend by the fire.

The Beast was silent for a long time, so long that Yeva's eyes began to play tricks on her. His form melted back into the shadows cast by the lantern, and she began to wonder if he was even still there. When he spoke again, she nearly jumped.

"You promised not to run," he murmured. "You did not promise not to try to kill me."

"No," Yeva agreed. "I didn't."

The Beast stood in silence again for a few seconds. Then came the oddest, most unexpected of sounds—a bass rumble, a quick burst of rich velvet, lacking the somber chill his voice usually carried.

He was *laughing.*

Before Yeva could react, the Beast was gone.

BEAST

She believes she can kill us. She wants to avenge her father's death, letting hatred and fury fuel her. Her word not to run comes easily because she has no desire to flee—not until we are dead.

She has a fire to her that we have not seen, have not felt, in a long time. That the fire wants to consume us makes no difference— that passion will make her stronger, faster. More useful to us. That is all that matters. Fire cannot hurt us.

And yet, when we light her a lantern, there is a moment as we watch the wick flare in the darkness—a moment in which I want to touch the flame.

Just to see if I can still be burned.

TWELVE

YEVA DID WHAT SHE could for Doe-Eyes. After lighting a fire in the cold hearth from the flame of the oil lamp, she broke an arrow haft in two for splints, which she bound to the broken leg with strips torn from her tunic. If she'd had the medicines she'd brought with her, she could use the cypress salve she'd applied on her own ribs, but she had no way of summoning the Beast to return. Nor did she feel like pressing her luck with him further.

As Doe-Eyes heaved a noisy sigh and rolled onto her back, all four paws in the air and belly exposed to the fire, Yeva leaned against the edge of the divan and closed her eyes.

That laugh.

Beasts did not laugh. True, Doe-Eyes smiled at her—but it was not a smile the way most humans would recognize it. Yeva knew she was seeing happiness when her dog's mouth fell open and the tongue lolled out, and it translated into a smile in her mind because she knew Doe-Eyes, knew each twitch of her tail or flick of her ears, and what they meant. But the laugh from the

Beast required no translation, no learned interpretation of his body language.

The laugh was *human*.

It was one thing to wish to hunt down and destroy the animal that killed her father. It was entirely another to think that what had killed him was, in some small way, human. It made his death something else.

It made his death murder.

A rabid animal, a man-eater, deserves nothing more than a swift death to spare anyone else the fate her father had suffered. But a murderer?

That deserved a kind of vengeance that turned Yeva's heart to ice.

Behind her closed eyes, images played like light through colored glass. Fragmented, flashing so quickly from one to the other that her thoughts became as scattered as the light itself. The Beast's snarling maw, inches from her. The calm with which he spoke of her family's torture and death if she betrayed him. The anguish in his eyes when the blindfold fell away and she saw his face. The swath of trampled snow carving a path for her to carry her wounded dog with greater ease.

At some point the still images became moving scenes of things remembered and things imagined, and soon the scenes became dreams, and Yeva slept.

Yeva was awakened the next morning by Doe-Eyes's urgent whining and a cold nose digging into the crook of her elbow. Though she could not tell in the windowless room whether it was morning, she felt like she'd been asleep for days. But as she rubbed at her eyes, she saw that her bow was missing, and her quiver of arrows. He'd taken her weapons. Even the fletching knife that had lain on the floor ever since she'd stabbed him was gone, leaving only a spatter of old blood where it had been.

Doe-Eyes whined again and Yeva slipped off the divan and into a crouch, assuming she'd see her favoring the injured leg. Instead Doe-Eyes gave an awkward, urgent sideways hobble, which, after a moment of confusion, Yeva recognized with a burst of clarity.

"You'll have to hold on," Yeva told the dog, thinking with dread of the long flight of stairs required to reach the outdoors. "And promise not to wet my tunic if I carry you, because I only have the one."

The Beast had not forbidden her to leave the room, only to flee the castle entirely, but her hand trembled anyway as she reached for the latch. It gave under her touch, and the door swung outward. Doe-Eyes hobbled past her, galloping in a stiff-legged, slipping way up the staircase ahead of Yeva. At least she would not have to try to carry her and the lantern.

Yeva felt as wobbly as her dog as she followed in Doe-Eyes's wake. She found that the staircase was not as long as she'd remembered from the day before, that exhaustion had stretched the distance out in her memory. Doe-Eyes remembered the way, and as soon as Yeva opened the door at the top of the staircase, Doe-Eyes scrambled forth, making for the massive front doors.

They still stood open, and a faint spray of snow blown in by the wind glistened in the sunlight cast upon the floor. She had not noticed yesterday that the floor was a polished marble, smooth except for the places where the stone had cracked after centuries of the castle settling and shifting. Doe-Eyes bolted toward the sunlight, and Yeva trailed after her.

The clouds had cleared in the night, and the glare of the sun on the snow was so blinding Yeva had to stand just inside the doors, holding her arm across her eyes to shade them and squint to track her dog's progress. Doe-Eyes went only a few paces down the outer wall of the castle before dropping into a crouch to relieve herself.

Yeva turned her face toward the brilliant morning. The sun was only a few handspans above the far mountains, but it was still bright enough reflected on the snow to make her eyes water and nose itch with the urge to sneeze. She wiped at her eyes and scanned the valley, tracking the river from where it passed under the bridge before her, on toward where it vanished in the trees to the west.

There was no sign of the Beast. No new tracks led from the door except those Doe-Eyes had just made, and though it was difficult to tell new tracks from old, Yeva didn't think any of the churned frozen slush leading down to the cave was fresh. So where had the Beast spent the night?

Somewhere in the castle, Yeva knew, she'd find whatever she needed to survive. Kitchens, latrines, perhaps even some room not too badly decayed for her to sleep in. The Beast might prefer to live deep underground, but Yeva could not bear the thought of spending one more night with the weight of all that stone over her head. And if nothing else, it would be impractical to bring Doe-Eyes up and down those stairs every time she needed to go out.

Yeva decided to explore. A part of her shrank from the idea, uncertain what horrors she might uncover in a castle prowled by a cursed Beast. But the rest of her thrilled to the thought, curiosity settling in and overwhelming her fear.

Because there was another reason to search the corners of this crumbling, ancient castle. Somewhere, somehow, she would find the key to destroying this Beast. He was too fast and too strong for axes or bows, but she would find a way. She *would* discover the secret to killing him.

Now that her urgency had eased, Doe-Eyes was moving much more stiffly on her wounded leg. But Yeva could not order the dog to stay put. Whenever she tried, Doe-Eyes would drop down onto her haunches, tail wagging furiously—and then, as soon as Yeva turned her back to leave the great foyer, she'd hear Doe-Eyes's toenails click-clicking against the marble and then feel her hot breath on the backs of her calves.

"Fine," Yeva told her finally, in fond exasperation. "You can come along. But don't complain to me when your leg hurts tonight."

Doe-Eyes only grinned at her, hobbling along, lolling tongue jouncing with every step. In truth, Yeva was glad for the company.

She kept her explorations to the ground floor for Doe-Eyes's sake. She found room after room of faded tapestries and grand marble floors. One room held piles of rusted, ancient armor scattered at regular intervals—a display room, a decorative armory. Another room held a dining table so long Yeva could not have thrown a butter dish from one end to the other. Some of the chairs were missing—others were broken into pieces, or rent apart, their cushions spilling stuffing like entrails onto the floor.

She came to another hall, lined on one side with what had once been a series of stained-glass windows, most of which were smashed now. Snow had blown in through the empty stone frames, lying in wispy drifts in front of each window. Yeva crossed over toward one that still had some pieces of the original glass clinging to its edges. She reached up to trace her fingers over the vivid gold tips of a bird's wing. There'd been no illustrations in her father's book of tales, but Yeva had always imagined the Firebird this way: wings outstretched, golden, shining even in the palest winter light. She felt a sudden pang of loss for the images the windows had once held.

Her boots squeaked against the blown snow as she turned, but the sound made her pause. True, her steps had crunched against the snow, but not on the broken glass that should have been scattered everywhere if centuries of storms had blown the windows in. Yeva crept to the edge and gripped the window frame as she leaned out, peering down below. There was only the empty expanse of a snow-covered courtyard. But she knew that somewhere beneath the drifts of white would be the remains of these windows. Because someone had broken them from the inside.

Yeva left the snowy hall and moved on. She found the latrines, and the kitchen, covered in cobwebs, each pot and dish dull with dust and age. She found no bedrooms, for they must have been on the second or third floor, but she did stumble across enough sitting rooms with moldering divans and sofas that she could certainly make a bed for herself if she could stand the smell of mildew and age. Given a choice between the cleaner divan in the Beast's room underground and a pallet on the floor of a sitting room within reach of the outdoors, she'd choose the latter without hesitating.

Her stomach was growling unhappily, but Yeva had seen no sign yet of the Beast, or of food he'd left for her. She'd given her word not to run away, but did that include leaving the castle to find something to eat? He'd confiscated her bow and she had no wire for snares, but even in winter she might be able to find edible roots if she searched. Though roots would do little to satisfy her hunger.

If only she had some way of finding the Beast and asking for her bow.

As if the thought had summoned him, a roar echoed through the halls, vibrating through the soles of Yeva's boots. Her heart jumped into a flurry, and Doe-Eyes pressed in sideways against her leg, ears flung back flat against her skull. Yeva pushed the instinctual flash of fear down.

He needs me, she reminded herself. *He won't hurt me.*

And yet he'd killed her father.

The sound came again, and this time Yeva thought she heard words in it. *"Girl!"* the Beast was roaring. "Where are you? Come."

Irritation rose up, warming her where fear had frozen her feet to the ground. "Who does he think I am?" she asked Doe-Eyes. "Some quivering servant? To be summoned whenever he wishes?"

Doe-Eyes didn't answer.

"Girl!" the roar came again. "COME."

Yeva's hands balled into fists, and she took off back the way she'd come. From the many-faceted echo of the Beast's roar, she guessed he was in the grand foyer. She burst into the hall, Doe-Eyes skittering along beside her, and drew in a breath to shout back at the monster as soon as she saw his great bulk silhouetted by the pale light coming from the open door.

But the Beast was laden with something, leaning backward and dragging a large burden in his teeth. He stepped sideways, ears flicking straight up as he heard her footsteps, and halfway turned. The thing he was dragging was a deer, glassy-eyed as its head lolled toward Yeva. The Beast stopped, his great red-gold eyes rolling toward Yeva, his teeth clamped around the base of the young buck's neck. He opened his mouth to drop his burden, working his jaw for a moment as if relaxing the muscles there.

"I have brought you food." The Beast staggered a step to the side, then dropped onto his haunches, jaw still hanging slightly open as he tried to conceal his quicker breathing.

Yeva was struck so suddenly and so vividly by a memory that her own mouth fell open. He looked so very much like Pelei, her other dog, whenever he brought home a dead squirrel or rabbit he'd caught—where Doe-Eyes was tidy, Pelei would bring the mangled carcasses straight into the house, deposit them on Lena's clean rug, and then stand there amid the blood and the fur, panting and grinning proudly as if to say, *Aren't I a good dog?*

The Beast was still watching her, clearly waiting for some response. When Yeva didn't say anything, his face darkened, the brows lowering and his jaw closing. "Well?" he demanded.

Yeva's breath caught up with her and she frowned. "Well, what? Do you expect thanks? You've made me your prisoner. I'm not going to thank you for feeding me."

"Eat or don't," growled the Beast. "I care not."

Yeva took a deep breath. There was no question: no animal could be this temperamental, this . . . childish. There was *without a doubt* an element of humanity, however deeply buried, within this Beast. "You care because you have gone to all this trouble to catch and train me, for whatever purpose you won't explain."

The Beast just snarled at her, and turned to stalk away, toward the opposite side of the castle from the one she'd explored.

"Beast!" Yeva called. "Wait!" And when the Beast paused, she did as well, gathering her thoughts. "Do you know how to dress a carcass, or only how to devour it?"

"I am not your servant," the Beast replied, glaring at her over his shoulder.

"No," Yeva agreed. "But I have no knife, nothing with which to carve meat from these bones. I cannot simply rip off chunks with my teeth as you would do."

The Beast was frowning still, but his aggravation turned to

consternation. "If I give you a knife, you will try to kill me."

Yeva's stomach growled again, and she could not help but roll her eyes. Just now, killing the Beast was not foremost in her mind. "I won't try to kill you when I'm hungry."

The Beast stared at her. She stared back at him. Doe-Eyes looked between them, still ill at ease in the Beast's presence and pressing close to her mistress. In the end, the Beast grumbled low in his throat and led Yeva outside, lugging the deer with him, dropping it in the snow some distance from the door. He vanished and then reappeared some time later with her pack, in which Yeva found everything she'd brought with her. Though the food stores were nearly gone now, and the willow bark too, the other medicines were there, and her wire for snares, and the fletching knife as well.

Dressing squirrel and rabbit was one thing—butchering the carcass of a deer was another. It was always her father who'd done this work when she was a child, and by the time she had its innards in a pile beside the carcass, she found she wasn't hungry anymore after all. Her bloody hands shook, and she wiped at her brow with her sleeve to buy time. She would not show weakness in front of the Beast, who stood some distance apart, watching her carve up his offering.

Doe-Eyes, who'd been snatching up various organs and then hobbling away to gulp them down with one wary eye on the Beast, finished eating the deer's liver and skipped back to press against Yeva. She paused before reaching to scratch at the dog's ears, her eyes on her blood-coated hands.

The Beast gave a low rumble. "You are inefficient."

"Yes, with you staring at me," Yeva mumbled back, too worn out and drained by the task to worry about angering him.

"Return indoors," the Beast ordered.

"I need to finish—"

"Return!" the Beast's voice rose, and he drew himself up taller, looming so that Doe-Eyes wheezed an inaudible whine against Yeva's arm.

Yeva fought the instinct to flee. "I have to eat!"

The Beast drew one deep breath, then two, and Yeva realized she had too. *Patience,* she thought. *That's what I'm reaching for with each breath—could he be doing the same?*

Finally, the Beast dropped his head. "I will finish your task," he said slowly. "That is what I meant."

"Then say that. Don't command me as if I were your property."

The Beast growled low and dangerous. "You *are* mine."

"You may have me captive," Yeva said. "You may control when I can leave and what I eat and how long I'm allowed to live. But you don't own me." She paused, then added with irritation, "And don't call me *girl,* like I have no name."

The Beast's tail flicked aside, twitching with anger. "You call me *Beast.*"

"That is what you are. Have you given me reason to call you anything else?"

The Beast hesitated, scowling across the blood-soaked snow at her. "I will call you Beauty then," he said. "For that is what you are."

Yeva remembered her stories, and her decision to call her invisible friend Ivan, and her thoughts could not reconcile that name with the monstrous visage a few paces away. Her father's nickname for her sounded strange from this creature, this thing that had murdered him. And yet she could imagine him calling her nothing else. From someone else it would be flattery, but there was no falsehood in the Beast's face. Yeva wouldn't have been surprised if he were incapable of lying, if his animal nature kept him to the truth at all times.

The compliment caught her so off guard that her response came before she could stop it. "Thank you," she mumbled, dropping the knife to wipe the blood from her hands against the snow.

BEAST

She calls you Beast, for that is what you are.
And Beauty.

The surprise is not the compliment, not the truth, that she is beautiful. The surprise is not that we wish to help her. The surprise is not even the electric warmth that rises at the sound of her voice, even when she is shouting.

The surprise is how much I long to hear her call me, just once more, Ivan.

THIRTEEN

FROM THEN ON THE Beast brought her meat that had been dressed and carved. She didn't know how he managed such delicate work with only claws and teeth, because he never let her watch. Sometimes she killed the game herself, as he continued to take her into the wood to practice her skills. Other times, when her game was scarce, he'd go out on his own. He never failed to bring something home.

She cleared a space of dust and cobwebs in the vast kitchen, and cleaned out one of the four hearths so she could use the roasting spit. A few of the pots and pans she scrubbed clean, and a few plates and bowls as well. One of the sitting rooms she took as her own, and the Beast did not object when she began to sleep there instead of in his lair below. She imagined she was carving off a piece of the lifeless castle itself for her own use—or else bringing that tiny piece to life again. All around her was the dead, decaying carcass of whatever court had once existed here, and she was only living in a tiny corner of its shell.

With Yeva's cypress salve, Doe-Eyes's leg began to heal as the days stretched into weeks. She still hobbled, due to the splints keeping her leg straight, but she could move much faster, and no longer favored it the way she had been. Yeva could bring her along when the Beast took her hunting, and though Doe-Eyes was still too slow to catch anything herself, she delighted in galloping after the little scurrying things in the brush that caught her sight, and she slept much more soundly for the exercise. She bore up far better against the cold than Yeva would have thought, although that might have had as much to do with the dog's loyalty as her hardiness.

Yeva tracked the days with a bit of charcoal on the wall. Though she could not know how long she'd been down in the cell, she estimated it had been at least a month. Which meant that by now, her sisters must think she'd met the same fate as their father. And Solmir must believe the same. How long would his word last? She knew him to be a good man, but if he came to understand that Yeva would never return to marry him and repay him for taking care of her family, how long would he continue to do so? Her sisters had never learned to hunt as she had, and Albe certainly knew nothing about it. How would any of them survive without her?

She remembered her sister's words to her as she prepared to rush into the wood in search of their father, the words she'd ignored without a second thought. *We need you here.* And she'd abandoned them anyway.

No. *No.* She would not think of them. Not until it was done, and their father's death was avenged. She couldn't afford to. She forced her heart to harden, pushed her sisters from her mind.

It was two weeks after she'd moved into the castle above when the Beast came as usual to fetch her for the day's work. This time, however, he stopped at the far edge of the bridge and sat down, fixing his eyes on Yeva.

She fingered the bow over her shoulder and eyed him back, uncertain at this change in their routine. "What is it, Beast?"

"Your skill at hunting in your wood is sufficient," the Beast announced. "Now you will begin hunting in mine."

Yeva's brow furrowed. "Yours? I don't understand."

The Beast hesitated, his gaze sliding toward the forest beyond the overgrown road leading to the castle. "It is difficult to explain without—" He stopped short, as if someone had stolen his breath.

Yeva's pulse quickened, curiosity tingling its way up her spine. "Without violating the terms of the spell?"

The Beast's jaw fell open, and if it weren't for the number of sharp, menacing teeth his mouth held, Yeva might have laughed at the shock written across his animal features. He went absolutely still, even the tip of his tail that was usually so expressive. For an instant he was so like one of the crumbling gargoyles on the battlements of the castle that Yeva thought maybe just speaking of his secrets had turned him to stone.

But then he heaved a breath and dropped lower to the snow, crouching like a wounded animal, forelegs bent and breath stirring the top flakes with each puff. "You are clever," he mumbled.

"I know stories," Yeva corrected. "The bespelled can never speak of what afflicts them—that is always part of the curse."

The Beast's eyes flicked up. "You believe I am cursed?"

It was Yeva's turn to hesitate. Her mind still could not decide whether he was a man who had murdered her father or a beast who'd given in to animal instinct and torn him to pieces. And it still couldn't decide which would be worse. Either way he would have to answer for what he'd done.

"I know you aren't natural," she said finally. "And you can clearly hunt far better than any human hunter could, so your need for me must mean you have a task you cannot complete on your own."

The Beast said nothing, didn't confirm her guesses. But neither did he deny them.

"And this existence is clearly . . ." Yeva paused, swallowing. "It's clearly miserable."

The Beast stayed silent.

"So, yes." Yeva took a deep breath. "Yes, I believe you are cursed."

Still the Beast gave no reply, which gave Yeva time to study his face. Though he'd dropped his eyes again, there was something about his features that caught her attention. He seemed different today, and not only because he'd changed their routine by halting at the end of the bridge. His muzzle seemed somehow less elongated, his eyes less bestial, his mouth more expressive and less fanged. The longer she stared at him the more it seemed, in the sun-dazzled glare, that he was somehow also a man kneeling in the snow. She blinked, and blinked again, and could not dismiss the image.

"Enough," the Beast said abruptly, giving himself a shake that seemed to cause that humanity to fall away like shed fur. "It is enough for you to know that there is another world inside these woods, one you have not been trained to see. It is in this world that you will find your eventual quarry, so it is this world with which you must become familiar."

"Another *world?*" Yeva glanced out toward the wood as the Beast had done.

"The easiest way to explain is . . . think of your stories." The

Beast's face was turned aside, revealing only a sliver of his profile. "The stories you told of Ivan. That is the world you must learn to see."

Yeva found herself clutching at the grip of her bow, not in fear but in a sudden thrill of excitement. Her father had mentioned seeing flashes of things that could not exist—he'd told her of spirits and demons and creatures that had no names. But all children were told such stories, and all children grew out of them. She had never imagined the things her father told her might be reality.

"So what am I hunting today?" Yeva asked, a million imagined images flashing before her eyes. She thought of the glass wing tips still clinging to the window frame in the long, shattered hallway.

The Beast's lips pulled back, and Yeva could not decide whether it was a smile or a snarl. "Today," he said, "you will be hunting me."

Yeva felt like throwing her bow down in frustration. After three days of hunting the Beast, she could find no trace of him until he appeared close to sundown to bring her back to the castle. She knew now that it had to be magic, and her thoughts screamed at the unfairness of it. After all, she was human. Only a girl with a bow and a pair of strong arms and eyes. And none of those things could help her when tracking a magical creature through a forest that, for her, held only squirrels and deer and jays.

She'd been so sure this was a step toward achieving what she needed to do, that learning to track the Beast would be part of learning how to kill him. But that seemed farther away than ever, now that she knew how truly impossible it was to get the advantage on him.

The Beast was as frustrated as she was. She could read it in the gathering tension in his voice each day when he ended the hunt by revealing himself to her. So when, on the fourth day, he appeared early—no more than an hour or two after midday—Yeva's heart flickered with a beat of panic. Was she to be punished?

But the Beast merely sat there, appearing from behind a tree as she walked. He stared at her, contemplatively, and for once, Yeva refused to let the stare unsettle her. Instead she stared back, fingering the fletching on the arrow she kept nocked to her bow.

"Come," the Beast said finally.

"Come where?" Yeva asked warily.

"Here, to me."

Yeva didn't move, only gripped the bow more tightly and eyed the Beast sidelong, swallowing down fear.

The Beast's brows lifted. "I will not harm you."

"Your word?" Yeva asked.

"My word."

Yeva's hands shook as she returned the arrow to her quiver, and she stepped closer to the Beast. She stopped when she was near enough to feel the heat of his fur in the cold, near enough to smell that wild smell and see the flecks of red that gave his gold eyes their hue.

The Beast inclined his head, a melding of nod and bow that left Yeva more confused than before—a courtly gesture, so familiar from her time among the baronessa's retinue, but so alien from this creature. "Turn around."

Yeva did as he asked, though every nerve in her body told her not to turn her back on him, told her that she was mad to let such a predator so near.

She heard the Beast move closer behind her, and a warm paw

came to rest in the center of her back. She suppressed the urge
to shiver, certain at any moment she'd feel his claws. Instead she
heard his voice.

"Close your eyes and listen." His voice was very quiet, and
despite the vast open wood all around, his words felt intimate,
private. Yeva thought that even if someone were standing a few
paces away, they wouldn't hear him. It was as though he was
speaking directly into her ears. "Tell me what you hear."

"I hear you," Yeva replied. When that got no response, she
took a long, slow breath and let her attention move outward. It
was difficult to listen with the reminder of the Beast right behind
her, but as the sounds of the forest settled into the quiet she
almost forgot about his touch.

"I hear jays," she whispered. "Calling to one another. There
is a wind some ways to the east, making the trees sigh against
each other, but it's not coming our way. Snow sliding from a
branch."

"Is that all?"

Yeva, eyes closed, felt her brows knit. "What else am I
supposed to hear?"

"Listen."

Yeva listened. She listened until her ears started to ring
in the quiet. She was about to speak, and drew breath to tell
him she heard nothing, when something made her stop. The
skin at the back of her neck prickled, and not from the Beast's
presence. She felt her head turn, making the prickling stronger.
"I hear . . ." Her thoughts emptied as she tried to name the
sensation. Something was pulling at her, drawing her attention
northwest, and it *was* a sound. Except it wasn't a sound, at the
same time. "I hear . . . music."

The Beast's breath caught, then started again. "Music?" he

repeated, sounding surprised.

"I can't describe . . ." Yeva's ears strained. It wasn't music, not really. But her mind could not interpret it any other way, this feeling, this sweeping, rhythmic pulse that kept drawing her attention off through the woods. "It calls to me the way music does."

"Music," the Beast echoed again, his voice low and musing, almost wondrous. "That is not what I hear."

"What do you hear?"

"That is not important. For now, just concentrate on the sound."

Yeva wanted to know the answer to her question, but she wanted to listen to the music more. Though the sensation was new and alien, it also felt strangely familiar. *I've heard this sound before*, she realized, her entire body tingling. She'd caught glimpses of it, like a distant haunting refrain, in her deepest moments of silence in the wood. When the long days stretched timelessly on, and her mind emptied of thoughts until there was only her footsteps in the snow, only the feel of the bow in her hand, the bite of cold on her cheeks. When everything else faded away, this sound was what was left.

What is it you're looking for out there? Asenka had asked her.

"I hear it," she whispered, mesmerized.

"Hold the sound in your mind," the Beast murmured in her ear. "Imagine that it is not only a sound, but that it is a vision as well. Imagine that you will be able to see it when you open your eyes."

She instantly saw colors playing against the backs of her eyelids, pulsing in time with the not-quite-music. Blue and white and green streaks of light shot across her vision. She did not dare breathe to speak, but nodded instead, slowly, as though moving too quickly would jar the vision free.

"Now," the Beast whispered. "Open your eyes."

Yeva did as she was told. All around were the trees, and the snow, and the underbrush, and the light in her mind's eye was transposed against the scene. There was a focal point, a spot from which the light seemed to emanate, and Yeva stared at it. Suddenly a woman stood there, leaning against one of the trees. Her hair was long and raven black, and she was naked, as though the cold meant nothing to her. Yeva felt her face warming, suddenly all too aware of the rough wool on her own skin, and of the Beast's presence behind her. The woman was beyond beautiful, and she stood running her long fingers through her hair like a maiden waiting for a lover. Then she paused, and turned her head. She looked straight at Yeva, and when their eyes met Yeva felt something inside her shatter.

She cried out and stepped back, falling against the warm bulk of the Beast. She fumbled with the bow at her shoulder, trying to grab for an arrow but getting only handfuls of the Beast's fur. She gasped for breath, fear coursing through her veins, and looked back at the woman—and she was gone. There was only a pair of startled thrush that burst from the underbrush, crying and fluttering off into the distant wood.

Yeva stood, heart pounding. All at once she noticed how much she was leaning against the Beast, and that all her fear was for the strange woman in the wood, and that rather than terrifying, the Beast's warm presence behind her was reassuring.

She had forgotten for an instant that the Beast was her enemy, that she existed now only to kill him. It had been only a few heartbeats, her thoughts flooded with the music of this strange other world, but she'd *forgotten*. Her stomach lurched, sickened, and she stumbled away from him.

When she turned, he was calm, watching her as though nothing strange had happened.

"What was that?" Yeva fumbled with her quiver strap to adjust it, disentangling her cloak from about her, trying to compose herself.

"Her name is Lamya," the Beast said. "She and her sisters live in the next valley but they travel often, and Lamya prefers lying by the side of my river to shed her skins in the sun."

"Shed her . . ." Yeva blinked, trying to understand. "Shed her *skins?*"

"She is a dragon." The Beast's brow furrowed. "Have you not seen a serpent's shed skin before, in the wood?"

"But . . . but she was a woman, not a serpent at all."

"She is that too."

Yeva stared into the trees, trying to summon back that burst of color and music. She thought she heard a distant, rhythmic pulse, like the leathery flapping of great wings, but then it seemed nothing more than a far-off gust of wind. Yeva's head spun. "Beast, what . . . what is this?"

The Beast sank down on his haunches. "This is my world."

"The . . . the thing you need me for," Yeva said. "You want me to hunt a creature from this world, your world."

The Beast nodded.

"Lamya?"

"No, not Lamya."

"But you won't tell me what it is?"

"I cannot."

Yeva let her breath out in a rush. "How can I hunt a thing if I don't know what it is?"

The Beast was silent. Yeva had come to know him well enough to see from the set of his face that he was troubled. "I . . .

I do not know," he said finally. "But if you can see Lamya, then you will be able to see her, too."

Her.

Yeva filed the tidbit away, tying it down in among the other scraps she'd collected. For now they were shreds of next to nothing, but perhaps, if she gathered enough of them, she'd be able to stitch them together into a tapestry with answers. For now, she would wait and listen for that far-off music. For maybe, somewhere in its rhythmic pulse, in the way it seeped into the empty spaces of her heart like warm honey into dry bread . . . maybe in that music she'd find the way to kill the Beast.

"Beast," she said, making her voice steady, letting it warm.

"Yes?"

"You said that you didn't hear music." Yeva watched his face. "What do you hear?"

"For me," the Beast replied, "it is like a heartbeat."

Yeva fought a smile pulling at the corners of her mouth. "The heartbeat of the forest."

The Beast gave himself a little shake, then tilted his head eastward. "That is enough for today. We will return now."

As he turned to pass her, the Beast moved on top of the snow, his paws not even stirring the loose snow dusting the icy crust. Yeva's boots crunched through, but he moved like wind, like spirit. He was showing her how he could travel through the forest without leaving a trace, and Yeva watched each step as if hypnotized.

"It is the same sound I heard," the Beast said as he passed her, "when I first saw you."

BEAST

We remember a time of such clarity. We were Beast, we ran with wolves and hunted prey, we lived on the wind and breathed the forest. We wanted nothing but to be, to run, to endure. Want didn't exist.

And we remember another time, too, a time of longing and desire, where we existed as nothing but want . . . always the next unattainable thing. There was no joy in what we had, only in what might come.

And now these two selves, these two minds cursed to exist as one, every day grow more at odds. We return to our den to pace and end up railing against the darkness and the dirt—we lie before the fire in our room and itch at the confines of stone and mortar.

Only she frees both of us. She moves like beauty, she whispers to us of wind and forest—and she tells us stories, such stories that we wake in the night, dreaming dreams of a life long past. She reminds us of what we used to be.

She whispers to us of what we could be.

FOURTEEN

YEVA AND THE BEAST fell into a pattern as the weeks began to stretch. Though she still could not track him through the forest, even as she developed an ear for magic, she discovered other wonders living in the Beast's valley. Trees that had faces, voices, peeping at her one instant and gone the next. Lights dancing in the distance, riding the storm winds, laughter calling her to join them. A fox that stopped and smiled at her. Birds that flocked together this way and that on the wind, painting shapes in the sky over the meadow: a face, a cresting wave, a herd of running deer.

She asked the Beast about them all. Sometimes he had names for them, and sometimes he did not. Sometimes, very, very rarely, she'd tell him of a creature even he had never seen. Yeva thought, privately, that those moments seemed to delight him. She asked him each time, at each new wonder, whether that was what she was meant to hunt. Each time he said no.

It was nearly two months after moving into the castle, by her charcoal tally on the kitchen wall, that she woke to find the Beast crouched in the corner of her room.

At first she didn't see him, and rose half sleeping from her nest of blankets to add a few logs to the fire so the room would heat while she woke the rest of the way. Doe-Eyes never bothered to wake when she did, grumbling happily from her part of the pallet until the fire drew her out to bask in its heat. Yeva wrapped herself back up in her blankets and jiggled her knees up and down to bring the blood back to her toes, and waited for warmth.

The shadows in the far corner moved, and Yeva let out a shriek before she could stop herself. She'd seen dark, frightening things in the musical wood, and her dreams had been more troubled since she'd begun to see this other world. She reached for the fire poker before she could think.

The Beast stepped forward into the light and blinked his round eyes at her. "We did not mean to frighten you."

Yeva gulped back her panic, her pounding heart starting to calm as she saw it was only the Beast and not some monster from her dreams.

It was only the Beast? When did that happen?

"You can't come in here like that, while I'm asleep," she gasped, lingering fears prompting irritation to sharpen her voice.

The Beast's brows lowered. "Why not?"

"It's not polite," Yeva retorted, then took a breath as the ridiculousness of that sank in. What were manners to a Beast?

But as she struggled for a reason he would understand, the Beast merely tilted his head a fraction to the side. "Very well. Do you wish us to leave?"

Yeva's voice sputtered to a halt. *Yes,* she thought. *Or else let me kill you and end all of this.* But aloud, she said only, "What do you want?"

"Polite," the Beast echoed, murmuring the word as if to himself. But there was a wicked gleam in his eyes that made Yeva stop short, a realization snapping into her mind like a spark from chafing wool.

He was *teasing* her.

"It is time for training."

Yeva's head ached. She was weary, but more than that, she was frustrated. The more she understood of this world the Beast had shown her, the more she saw how little hope she had of avenging her father unless she could discover a weakness, some secret that would give her the upper hand.

But it was clear she would not find the Beast's weakness by ordinary means, and she could not afford to keep growing complacent, to let the days slip by unmarked. She would track these creatures in the wood, the ones she'd learned to see with the Beast's help. One of them had to know something, anything, that would help her kill the Beast. And she'd hunt down every last one of them if it came to that.

Quickly, she rose to her feet and crossed the room to splash frigid water from the basin onto her face. "Beast," she said, earning herself a faint grunt in response. "I want to go into the forest on my own today."

The Beast's brows lifted, but he said nothing, clearly waiting for an explanation.

"I need to be able to navigate this world of yours alone, without your guidance." Yeva could see the Beast shift his weight from one side to the other, see him start to reply. "And," she added quickly, "whatever quarry I'm meant to find, we haven't found it yet. Perhaps it won't reveal itself to you. But maybe it will to me if I'm alone."

That brought the Beast up short, and he gazed at her with

those steady eyes, tail swinging side to side like a slow, gentle pendulum. He stared at her so long that Yeva's own eyes began to water with the effort of not looking away. When he spoke, his voice was low and careful. "I still have your word that you will not attempt escape?"

Yeva swallowed at that reminder, bitterness on her tongue. "You still have my word. Since you will kill my family if I do."

Silence again, broken by the hiss and intermittent pops of the fire in the hearth. "Yes," he said finally.

Yeva hesitated. "Yes, you will kill my family if I escape? Or yes, I may go alone?"

"Both." The Beast's brows lowered. "I accept your word. If you were given to lying, you would have promised not to kill me at the start. Since you did not, I believe you when you say you will not flee."

His voice was so low, so bitter, so full of loathing, that Yeva almost took a step back. The fire no longer seemed to hold any warmth for her, and she shivered. "You killed my father," she whispered. "I can never let his death go unanswered."

The Beast's eyes were flat and dull. "And that is why you stay. Not because of threats or fear. Because you believe one day we will drop our guard, and you can avenge him."

Yeva's jaw clenched. She had little hope of convincing him otherwise, not when he saw through her so easily. So let them be enemies. She'd find a way to destroy him regardless. "Yes."

The Beast's tail stilled. The flat eyes softened, his face suddenly so human that Yeva *knew* he had changed, that it was no trick of the light or her own eyes. He seemed torn between two warring natures, and whichever ruled him at any given time, that aspect took over.

Just now, his face, his expression, was so full of anguish that

Yeva's fury vanished and her heart ached so much that she bit her lip.

"We did kill him," the Beast said after an eternity, and his face closed over again as he looked away toward the door. When he looked back, he was the Beast once more. "And maybe one day we *will* drop our guard. Then you will get what you most desire."

He turned and was gone.

Yeva fought the instinct to wipe the frigid wash water from her face. She wanted to hold in the chill, wanted to remind herself she could not, *would not* be comfortable here. She was a prisoner in this decaying castle, tied to the thing that had destroyed the person she loved most in all this existence.

But something, an ache that Yeva would not name, stirred deep in her heart. With those words the Beast had renewed her dedication to vengeance, shored up her determination to remain here. Even if he said she could go free tomorrow, she would stay, and wait, and find a way. . . .

With those words he had ensured she would not try to leave him. It was a human thing to tell a person what they want to hear. A human thing to manipulate and hide the truth to serve one's own ends. A human thing to lie.

And in the moment he admitted to killing her father, he had seemed so very human.

Though the sky was clear and sunny, the air was bitingly cold, and Yeva set a brisk pace to keep her blood pumping. Doe-Eyes trotted at her heels, her leg so improved she could accompany Yeva all day if necessary. Her father's bow at hand, her pack filled with her own gear, Yeva felt more at home, more truly free, than she could remember ever feeling. Even without the Beast's threats against her family, she would return to his castle by choice. Vengeance, not fear, would bring her back. And if all went well, she would return armed with knowledge of the Beast's weaknesses.

She could hear the music always now, a constant thread that lingered in the very back of her mind, unless she summoned it to her attention. It was not unlike the way she'd always heard the forest before, its tiny noises and breezes weaving together automatically to paint a picture beyond what she could see. It unnerved her, how easily the music became a part of that picture.

She shoved those thoughts aside and concentrated, turning her head this way and that to locate the different threads of magic, like scent trails. She twisted toward the nearest, giving Doe-Eyes a sharp whistle to stay close, and set out.

Yeva had learned from her excursions with the Beast that the creatures in this wood were rarely evil—and neither were they good. They simply *were*, the way animals were. Spirits that led travelers astray could also help them find the road again. Birds that warned of dangers ahead could also cry out and betray a person's presence to waiting beasts.

This was a world governed by balance. Evil deeds begot evil consequences. Blessings used for ill purposes could quickly become curses. Though Yeva would tread carefully, and knew any information she sought would require some kind of payment, she felt certain that even in this realm she could only be rewarded for seeking to destroy the Beast.

She was several hours out from the castle, over the ridge and into the valley beyond it, when a movement caught her eye and made her stop. She put a hand on Doe-Eyes's head, signaling silently for her to be still.

Just ahead, mostly hidden by the trees, was a face. An old man was watching her, as still as the snowy world around him. His skin was lined and grooved like bark, his hair long and tinged green like moss, his eyes the pale blue of an icy pool. She had never seen him before.

She took a breath and moved forward a step, but the instant her weight shifted the face vanished behind the tree again.

"Wait!" she called, breaking into a run, eyes scanning for a shape darting through the woods. But when she reached the tree behind which the man had been standing, she found a fox there, sitting calmly in the snow and gazing up at her.

Yeva, breathless, stared at it, and it stared back. At her side, Doe-Eyes sniffed interestedly—but didn't go stiff as she would have done had an ordinary fox appeared in their path.

"Well?" said the fox.

Yeva yelped, and couldn't help but take a step back, half lifting her bow. She caught her breath, noticing the fox had the same pale-blue eyes the man had had. She swallowed. "What are you?"

"I am Borovoi."

Yeva shifted her grip on her bow, forcing herself to relax lest the fox—or old man, or whatever he was—sense her nervousness. "Is that your name, or what you are?"

The fox's head tipped to the side. "I am Borovoi. What a waste of a question. You only have one more."

Yeva's mouth opened to protest, but she stopped herself before she could speak. In her father's tales, the number three was always important. Three sons, three wishes . . . this world was ruled by the laws of those stories. She took a deep breath, choosing her words carefully, and asked, "Can you show me how to destroy the Beast?"

The fox paused for a long moment. Then his lips drew back into a wide, toothy grin, and he whirled with a flash of his red tail and darted off into the forest. Yeva broke into a run without thinking, shoving her bow onto her shoulder and sprinting as fast as she could. She could see no tracks, but the fox was always just ahead of her, visible as a flash of red fur against the white canvas of snow. She ran until she stumbled into a dense thicket, which tangled about her legs; her momentum tried to keep her moving and she went crashing down into the dry, leafless branches.

Gasping, she crawled forward, detangling herself as best she could, ignoring the scratches on her face and the branches snagging her hair. When she finally stumbled free, she found herself in a snowy clearing—and the fox, Borovoi, was nowhere to be seen.

Yeva stood panting, trying to catch her breath as Doe-Eyes came wriggling through the thicket after her. Tongue lolling, gap-jawed, Doe-Eyes gazed up at her mistress as though to say, *What fun! Again!* Still winded, Yeva dropped into a weary crouch. She rubbed at Doe-Eyes's ears as she scanned the clearing.

There had to be a clue here, some importance to this section of the wilderness. Though tricksters were everywhere in fairy tales, they rarely lied—any misfortunes were always the fault of the hero or heroine, misunderstanding what was really being said. So Yeva doubted she would find some weapon buried beneath the snow that could kill the Beast, but she knew some piece of the answer must lie here.

She set off across the clearing, steps cautious, eyes scanning. It wasn't until she was nearly halfway across that she noticed a flat expanse that was lower than the rest, and mostly clear of snow.

When she drew closer she found that it was a pool, a woodland spring that had frozen over in the cold. Yeva strode halfway around it, peering at the ice, which showed little but black water beneath it. Ordering Doe-Eyes to stay put, Yeva gingerly stretched a foot out to test the ice's surface. It gave only the tiniest groan in response as she shifted more of her weight onto that foot.

She was about to take another step when a flash of gold beneath the ice made her stop short. Heart pounding, she stared into the black depths, hoping for another glimpse. It came again, a sweep of fire gold, and then abruptly it was there.

The Firebird.

Yeva gasped and threw herself down onto her knees to stare beneath the ice. The Firebird was trapped there, its golden wings outstretched, beating futilely against the ice's surface. With a cry, Yeva drew her fletching knife from her boot and chipped at the ice—she forgot about Borovoi, forgot about her reason for coming to the wood alone, forgot even the Beast himself. She could see only the Firebird, hear only its muffled cries, each one a stab at her heart.

All her life she'd longed for the tiniest glimpse of this creature. She would not let it drown—she would free it, take it for her own, feel the heat of its fiery wings on her face. She stabbed down at the ice again and again, feeling it shudder beneath her. Each groan of the ice made her work harder, faster. Doe-Eyes's frantic barking at the pool's edge faded to a distant buzzing in her ears. All she heard, all she was, was the Firebird's song.

The ice gave a mighty crack, and a spray of water flecked Yeva's face. She moved so she could drive down at the hole with her boot, putting every ounce of strength she had behind it— and then the entire sheet gave way with a roar.

Yeva was in the water before she knew what was happening, air driven from her lungs and rushing back in a huge gasp before her head went under. For a long instant she felt nothing—no cold, no wet, no fear at the sudden darkness—only the need for the Firebird, the longing to touch it even once, even if it flew away and she never saw it again.

Something wrapped around her from behind and she turned, joy flooding her heart as she expected to see the Firebird at last, whole and in front of her, not obscured and blurred by the ice. Instead, a rotting face loomed out of the blackness at her, bony arms pulling her close. It had once been a woman, her long hair still clinging to what remained of her scalp, and the flesh of her cheeks had sunken and rotted so that Yeva could see her teeth in profile as the thing leaned forward to whisper in her ear.

"Stay with me," the dead woman sighed, holding on to Yeva with unnatural strength. They were sinking, down into darkness, far deeper than a meadow pool should be. The thing's hair curled around Yeva, wrapping around her neck, slithering along her skin beneath her clothes.

Yeva tried to scream, but all that came was a torrent of bubbles. The spell broken, her longing for the Firebird gone, Yeva's body struggled for survival. Her lungs were burning even before she'd wasted air trying to scream, and she struggled to pull one of her arms free from the thing's grip. When she'd hit the cold water her muscles had seized, and in her hand was still the knife she'd been using to chip at the ice. Yeva's mind felt slow and sluggish, and every second they sank deeper made it harder to think.

She lifted her head and saw the distant glimmer of the pale winter sun, and with a wrenching effort that drove another flood of bubbles from her lungs, she tore her arm free of the dead thing's grasp. She stabbed the knife down as hard as she could, driving it into the thing's shoulder until it grated against bone. It howled, a cry as much of grief and despair as of pain, but its grip only tightened. Yeva stabbed again, her vision growing blurry, and again, and again—finally the knife crunched through the thing's skull, and abruptly its arms fell away. Yeva tried to swim upward, her own body barely responding to her mind's commands. When she looked down, all she saw was a ghostly pale form sinking slowly, quietly, into the black depths.

She clawed her way up, the glimmer of light above her seeming farther with every stroke—but eventually her arms remembered how to swim, and just as her lungs readied to breathe water if she could not find air, she broke the surface with a gurgling cry.

The pool itself was small, and though the ice was too thin for her to climb on top of it, she could make her way to shore, the ice shattering around her. She fell into the snow, dizzy and shivering, sobbing for air. The roaring in her ears began to fade, replaced by Doe-Eyes's frenzied barking; Yeva opened ice-crusted eyelashes to find her dog dancing above and around her, nudging her from all sides. She couldn't even feel it when Doe-Eyes began licking the water from her hands.

All she wanted was to lie there in the snow and breathe and stare at the sky, which was turning gray with clouds. Some distant part of her mind knew, though, that this was wrong. She must move, or die from the cold. With a moan, she rolled over onto her side and drew her knees in close to her body, then slipped her pack from her shoulders. Most of her supplies were wet, including her tinder for starting a fire, but she had no firewood or kindling anyway, and that wasn't what she was after. She kept her sleeping-roll blanket at the bottom of the pack, and the pack's leather and the layers of supplies had protected it somewhat. It was damp, but far drier than anything else.

She peeled off the sopping outer layers of her clothes, moving as quickly as her numb, shaking fingers would allow.

Her shivering began to slow, but rather than making movement easier, it seemed harder and harder to move. She knew that was bad—that all of this was bad—that she would die of exposure. She wondered what would happen to her family, whether the Beast would kill them for her failure, or if they'd simply go on living in that cabin forever. She imagined Lena learning to hunt, then found herself laughing at the thought of her prim sister trying squeamishly to retrieve an arrow from a deer.

It was a sharp bark from Doe-Eyes in her ear that brought her back to herself, wrenching her thoughts from home with an effort. A surge of fear that she was losing her ability to think got her the rest of the way out of her cloak and clothes until she was only in her wool undershift—that she kept on, for even wet the wool would help her somewhat. Then she tried to call Doe-Eyes, her voice cracking and whispery thin. The dog tucked her body in close and Yeva wrapped herself around her, and the blanket around them both, and tried to think.

Her tinder was soaked but if she could make it to the forest perhaps the thicket she'd fallen into on her way to the clearing would have wood dry enough to ignite from sparks. If she could get her hands working she could shave curls from it with her knife. If she had a lantern she could warm some water to drink . . . she ought to ask her invisible friend to bring her one, to unlock her manacle, to let her out of the chilly cell and into the room with the blue divan, and the hearth. She curled more tightly around the warm body alongside hers and mumbled, "Asenka, your toes are so cold. . . ."

Doe-Eyes's barking roused her and she groaned, "Hush, it isn't dawn yet!" But there was light against her eyelids, and a shadow moving across them. She tried to open her eyes but her lids wouldn't listen; she tried to lift a hand to pry them open but couldn't tell if her arm was moving. "Where's my arm—I need that to shoot. . . ."

"Hush," said a voice in her ear, tense and deep. Not her father's voice. But familiar somehow. Warm like velvet. "I will carry you on my back. But you must hold on or you will fall off."

"I'm not a child," Yeva protested. The voice ignored her, and she expected to feel a pair of arms lifting her. Instead something clamped onto her shoulder, a firm pressure, and dragged her back and halfway up onto a soft slope.

"Climb," the voice ordered.

Yeva grabbed automatically, fingers closing around handfuls of fur. Her muscles seemed weak for some reason as she dragged herself upward, a task that should've been easy. The soft thing beneath her moved, staggering to the side and half knocking her upward. Then it rose, making her stomach lurch.

"Hold on." This time the voice came from beneath her, rumbling against her chest and cheek like a house cat's purr, or the stirring of distant thunder. The thing began to move, slowly at first, then faster and faster until Yeva pressed her face in against the spicy fur so the wind would not sting her cheeks.

As Yeva's consciousness slipped away, she heard the voice again, murmuring, *Hold on.*

BEAST

We are not afraid. We are never afraid. It has been centuries since we knew fear, even longer since there was any being, beast or man, strong enough to harm us.

And yet our heart pounds like thunder in our ears, echoing like a voice shouting at us to run harder, move faster. Our paws feel clumsy, and half the time we sink into snow that we long ago learned to cross without leaving a trace. Though we always know exactly how far we are from the castle it feels twice, three times as far as it ought to be.

The body against our back is cold. She is no longer moving. Only that she has not fallen, that her hands still grip our fur, tells us that she is still alive.

Hold on, Beauty.

Hold on.

FIFTEEN

YEVA WOKE BECAUSE HER skin was on fire. Her voice was cracked and she found she could barely move, and that when she did, it made her body burn all the more.

"Go slowly," said a low voice. She knew that voice. The Beast.

She opened her eyes to find him crouched several paces from her, his eyes narrowed onto her face. The tip of his tail twitched as she met his gaze, then twitched back as though he wished to hide that tiny hint of reaction.

Yeva was lying on the floor before the hearth in her room, on top of several layers of blankets, the uppermost of which was of soft fleece—and yet it scratched against her skin like burlap. Some detail prickled at her mind sluggishly, and it wasn't until she looked away from the Beast that she realized what it was.

She was naked.

Yeva gave a low, horrified cry and snatched up the blankets to gather them around her body. Her fingers felt clumsy and swollen, but she forced them to grip the blankets.

The Beast's eyes narrowed all the more, lips curling back. Yeva could not tell if he was snarling or smiling. "You are improved," he said.

"Did you *undress me?*" Yeva demanded, starting to shiver— the fire in the hearth had been warming her far more than the blankets around her were doing now.

"If I had not you would likely have died." The Beast's tail lashed once. "Would you have preferred death over preservation of your modesty?"

Fragments of memory were coming back now: the shocking cold of the icy water; the flood of terror when she turned to find not the Firebird, but a haunted wraith before her eyes; the smell of the Beast's fur as he carried her on his back. She gulped for air, remembering the burning in her lungs as she began to drown. Doe-Eyes was at her side, and crept in close—Yeva opened the blanket enough for the dog to crawl in alongside her, giving off heat like a furnace.

When Yeva didn't answer, the Beast gave a low growl and sat up, leaning back on his haunches so that he once more loomed over Yeva, prone on the floor. "What should it matter? I am a beast no different from the hound at your side."

Yeva clenched her jaw a moment, gathering Doe-Eyes in against her body and then glaring up at the Beast. "We both know that's not true," she snapped.

The Beast's hair lifted along the ridge of his spine, a crest of irritation Yeva had come to recognize as plainly as the furrow in a man's brow or the thinning of his lips. He turned toward the door.

"Wait." Yeva's breath caught as the Beast halted. She knew she ought to thank him for saving her, but the words stuck in her throat. To thank her father's murderer? Her captor? He had only saved her because of his need for a hunter, and yet she'd felt the urgency in the Beast's gait as he ran, the raggedness of his breath as he pushed himself harder, faster, to get her back into the shelter of the castle.

Thank you.

But when Yeva opened her mouth again, she said only, "What was it? The thing in that pool?"

The Beast turned back, eyeing her before settling onto his haunches again. "The pool belongs to one of the Rusalka, a girl killed long ago by a lover or a father or brother. She appears to men as their heart's desire to lure them to their deaths."

Not just men, Yeva thought bitterly. "And what of Borovoi?"

"Borovoi?" The Beast's brows lifted in that expression so like surprise that it almost made Yeva forget about the teeth, the eyes like a wolf's, the ears that pricked toward her when she spoke. "You met him? He rarely shows himself."

"He brought me to the Rusalka's pool."

"Borovoi is one of the leshy, the forest spirits. He grants answers, though the answers he gives often lead travelers astray. What did you ask?"

Yeva's lips pressed together. She'd asked him how to destroy the Beast, but if she was to have any hope of lulling the Beast into lowering his guard, she certainly could not tell him that. "I . . . I cannot remember."

The Beast was silent for a time, long enough that Yeva wondered if he might know she was holding back the truth. But then he bowed his head and took a step backward. "I will let you recover. You will not have to train tomorrow."

Yeva, still shivering despite Doe-Eyes's trembling warmth, watched as the Beast padded softly toward the door, tail sweeping gently behind him. She'd asked the leshy how to destroy the

Beast, and it had brought her to a place that, had it not been for the Beast, would have been her death. She knew that the Beast needed her skills as a hunter, that he hoped she'd play some part in unlocking his curse. But her death would hardly destroy him, only delay his freedom until he found some other hunter to use.

The Beast paused in the doorway for a few seconds before glancing back over his shoulder. "What did you see?" he asked quietly. "In the Rusalka's pool. What was your heart's desire?"

Yeva's pulse sounded quick and loud in her ears. She could still see the Firebird there, its great gold wings sweeping against the ice, calling to her. "I—I saw my family." The lie came so haltingly she felt sure the Beast would see it.

But he only inclined his head once, eyes dropping to the floor before he vanished, leaving her alone.

Yeva crept closer to the hearth, making sure the Beast was gone before opening the blankets to let the fire warm her. She shouldn't have had to lie. She should have seen her family, or Solmir, or her father alive again. She should have seen home, her old life, the comfort of a world without monsters and curses and Beasts. But instead, she'd seen the one thing that most symbolized the world she'd dreamed of as a child.

Instead, she'd seen magic.

As if the Beast could somehow control the weather, no sooner had Yeva recovered enough to venture outside again than the dead of winter hit like an iron fist, and it was no longer safe for Yeva to brave the woods. Blizzards howled through the castle, forcing her to shut up the doors and huddle with Doe-Eyes close to the fire. She half expected to find the Beast waiting behind her, as he did in the wood when she hunted, but he never came. She did return once from the kitchen to discover that layers of tapestry had been fixed over the high window frames, which had been letting in the cold. She could not think how the Beast could have reached them, and for an instant the image of him trying to climb a ladder with four paws and a tail made her want to laugh. But her room was much warmer, and she'd fall asleep on the rugs before the fire gazing up at the high tapestries and imagining what stories lay hidden beneath the centuries of fading and dust.

She saw very little of him during those dark weeks. For a time, the only sign he was even there was the occasional refreshed store of game in the larder. Every now and then she'd catch a flash of red-gold eyes vanishing into the shadows as she explored the castle, or a glimpse of a tail disappearing around the corner, but he never stayed or sought her out.

Doe-Eyes was her constant companion, following her everywhere. Even if the dog was dead asleep, rolled over on her back in front of the fire, if Yeva rose so much as to visit the latrines, Doe-Eyes would wake, scramble to her feet, and trot along at Yeva's side. Her leg had healed almost as good as new, only a slight limp left behind when Yeva failed to keep the fire burning hot enough and the cold crept in. Yeva was glad Doe-Eyes had found her so miraculously in the wood that day, saving her from the ache of loneliness.

And yet, despite her dog's warm body leaning against her as she slept, something twinged deep in her psyche, a discontent that Yeva could not—or would not—name. She'd watch the windows as she wandered the empty castle, the landscape sometimes obscured by storms, sometimes a white, crystalline stillness. Once she saw the silhouette of a distant bird of prey circling the wood—then saw it turn, and the flash of a long, forked tail made her breath catch. *She is a dragon,* the Beast had told her after her brief encounter with Lamya in the wood. Now, as

Yeva blinked, and the silhouette stooped into a dive after some prey unseen behind the next ridgeline, she could not be sure of what she'd seen. Cooped up indoors, surrounded by snow and emptiness, her eyes could easily play tricks on her.

I miss the outdoors, she told herself, turning her back on the window. *I miss hunting. I miss my family.*

Only occasionally, when she let herself dwell too long on the feeling of being unsettled, incomplete, did she remind herself, *He killed my father. He is a murderer. He is a Beast.*

I do not *miss his company.*

The castle itself was enough of a mystery to keep Yeva's mind occupied during the long, dark weeks of winter as she waited for her chance to roam outside again. With Doe-Eyes at her side, she took to exploring by lantern light the endless corridors and rooms. Some, especially on the top floor, were in such disrepair that the roof had caved in. In those places all was snow and rubble and it was impossible to tell what the room had once been used for. Others were almost entirely intact, and but for the centuries of dust and cobwebs, could have been abandoned only yesterday.

From the look of the pristine, freshly fallen snow outside the castle doors each morning, she could tell the Beast was not spending his nights in the lair beneath the castle. Yeva supposed he could be concealing his tracks, but he'd never done so before on his way to the cave, so she couldn't think why he would now. She assumed he must be living in the castle, but the room down the long spiral stair where she'd convalesced and told her stories was empty, and the hearth cold.

She told herself she was searching for his new lair so she'd be able to keep an eye on him, monitor him, perhaps even catch him unawares while he was asleep. But as she turned each corner, stepped through each doorway, it was curiosity that drove her. And while it was a softer, gentler flame than fury, it burned far more slowly and never guttered out.

Yeva knew that the Beast was cursed in some way, and that the answer to his curse involved capturing or killing some creature that lived in the magic world of the wood. Though she imagined that he'd once been human, sometimes her certainty faltered. The ferocity in his gaze when he'd drag home the day's dinner, the alien stare of his eyes as he surveyed the wilds, the moments of utter abandon when he ran through the trees.

Perhaps instead he'd once been an animal, cursed now with human traits. Either state must be a torment. For an animal to be haunted by human conscience, human guilt, human loneliness and fear and desire, would be maddening. And for a man to have his humanity stripped away by the endless onslaught of animal instincts and predatory impulses would be heartbreaking.

The mystery of the castle *was* the mystery of the Beast, and she roamed for days on end with Doe-Eyes's toenails clicking on the cracked marble at their feet.

Though it was nowhere near as large as the castles depicted in illuminated stories and fantastical tapestries, Yeva kept discovering new rooms that she had somehow missed in her previous wanderings.

She found the remains of an old workroom, full of spools of faded thread and a loom and spinning wheel draped in cobwebs. A single gray thread still ran from the rim of the wheel through the spindle, but when Yeva reached out to run her finger along it, it crumbled into dust at her touch.

She found a vast suite of rooms clearly meant for the master and mistress of the castle, with a bed so large she could have lain down crosswise upon it and not reached the edges even if she stretched her fingertips over her head. The bathing chambers held a tub sunk into the marble floor and a chute in which to dump coals to keep the water warm for hours on end. Yeva had never had such luxury—even at the height of her father's wealth, she and her sisters would draw straws as to who would get the tub first, and get the hot, fresh water all to herself. Yeva almost never drew the longest straw, and often shivered her way through her bath. Without servants to draw water, it would take her hours, if not days, to bring enough water to fill this tub—but the thought of it made Yeva smile. She'd been bathing with cloth and buckets of water, and the idea of submerging in warmth, of being entirely, utterly, totally clean . . . she sighed and moved on.

It was on her third or fourth survey of the castle that she stumbled across the library.

She stopped dead and lifted her lantern high to illuminate every shadowy corner. Yeva and her sisters all knew how to read, and though Asenka was certainly the most learned of the three sisters, Yeva had always loved to be read to. Most of her father's books were scholarly texts, but one of them held some of the old stories he'd told her when she was a child, and though she could read the words herself, there was a magic to having them spoken aloud to her, so she could close her eyes and simply listen, and weave images in her mind as the stories unfurled.

Her father had owned over a dozen books, the most of anyone in the town including the baron himself. And as Yeva scanned the walls, each one lined with shelves and each one full of leather-bound books, at least a hundred books, more than she knew existed in one place, she felt her heart might simply burst.

The room itself was dank and cold. It was an interior room with no outside windows, but leaks in the ceiling had allowed moisture to drip onto the floor, and Yeva's nose filled with the smell of rot and mildew. But even that couldn't dim the flare of excitement as she hurried across the room to set the lantern down on one of the end tables in order to reach out and pull one of the books from the shelf.

Its spine crumbled at her touch, and she lifted the cover gingerly. It broke apart in her hands, and the page beneath was so stained with rot that she could not make out any of the text. She set it aside and reached for another, and another—but each one had been so tainted with age and damp as to be unreadable. Yeva was so unprepared for the swell of anguish at the thought of the knowledge lost in this room that she sat down hard on the floor, gasping for air. Doe-Eyes pressed in against her—though she didn't know why, she knew her mistress was upset, and gave her ear a tentative lick.

"You are unhappy." The somber voice came from behind her, but Yeva had grown so accustomed to the Beast's abrupt appearances that she felt only a flicker of surprise.

She turned to see him filling the doorway, a large shadow with gleaming eyes. She wiped at her face and cleared her throat. "I'd hoped to be able to read these," she said quietly. "I used to love hearing my father—" Her voice stuck, and as she gazed back at the Beast, a dull flicker of that angry despair rose up. She'd never hear her father read to her again.

The Beast let the silence stretch, the only sound the gentle scrape of his paw on the stone as he shifted his weight from one foot to the other. "Come," he said, and without waiting for her to answer, turned and vanished from the doorway.

Yeva considered ignoring the order out of spite, but she'd begun to sense differences in the Beast's voice. Sometimes his orders were heavy and sharp and designed to make her feel small and helpless. But at other times, like this one, there was a plea evident in the tone, and though he never said "please" or "will you" or "might I suggest," there was nonetheless room in his voice for her to refuse.

So she rose to her feet, one hand on Doe-Eyes's back to steady herself, and followed the Beast out into the corridor.

He led her clear to the other side of the castle, walking in silence. Yeva's lantern didn't cast its light far enough to illuminate his path, but the darkness didn't seem to bother him. He never put a foot wrong or hesitated or clipped a wall.

He padded into the master suite of chambers, which had no other exit as far as Yeva was aware. But instead of coming to a halt, he crossed toward one of the tapestries. An instant before he reached for it, Yeva saw that it was brighter and cleaner than the others, having collected less dust—and when the Beast lifted it aside, she realized why. It concealed a thick ironbound door that swung soundlessly inward at the Beast's paw.

The secret door led to another stair, and as Yeva transposed her mental image of the castle as seen from the ridge above the valley onto the corridors she'd begun to learn, she thought they must be ascending into one of the thick round turrets. The Beast climbed the stair ahead of her, always just vanishing around the curve of the wall as she glimpsed him, but she saw enough to discover that he was climbing the staircase on two legs, not four, and her heart began to slam against her rib cage. Though the joints of his legs were all wrong, and his tail still swept after him, and his fur still caught the lantern light, to see him walking like a man caused all her questions to surge up again until she almost forgot the lost library below.

The stair led to another door, and this time the Beast stopped. He dropped back down onto all fours as Yeva approached, and he paused. His eyes flicked back over his shoulder at her, and she saw indecision written there, recognized his hesitation as clearly as she would've on one of her sister's faces. Then he gave himself a shake and reached out with one paw toward the latch.

She'd never quite seen how he managed many of the things he did—though it'd become quite obvious that no one else lived in the castle and that the Beast must have cooked her food while she was in the cell, lit her lanterns, locked and unlocked her chains. No beast with only paws and teeth could do such things, and Yeva had to admit the role that magic played in every aspect of the Beast's existence. Perhaps he merely did it with a wave of his paw, the same way he simply walked on top of the snow as if it were solid ground, or turned his own scent off like a tap to hide himself from nature.

But this time, as she watched, he *changed*. His paw seemed to shimmer before her eyes, rippling like hot air escaping a door into a frosty morning. Her eyes ached with the need to look away, but she forced herself to watch, ordering herself not to miss it this time. The furry toes lengthened, the claws shortening, the whole wrist joint shifting up. It was not a hand, nor a paw, but something in between. And it held a key.

He unlocked the door deftly, and the key vanished somewhere about his person. By the time he put his hand back down it was a paw again, and he glanced back at her as if nothing strange had taken place. "Come," he said again, more gently this time.

She followed him into the room.

The room was round and held four windows, shuttered tightly against the winter outside. The ceiling above was peaked, supported by wooden crossbeams that had been repaired and replaced over the years, each one stained a slightly different shade by time. Like the one below the castle, this room was obviously lived in. Unlike that one, however, the furnishings here were not cobbled together from whatever bits and pieces were least destroyed throughout the castle's many rooms—here they were of a kind. A low daybed divan stretched along one wall below a shuttered window, bordered on each side by matching end tables. Odds and ends scattered their surfaces: a rabbit's skull hung with beads and feathers; a tiny box inlaid with mother-of-pearl; a small stone figurine of a knight such as a child might play with, worn shiny with use. Rugs of thick blue shag covered the floor, and the hearth at the far side of the room glowed with fresh coals.

The Beast turned to a wardrobe that stood near the divan, and sank bank on his haunches so he could reach with both paws to open the wardrobe doors. The air shimmered again, but this time it was easier to watch as he shifted enough to grasp at the door handles. She expected to see what one normally finds inside a wardrobe: cloaks, dresses, shoes, hatboxes—or else, she supposed, tunics and leggings, if the masculine decor spoke to the room's original occupant.

Instead the wardrobe was full of books.

Unlike those in the library below, the leather of these spines was bright with color, showing the original dyes, and their titles were stamped deep. Though the gold and silver leaf was worn from some of them, others she could read. Still others were written in languages she had never seen before.

She felt her breath leave her, and before she knew what she was doing, she came up beside the Beast so she could lift the lantern higher and scan the collection. There were maybe thirty or forty of them—nothing to how many were in the ruined library—but these had been cared for, protected and preserved against the years. And though they showed wear, cracked spines and corners rubbed such that the dye had faded, it was the kind of wear from use, the wear her own family's books had shown before they sold them. These books were read, many times. These books were loved.

The Beast shifted at her side, his fur brushing her arm and making her shiver. He was warm, warmer even than the coals in the hearth.

Yeva's mind spun. The spines that she could read bore the names of old knights' tales, the cataloging of magical creatures, adventures in distant lands she'd never heard of. No dry scholar's texts—all stories.

"You . . ." Yeva was so taken by surprise that she found it difficult to speak. "You—you saved these?"

The Beast's eyes slid from the contents of the wardrobe to Yeva's face, then back again. "Someone else used to live here," he said finally. "It was he who rescued these from the damp."

Yeva tore her eyes from the books so she could study the Beast's profile. When she looked again at the room she saw details she hadn't noticed before. The shag carpet lying before the fire was worn more than the others, flattened and thickened with fine pale-gray hairs, the same color as those coating the Beast's underbelly. The inside of the door was grooved with scratches, such as might be left by someone with claws before he remembered how to use a latch.

"You live here," she whispered, turning in a slow circle as her gaze flew about the round tower room. "This is where you stay when you don't stay in the cave."

The Beast's eyes fell to the floor. "Yes."

"But . . . why show me this now? These books, the trinkets . . . they're yours. Why keep it from me before?"

The Beast didn't answer. She could not see his eyes, for his head was dropped down and gaze fixed to the floor. The Beast remained silent for a time, and if it weren't for the way his chest rose and fell with increasing speed, Yeva would think he was ignoring her. But his emotions were rising, his breathing quickening, and she waited.

"You would not have cared," he burst out in a snarl. "We have no desire to change your opinion of us. You are our weapon. Nothing more. That you stay because you are waiting for the chance to kill us only serves our ends, to keep you here for our task."

Once, Yeva would have shrunk from his temper. Once, that snarl would have made her tremble. Now she just stared at him, a thousand questions spinning in her mind. Though her lips kept trying to shape the questions into words, there were too many for her to sort through, and she could only stand there, mouth opening and closing.

The Beast looked up finally to see her dumbfounded expression, and the too-human eyes faltered for an instant, brows lifting from fury into pain. Then he turned on his heels and stalked toward the door.

"Beast!" Yeva tore her feet from the ground and ran to throw herself between him and the door. "Wait."

The Beast paused, head dropping low, so low his muzzle nearly brushed the carpet. Yeva knew the body language from years of caring for Doe-Eyes and Pelei—shame. He regretted his outburst.

"Thank you . . . for showing me this," Yeva said.

The Beast's head swung round until he could fix those staring eyes on her, and this time they were round with surprise. Yeva had never thanked him for anything before, not since learning the truth of what he was. "You—" His voice deepened. "You may come here to read whenever you wish. I will leave the door unlocked."

Yeva's heart pounded as the Beast made his departure, his paw pads whispering against the stone as he went. She was wrong— she *had* thanked him once before, when he'd brought her a deer and called her Beauty.

She'd meant it then.

She meant it now, too. And that, more than the Beast's temper, more than the snarl of his fangs and the snap of his jaws, made her shiver. The reason he'd never shown her this room before was because he had no reason to do so. She was his captive, kept for his purpose. And he'd revealed this room now, this part of himself, simply because she had been sad . . . because he'd seen, in the way she looked at the ruined library, how much a room like this would mean to her.

Her vision blurred and she swiped angrily at her eyes. She ought to throw every one of these cared-for books into the fire. She ought to smash every keepsake and memento in this room. She ought to want to hurt the Beast in any way she could.

She crouched on the floor, burying her face in her arms. She couldn't stay here any longer. Each answer she found led her further from destroying this creature, this murderer, this thing that had killed her father. *He* was the reason she'd never hear her father read to her again. *He* was the reason her sisters must believe she was dead. *He* was the reason for everything. She could not let a place like this change any of that.

Doe-Eyes nuzzled at her elbow until she lifted her head, stroking absently behind her dog's ears. Her eyes fell upon the hearth, on the rug before it and its coating of fine hairs from the Beast's coat. She gazed at it for a long time, enough time for her thoughts to still and her pulse to quiet. The pieces were slow to connect, and she felt them sliding into place with something almost like dread.

For in showing her this room, the Beast had given her exactly what she'd been trying to find all these long months.

She'd known from the lack of tracks outside that he was not spending his nights in the dark den below the foundation. But she knew now where he slept in the castle, where he was at his most vulnerable.

She wasn't fast enough or skilled enough to kill him, not when he was awake and watching her, alert to her every movement. But if he were asleep . . .

Yeva forced herself to remember that moment in the forest all those weeks and months ago when she'd found her father's body. She forced herself to remember the surge of nausea when she realized that the Beast had killed him, that the blood spattered around that clearing was her father's. She made her mind flood with images of blood, and revenge, and hatred. She'd never hear her father read to her again, and the Beast had reminded her of it. Perhaps he felt guilty, and that was what prompted these little kindnesses, and there was a part of Yeva that needled her to think of using them against him—but she was stronger than the Beast, and she was harder, and she could outlast his guilt without caving to her own sympathy for his plight. She let the needles stab at her, again and again, until she felt numbed to their sting.

Because now she had the means to make everything right. She'd be able to go home, to her sisters and to Albe and to Solmir, though she could not think of them, not yet, not until it was done. It would not be tonight, nor tomorrow, but soon.

Soon she'd be able to kill the Beast.

BEAST

We see the way she looks at us. We are not blind.

She hates. When she forgets herself the hate retreats, like the river's waters in summer, but the damp sandy scars that stretch through the valley tell of the groundwater still there, still carving its course through the forest. And her hatred is still there, and its scars mark her face every time she sees us.

She must not know the truth. All we need is for her to stay, and complete her task, and if the thirst for revenge is what will keep her at our side, well, then we've thirsted enough to know she will stay until time robs her of youth and leaves her bent and trembling.

I wish just once she would look at me without hate.

But wishing is for men. Wanting is what brought us here. Desire and greed are human traits.

We are the Beast.

And yet . . . I wish.

SIXTEEN

WHEN THE STORMS RETREATED, the Beast began to take Yeva hunting again. Yeva had expected the weather to shift, for by her makeshift calendar she'd spent many months here, and spring ought to have begun creeping delicately in at the edges of the forest. But the valley remained blanketed with snow, a new dusting falling every few days to erase their tracks and give them a fresh canvas from which to work.

Yeva began to use that glimpse of magic the Beast had shown her, and slowly she became better at it. Soon she could track the Beast for leagues before she lost his trail, and the thrill of hunting prey that could outwit her, outsmart her, quickened her steps and sharpened the air in her lungs. She slept more soundly and deeply than she had in weeks cooped up in the castle.

Sometimes the Beast would spring from nowhere, shortly after she lost his trail, and demonstrate that he'd been two paces behind her for the last half hour, and Yeva would let herself laugh. The sound seemed to hearten the Beast, and Yeva felt his body language shifting, his manner warming. Spring had not come to the wood, but it was coming to the Beast's heart. And at the same time, she hardened her own.

It was no different from tracking him through the wood. Day by day she grew better, faster, more sensitive to the hints of magic that would alert her to his presence. And day by day, inch by grueling inch, he let down his guard.

One night Yeva returned to the castle after giving up on the Beast's trail to find that he had beaten her back, and had moved a number of pieces of furniture from the underground room into the one she'd chosen for herself. The blue velvet divan was there, and the table, and a big flat cushion stuffed with wheat husks and hay had appeared before the hearth. It was onto this cushion that Doe-Eyes sprang immediately and rolled around until she could stretch all four snow-covered paws out toward the fire, which crackled merrily.

Yeva stood in the doorway, fingering the tip of her bow, which she had not yet unstrung. She stared, feeling vague and uneasy, heart rebelling at how swiftly she felt at home here. This was not, could never be, home.

"Is there anything else you wish for?" The Beast spoke from a few paces behind her.

Yeva swallowed. "It's wonderful."

The Beast hovered just beyond the doorway. His gaze was on her hands, which still gripped her father's bow.

She took a deep breath and then slipped her leg between bow and string so she could bend it across her thigh and unstring it, there while the Beast watched. She set it in its corner and turned her back. She had to stop to remember how, and then, with effort, turned to smile at the Beast. "Thank you."

The Beast's ears flicked, flattened, then shot up again, which spoke to Yeva of surprise, then pleasure. He shuffled back a step, and before her eyes, he shimmered. It was the same eye-straining blur that occurred when he needed dexterity for locks or latches, but this time it was all of him, and for a moment he seemed like something else, some*one* else. Yeva heard a swell of music, like that she heard in the wood—only this was a song all his own, a thread she could separate and listen to and know.

Then the Beast shook himself and the mirage fell away like a shower of stray hairs. He took another step back.

"Good night, Beauty," he said, and quickly hurried into the shadowy corridor.

Yeva waited, controlling her breathing with an effort. She knew the Beast would hear the sound of her quickening breath if she let him.

"Sleep well," she whispered—then sat down to wait.

"Stay," Yeva whispered to Doe-Eyes, catching and holding the dog's gaze. She didn't like asserting her dominance, for it made Doe-Eyes unhappy and uncertain, but Yeva couldn't risk the dog coming after her anyway and alerting the Beast. Still, the fleet hound rose up, head cocked uncertainly, as Yeva moved toward the door. "Mind the house," Yeva said automatically, the command that had for years stood for two things: that Doe-Eyes must stay, and, most importantly, that Yeva would return.

Doe-Eyes sat back down and then, with reluctance, dropped her head onto her paws.

Yeva slipped into the corridor, knife resting comfortably in her palm. It was the blade the Beast had given her for butchering and carving, and if it was not quite as sharp as her fletching knife, it was much larger, and she'd grown familiar with it over the months. She let it hang from her hand beneath her cloak, easy to hide should the Beast be awake and spot her.

He could be watching her even now, from the shadows—but Yeva did not think so. She felt certain if he were near, she'd hear that thread of magic, that song that was all his own. If he were watching her, she'd hear the way that song quickened when he saw her, quickened to match the rate of her own heartbeat. And though her heart was racing now, she could not hear the Beast's song.

As she reached the hidden spiral stair leading to the turret, her heart pounded even harder. She wished she could control it as she could her breath, but she settled for controlling her speed, and moved quickly up the stairs and through the door. She slipped to the right and pressed her body against the side of the wardrobe. The room was lit dimly by the remains of a fire, and she saw the bulk of the Beast on the daybed along the wall. The steady rise and fall of his outline told Yeva that he slept.

Or pretends to sleep.

She'd thought of bringing her bow, so she then wouldn't have to risk crossing the room and getting close to the Beast. But even if her arrows could penetrate his hide, her best shot would be to perforate a lung, and it would take him far, far too long to suffocate to death. Enough time, certainly, to kill Yeva for what she'd done. Further, Yeva didn't know the extent of his magic, and whether he'd be able to heal such a wound. Her attack would have to be decisive, and brutal in order to be final.

If she could kill him from here, though, she would not have to see his face. And he would never see hers. Never know who had struck the killing blow. Never know it was his Beauty that had ended him.

She forced herself to shed those thoughts. She would have to be close to him when she struck. Her best chance was to cut his throat. He would kill her instinctively unless she penetrated deeply enough to nick his spinal column and deaden his movements. But even a Beast would bleed to death in seconds if she could open his jugular. Too quick for any magic he might summon.

She crept closer, watching for the slightest change in the rise and fall of his body. She breathed silently, forbade herself from taking any deeper breaths, forbade herself from swallowing her nervousness, for the tiniest sound could wake him. Something tickled at the back of her mind that the scene wasn't right, something about the proportions of the room that made her feel as though she were in a dream and watching the world distort. She felt too large, and the room too large as well. . . .

She realized what it was: the Beast was smaller.

And then he rolled over, and she saw why.

His form was human.

Not entirely human—it was as if the aspect of the wolf was laid overtop him like a costume. And like a costume, it didn't seem real. The ears and the teeth and the claws were but shadows. Yeva froze, staring down at his face with the knife clenched in her hand.

She'd long known that the Beast had two natures, and that they fought within him. She'd seen him use his hands, seen him shift a little when she treated him with kindness, saw the humanity in his eyes when he was at his softest.

He seemed to shift without thinking, without comment, and Yeva had wondered if it were possible he wasn't aware of it, or if his outward appearance shifted as involuntarily as the beating of his own heart. The knife felt like lead in her hand.

Do it, said the vengeful voice in her heart. *Before he catches your scent and wakes. Now! He is your father's murderer no matter what face he wears.*

Yeva lifted the knife.

The Beast's lips parted, his eyelids flickering. "Yeva," he mumbled. "Beauty."

She froze. He was dreaming about her. She swallowed before she could stop herself, body flooding with every ounce of uncertainty she'd been pushing into the dark, unseen corners of her mind where she wouldn't have to face it.

She swallowed, and the Beast heard it, and his eyes opened.

They met hers, still clouded with dreams, hazel-gold reflecting the firelight and holding no other hint of red. "Beauty," he said again, more distinctly, and his mouth was human, and Yeva could not move. His mouth. She couldn't look away.

The Beast's face cleared of sleep, and he blinked, and then he saw the knife. For an instant his eyes snapped back to Yeva's, shock and confusion and hurt mixing together, and in that moment he *was* human, and Yeva saw it, that only his human aspect could register and respond to this kind of betrayal.

She knew in another heartbeat he'd be the Beast again. And because she knew she'd die when he was, and because the animal instinct deep in her heart knew what to do, she struck.

The knife stabbed deep into his throat, and hit bone, and Yeva gasped aloud as she jerked the knife sideways, trying to slice. It wasn't quite sharp enough and it met with resistance, all the tissues and tendons in his neck fighting her. His gasp turned to a gurgle and to a whimper. And then the knife was out, and there was blood everywhere, blood on the rug and blood spattering the wardrobe. Blood spattered the pages of a book that had been left open by his bedside, as though he'd been reading just before he slept. Blood hissed and spat in the coals. Blood mixed with the tears Yeva suddenly found coursing down her cheeks and dripped, watery red and thin, onto her tunic.

The Beast moaned again, and he was once more every inch the wolf, except that Yeva thought she heard a word in the horrible hissing gurgle: "Beauty." Was it her name? Or was her heart searching for the word, somehow wanting to find it in that sighing death rattle?

A final breath. And then he was still.

Yeva dropped the knife, discovering that part of the moan echoing through the tower had been her own, and her voice petered out into a thin, reedy cry until she gulped for air. She staggered back and fell, landing on the plush carpet. The room spun as she lifted her hand to her face, and she inspected herself, because she could not be sure the Beast hadn't struck her before he died.

But she was whole.

She gasped again, the sound emerging hesitantly, like her body needed to confirm the Beast was really dead and she was really alive, despite the evidence before her eyes. Yeva could not look at the body and so stared at the bloodstained book until its image was burned into her eyes. She waited for a sense of victory. Triumph. Elation. Anything.

But she felt . . . nothing.

No, that was wrong. As the room quieted and her heart settled and her mind slowly, slowly began to uncurl itself and reinhabit her body, she *did* feel something. Hear something. Very faint, but growing with every breath.

Music. The song of magic.

The Beast opened his eyes.

Yeva cried out and scrambled backward until she hit the wall. The knife was out of reach, but she could not even think of it now. The Beast had been dead, she was sure of it, yet now she was staring at this impossible thing as it happened in front of her.

The Beast's gaping throat knit itself together neatly, as though she was watching a seam ripping in reverse. His lungs filled in one great, wet, rattling breath, and he coughed more blood onto the rug, and then he breathed again, and this time coughed pink foam, and then he lifted his head and, reeling as from a great blow, rolled onto the floor and onto his feet.

He gave a muted roar, sounding almost more inconvenienced and befuddled than furious, and stumbled forward a step. Then his head, still moving haltingly as the bones and tendons in his neck repaired themselves, swung over until his eyes found Yeva.

She could not even brace herself. She'd known he was magic, but this was sorcery beyond anything she could have imagined. This was nothing she could fight. She'd never felt so utterly helpless. The Beast would leap upon her soon and end it, and her terror was so real and so complete that she found herself praying that he would, and now, so that she would not have to feel this all-consuming fear an instant longer.

"Do not be afraid," he whispered, then fell over, sideways, and slumped to the floor.

Yeva sat gasping, staring at the Beast. She did not imagine him speaking to her instead of simply tearing her apart, and she certainly had not expected his words to be . . . *kind*.

She found her shoulder blades peeling from the wall. Her body seemed to move on its own, crawling on all fours closer to the Beast.

He groaned, and lifted his head. His mouth was half open, panting like an animal who's been too long in the sun and must cool itself—but these gasps were for breath, and Yeva knew there was still blood in his lungs, and that he'd fallen over from lack of air. "Do you think . . . ," he said haltingly, stopping to pant, "I had not tried . . . to end my life . . . already?"

Yeva could not speak, only stare at him numbly.

"I suppose . . . ," he wheezed, "it never occurred . . . to you." He let his great head drop onto his paws, exhaustion closing his eyes.

"What?" Yeva managed to whisper.

"That I am a prisoner too. And have been far longer than you."

Yeva was suddenly, keenly, brutally aware of her body; of the muscles strained and screaming; of the pounding in her own head from too much air, hyperventilated; of the way blood stuck her fingers together, the way it had somehow gotten inside the leg of her trousers, and was sticking the back of her knee to itself when she crawled. Her eyes burned, and she didn't know whether they held tears, or if some of the Beast's blood had gotten into them.

The Beast drew several long breaths, and each one slid a little bit more smoothly into his chest than the one before. "For a time—I do not know how much time—I tried everything I could think of. I threw myself from my tower. I opened my veins. I walked out into the cold and lay down in the snow and waited for the winter to take me, but it never did. I stopped eating, starved for months and waited to sleep and sleep and never stir again, but I woke every morning the same, emptiness within me. I begged Lamya, and the others, to kill me. But they also failed."

He stopped for another breath before opening his eyes to look at Yeva, a great sadness in them that cut through her shock, finally, and left her on the verge of weeping. "If I thought you would have succeeded I would have let you kill me that day in the forest, when you found your father, and followed me into my trap."

"Why?" Yeva trembled, her voice as raspy as if it had been her throat slashed. "Why forbid me to try to kill you, why threaten my family . . ." She swallowed. "Why lie?"

"Because we know wanting. We know desire. We know need."

"Need . . ."

"You needed to believe you had a purpose. You needed to believe that you could kill me. You needed . . . hope." The Beast watched her, the great sad eyes empty of all that rage, all that bestial ferocity that she'd seen that first day in the wood. "Now you understand that there is none."

They stared at each other across the bloodied rugs, the spattered pages of the book, the glinting, sticky knife. The coals in the hearth glowed steadily, and outside the winter wind sang through the mouths of the gargoyles and blew snow against the castle stones, and somewhere down below Doe-Eyes waited, ears pricked and eyes closed, for the sound of Yeva's footsteps returning.

"Tell me," the Beast said softly. "If you had known, from the start, that I could not be killed, that you would never have your vengeance . . . would you have stayed?"

Yeva didn't answer. She could not answer. Her heart had emptied. Her desire for revenge had nowhere to go. Without it, what did she have? What was she? What had she become?

But the Beast's words had stung her, touching a buried current she'd been ignoring for days. For weeks. Ever since he'd brought her a deer and, over its carcass, had called her *Beauty*.

"Beast," she whispered, numb. "Did you kill my father?"

His eyes flickered, the ghost of something passing before them so that for a moment he wasn't looking at her anymore, but at some memory, some thought she could not see. He didn't answer, but rose unsteadily to his feet. Before she knew what she was doing, Yeva stood as well and crossed to his side.

The Beast froze. His gaze dropped from Yeva's face to where

her hand had come to press against his chest to keep him from leaving.

She swallowed, abruptly aware of how infrequently she touched him, and forced herself to fight the instinct to withdraw. He moved as if to brush past her, but Yeva didn't take her hand from his chest, and dug her fingers into the soft fur.

"Let me go," the Beast said quietly. Then, so soft she almost missed it: "Please."

"He was already dead, wasn't he?" Yeva said. "When I came upon him in that clearing. You were coming to find him, to track the hunter you needed for your task, and you came upon his body moments before I did. The scavengers had gotten to him. He was already dead, wasn't he?"

The Beast shifted, the muscles stirring beneath her hand, reminding her that if the Beast truly wished to leave, he could brush her aside with an easy swat of his paw.

He did not answer. There was no need.

"Why take me?" Yeva asked.

The Beast's eyes closed, as if it might be easier to speak without Yeva's face before them. "Because I thought hunters like your father would come after you if you disappeared. I thought I could take one of them for my task. I knew I had to find someone else, someone younger, but still possessing his skill. I did not know then that you . . ."

The Beast's breath hitched. Yeva could feel it under her hand, and the beat of his pulse, so very like the music she heard in the wood. For the first time she understood how the Beast could hear it as a heartbeat.

"I did not know," he began again, "that you were the one I'd been searching for."

Before she could respond he slipped past her. Yeva could hear his steps for once, halting as he continued to recover from the mortal wound she'd given him, fading down the long curved stair of the tower. She thought they sounded like the rhythm of two feet rather than the gallop of four.

Nothing in her body was working, not her lungs nor her legs, and Yeva dropped to the floor with a feeling like knives in her chest. She began to sob so violently her body felt as if it might shatter. The fury that had sustained her, the burning need for revenge that had kept her alive in the cell, that had driven her in the wood to hone her archery and her tracking—what did she have now? Her fire had gone, and she felt its loss as keenly as if she were mourning a death.

And she was. When her father's death had been a murder, when he'd died because a savage Beast had ripped out his throat, she didn't have to grieve. She could find his killer and destroy him, stand over him, watch him die. She could have shaken the very earth with her vengeance and filled the gaping hole in her heart with blood.

She could have killed death itself.

But all that was gone now. Instead her father had died an old man's death, from a weakened heart and an unsound mind. He'd died cold and alone in a wood that he no longer knew. And there was no one who could pay for it, no one whose blood could dilute Yeva's grief.

She lay there on the floor, weeping into the blood-soaked rug, surrounded by the books her father would never read to her, the castle he would never see, the approaching spring that, for him, would never come. And as if by the same magic that had transformed the Beast, she became nothing more than a little girl who'd lost her father.

BEAST

The sound of her weeping follows us to the farthest reaches of the castle, even into our den below, back, back into the earth and the deep. We curse our animal's hearing and we curse our man's knowledge of what grief is and we curse the unfamiliar ache of regret that creeps ever deeper, ever deeper.

We curse everything, for we are cursed, and we have no arms to shelter her and no lips to press to her hair and above all no words to tell her that we know loss and we know pain and if they were monsters we could fight we would have slain them in her name long ago like the heroes of old.

But we are not a hero. We are cursed.

SEVENTEEN

EVENTUALLY YEVA'S WEEPING SLOWED, for though the lancing pain in her heart remained, her eyes could produce no more tears. She could not bring herself to stand, feeling as weak as if she'd been in bed for weeks—instead she crawled to the divan and slumped into its velvet cushions.

She slept.

Later she woke to a tiny sound, no louder than a whisper, but a sound she knew so well. A single footstep, the slip of paw pads against stone. The Beast was on the other side of the door. She waited, but he did not speak, and did not enter. After a time, she heard his footsteps retreating again, and she rose shakily to her feet. When she opened the door, she found food and a water skin and, wrapped in a roll of faded linen, her arrow-making supplies—and Doe-Eyes, having grown anxious waiting for her below, hoping to be allowed inside.

And then she found she could still weep, for the Beast who knew she did not want company and gave her that solitude, for the Beast who could not know how badly she *wanted* him to speak with her, about anything other than her father, and nothing but her father. She wept because she did not know what she wanted, and because she wanted everything, and because her father was dead.

She could not eat, so in time she slept again. This time hunger woke her, and Doe-Eyes's nosing at her elbow. Yeva stumbled toward the bowl of stew the Beast had left for her. It was cold now when she uncovered it, but she ate it anyway, ate until she forced herself to stop so she could offer the rest of it to Doe-Eyes, who sat at her feet trying not to stare longingly at the food in Yeva's hands.

Yeva sank back down onto the divan to the sounds of Doe-Eyes noisily cleaning out the rest of the bowl. Her eyes fell once more upon that book, the one the Beast had been reading where he slept, the one whose pages were stained with his blood. Her mind felt numb with the truth.

The Beast had not killed her father.

She had no more reason to stay, for each time the Beast had repeated his threat to punish her family if she escaped, she had believed it less and less. Now, as she thought of the pain in his eyes as he finally told her the truth, she knew he would not harm them, as surely as she knew the rhythm of her own heartbeat. She could leave. She could walk now out the door and down the bridge and out of the valley and never look back. She could go home.

As if the thought of them had summoned their spirits, Yeva felt the absence of her family so keenly, so abruptly, that she bent over at the waist and rested her head on her balled fists. She wanted Asenka, and her warm smile, and the feel of the wool between Yeva's fingers as Asenka knit. She wanted Lena's energy and spirit, and even her scolding, and could not help but imagine what she would say of Yeva's appearance if she could see her now, bloodstained and thin. She wanted Albe's fumbling attempts at kindness, his endearing grin, his devotion to the family that had raised him from childhood. She even wanted Solmir—the simplicity of him, how easy it would be to go with him back to the town to be his wife and ride horses through the trees and have servants to draw her baths, and books, and her sisters, and her dogs, and a life without magic and mysteries, and in that instant she knew she *could* do it. She could live that life. And just now she wanted it more than anything else.

She left the high tower room. She descended the twisting spiral turret, and walked through the master bedroom suite and into the long corridor, and down the next staircase and into the foyer and down the wide marble steps onto the wide marble floor. She pushed against the broad doors until they opened enough to send her stumbling and gasping and blinking into the harsh glare of the sun and the snow. She went sliding and stumbling down the snow-covered slope until she stood at the mouth of the Beast's cave, breathing hard, breath steaming the air, and sun-dazzled eyes conjuring wraiths out of the gloom to swim and twist beyond the edges of her vision.

"Beauty." The voice came from the depths of the cave, low and soft, velvet bass that echoed in the same place deep within her that heard the music of the magic wood.

"Beast," she answered, still breathing hard. "I must go."

Silence. She could not see him, only darkness, but she knew he could see her silhouette against the daylight at the mouth of the cave. Then, softly, his voice came again. "I know."

Yeva's heart shrank. It would have been easier if he'd roared at her, if he'd knocked her to the ground, locked her up, given her reason to hate him again. It would have been easier if he'd been the Beast. She swallowed. "My family. They're all alone. I have to go to them."

"You do not have to explain."

But I want to. Yeva stood, hands twisting in the fabric of her cloak, listening to Doe-Eyes pace around behind her, uncomfortable so close to the Beast's den.

Some part of the shadows moved, and she saw his eyes, gleaming briefly with reflected sunlight—then he moved again and the glimpse was gone. "Will you give your word to return someday?" the Beast said, so softly Yeva could not be certain she hadn't imagined it.

Yeva's mouth opened, but all she could think of was the echo of the conversation they'd had long ago, when they first stood face-to-face. "I will give you my word I won't try to kill you again."

"You did not promise to come back," the Beast said, and his voice was a lament, so shattered that Yeva almost began to weep again.

"No," she whispered instead. "I didn't."

She closed her eyes and listened with her soul, and from deep within the hollow of the cave she heard the Beast's song, the pulse of magic he'd taught her to hear. It was low and sweet, heavy with pain and age and the blurring of time. It held hints of things long forgotten, of stories and words and dreams and, most of all, desires.

The song *wanted*. It wanted in the way Yeva had always wanted, wanted not so much a thing as *everything*, something beyond naming, something *more than*, different, deeper. It was the want that kept her from saying yes to Solmir, though he offered her everything she could have named aloud; it was the want that brought her to the woods each day, the want that filled her dreams of some other life, something beyond what others desired; it was the want that screamed to the sky that she'd give everything, all of herself and all she'd ever be, to live one moment of that other life, the one she could not explain, not even to herself.

She closed her eyes and listened to the Beast's heart.

And before she could begin to weep again, she turned and she ran.

BEAST

Beauty. We feel her running, the spark of her life in our senses speeding southward, but growing no less dim for distance. We feel her like a star in the thick darkness of our valley, but she draws near its edge.

We thought we would have more time.

We should not have let her go.

We had to let her go.

Beauty. Beauty.

Hunter, hunted. We no longer know which she is, which we want her to be, which we need her to be. We know only that we need her. We must bring her back.

You must bring her back. You desire her. You want her.

Yes. But she is Beauty. She will be free. I wish her to be free.

The spark of her teeters on the edge of our senses, the edge of the valley, and then twinkles out. In every direction there is only the long, dark cold of winter.

Beauty.

Beauty.

Beauty.

EIGHTEEN

FOR A LONG TIME Yeva was only aware of the pounding of her feet and the soles of her boots and the crunch of the snow, and the icy air cutting deep into her lungs with every breath, and Doe-Eyes's joyful panting as the dog ran at her side. If she had not been training with the Beast almost every day she would not have been able to breathe the frigid air so easily, but she'd hardened her lungs against the cold and she ran like a deer, like a wolf, like Beauty.

Eventually the ache in her thighs and the tightening of her lungs slowed her, until she walked, numb, her muscles crackling with energy and pinging like red-hot metal cooling slowly after being pulled from the blacksmith's forge. Then, abruptly, she stopped.

She was sweating. The sun was warm on the top of her head, through the dappled leaves—*leaves?*—and she was no longer wading through snow.

There *was* no snow. Anywhere.

There were leaves on the trees.

It was spring.

No—she blinked, then blinked again, then stared upward, uncomprehending. The leaves overhead were golden and red, and fire orange, and her feet crunched as she walked, but not from snow. The toes of her boots disturbed piles of fallen leaves, and through the long arcs of the trees she saw a shimmer of gold here and a flash of red there as individual leaves tumbled and fell here and there in the still, autumn air.

Autumn.

Yeva's heart shrank.

She realized that time, like so many things in the Beast's valley, did not work there as it did in the outside world. But what she didn't know, what she could have no way of knowing, was how much time had passed. Had she missed only one summer? Or had a thousand years slipped away, so that her sisters' children, and their children's children, had all long since crumbled to dust?

Doe-Eyes, heedless of the strangeness of winter becoming autumn on the other side of the mountains, was leaping from leaf pile to leaf pile, sinking up to her shoulders and then bounding free, tongue flying from her gap-jawed grin.

But none of that could lift Yeva's heart, which felt small and tight and cold in her chest.

It took her days to find a familiar landmark, and it was no more than the proximity of a rabbit's den to a particular evergreen that triggered her memory. She'd seen that burrow before, many months—or perhaps many centuries—ago. She knew the forest in the Beast's valley now better than she'd ever known the one surrounding her father's cabin, but as she stood, turning slowly in a circle, she felt her instincts click a sense of her surroundings into place.

Home is that way.

Another two days, and she and Doe-Eyes found the stream that ran to a fork around the clearing. And as the sun set, they emerged into the clearing and saw the cabin.

It was empty.

Yeva's breath caught and for a while she merely stood there, blank, her thoughts coming in strange fragments. She was too tired to put them together with sense. But as Doe-Eyes began to sniff around the cabin, then sniff more urgently, then paw at the door with enthusiasm, a few things began to settle.

The clearing was still clear, and bigger than it had been, with only a few leaf-covered lumps to tell of the trees that had been hewn down for firewood. The wagon was gone, and as Yeva opened the door, she saw that much of the furniture was as well. And the floor, but for a few cobwebs in the corners, was tidy and clear.

The cabin might be empty, but it was emptied recently. Yeva strode back out into the clearing, scanning the ground for any sign of the wagon, or of horse tracks. But while the tidiness meant that the cabin had not lain abandoned for more than a few months, it would have taken only a few weeks, or even days if there was rain, for all trace of her family's path to vanish.

Yeva spent that night in the cabin, shivering in front of a small fire not because the air was cold, but because her heart was, and she could not warm it up. She resolved to return to the town, and ask if anyone there had heard from Tvertko's daughters, or knew in what direction they'd traveled, or of anything that had become of them.

For all she knew she *had* been gone centuries, and it was some

other family, some other wagon, some other life that had moved
away from this cabin and given her hope.

Hope, the Beast had said.

Yeva clenched her jaw and refused to think of him, and of the
great sadness in his eyes, and of the way he'd simply let her go,
because he had nothing else with which to hold her.

But while she could control her thoughts to some degree, she
could not control her dreams once she fell asleep, and while her
guard was down every thought was of the Beast, and her ears
rang with the song of magic, and the beat of wings, and she woke
sandy-eyed and weary at dawn.

She stopped at the first farmstead she reached and traded
a brace of rabbits for some brown bread and apples and a
mug of cider, and though the farmer's wife stared at her and
surreptitiously made a sign to ward off evil, Yeva asked them
nonetheless what year it was, and found that only one year had
passed since her father's ruin, and that she hadn't spent a century
in the Beast's company.

She moved on, and paid for a night in an inn with a handful
of quail's eggs and an archery lesson for the innkeeper's son, and
was so thrown by the feel of sheets and linens against her skin that
she ended up sleeping on the rug before the fire with Doe-Eyes.

She reached the outskirts of town on a gray afternoon, fits
of rain bursting from the sodden clouds to wet Yeva's hair and
weight her cloak. She was aching to find someone who might
know of where her family went, or what had befallen them, but
after the farmer's wife's reaction, she did not want to start rumors
of a crazy madwoman associated with them—for on the chance
that her family was alive and well, she wanted them to stay that
way.

It wasn't until she spotted a familiar face that she darted out from the alley into the street. "Galina!" Yeva exclaimed, shocked by her old friend's face. She looked so young, her skin so light and clean, not a hair out of place. Even the line of mud edging her skirt from the street was orderly, and civilized—everything Yeva had lost over the past year.

Galina jumped, startled, and then stumbled backward upon seeing Yeva. Yeva knew she must look alarming: muddy, scratched, weatherworn, and wet. Her arms and legs were lean with muscle now, and her hair was coarse with its own oils and dust from leaves and wind. Her clothes were still the bloodstained ones she'd worn when she'd tried to slay the Beast, and though the stains were old and brown, they were not hard to identify. The dog at her side was as wet and muddy as she was, and stiff with the tension she was picking up from her mistress.

"I—I carry no money," Galina said, fear written clearly across her face. "Please, I am with child—for his sake, don't . . ."

Yeva blinked and lifted a hand, freezing when the movement seemed to frighten Galina more. "Galina—" She stopped, registering the utter blankness with which her old friend regarded her. She didn't recognize Yeva at all. She swallowed. "You're married?"

Galina nodded, wide-eyed, arms hugging herself. "This past spring. Who—"

"I mean you no harm," Yeva said. She wondered who Galina had married, tried to think if she'd ever mentioned a passing fancy. With a pang, Yeva realized she knew very little about her friend, and almost nothing about the secret desires of her heart. She'd always been so eager to get away from the baronessa's entourage that she'd never truly gotten to know Galina. She tried to stifle the sting of regret and softened her voice. "I only want information."

Galina's fear had subsided only enough for her to breathe. "How do you know my name?"

"I . . . I asked someone." Yeva thought quickly. "You look about the age of the people I seek, and I thought you might have heard of them. Do you remember the merchant Tvertko, who lived here until last fall?"

"Of course," Galina said, the fear ebbing and leaving room for sympathy. "But I am sorry to tell you that he is dead."

Yeva's heart flinched. "I know. I wanted to ask if you knew where his daughters went. After the cabin. They went to the cabin, Tvertko's hunting cabin, and then . . . ?"

Galina's brow furrowed as she inspected Yeva, this dirty, bloody, wild thing that had stepped from the shadows and onto the bustling street, and who was attracting stares and oaths from passersby. "Two of his daughters live here, in town. They live in Tvertko's old house, up on the rise." Galina swallowed, face flickering with an old, remembered pain. "The other, his youngest—she is dead, too."

Yeva stared, too numb and dumbfounded to answer or to conceal how much Galina's words had affected her. So her sisters believed her dead. Not surprising, given Yeva's disappearance in the middle of winter with no sign of her for nearly a year. But to learn that they were alive and well, and living in their old house again, was beyond what Yeva could have hoped for them. She felt her eyes filling, a little of that tight, cold, hard thing in her chest easing.

When she saw the tears, Galina leaned forward, her breath catching. "Why do you ask me these questions? Who . . ." She trailed off, her brow still furrowed. A spark, the tiniest flicker, of recognition ignited behind her blank gaze.

"Thank you," Yeva mumbled, and hurried away with Doe-

Eyes at her heels before Galina could have a chance to see through the months of wilderness and cold stone floors to find the girl beneath. She didn't know why she ran—except that it would be hard enough to face her sisters, who believed her dead and had been mourning for her and her father both all these long months, and she did not want to run through it first with Galina.

Walking up the rise to their old house left Yeva with the most curious quiver in her heart, a mix of fear and anticipation that made her hands jittery. She wanted to reach for her bow— her hands kept twitching with the desire to pull her weapon off her shoulder—but there was no enemy to fight other than her own nervousness. Doe-Eyes seemed to remember the way, her steps growing lighter with excitement.

Yeva halted several paces from the door, her eyes sweeping the house as Doe-Eyes investigated the shrubbery lining the path. Her father's home looked exactly as it had a year ago, spent peonies littering the ground cover by the kitchen door, vines climbing up the trellis by her old bedroom window. Instead of reaching for the door knocker she stepped off the path and peeked in a window. There was the furniture they'd brought from the cabin, though some of it had been replaced with newer, nicer pieces. She saw someone move from one room to the next—a servant, she thought, but could not tell who. She circled the house, peeking through window after window until, without warning, her sisters were there.

They were in the kitchen, and they were baking bread. Lena was humming—though Yeva could not hear it through the warped and rippled window glass, she could see from the rhythmic tilt of her head to and fro that she was hearing music as she worked. Asenka was with her, her shoulder brushing Lena's from time to time as they worked. She had flour in her hair.

Lena reached for the mix of herbs to roll the dough in and Yeva's eyes swam with unexpected tears. Crusting the loaf with herbs had been Yeva's job since childhood, and to see her role in the family so neatly eliminated—she fought for breath and dashed her arm across her eyes, her cloak so heavily weighted with rain that she nearly sank to her knees.

They'd had no choice but to try to carry on. They believed she was dead. Yeva knew this. But here they were, happy and settled in the house they loved, clearly the recipients of some immensely good fortune. Perhaps Yeva should not walk back into their lives—perhaps it would be better if they simply went on as they were.

She stood, indecisive, the image of her sisters side by side rippling with tears and distorted glass.

Then a voice behind her demanded harshly, "Don't move." It was a man's voice, and Yeva froze. She was still so unused to hearing any voice but the Beast's that she felt a thrill of fear. "What are you doing there?"

"I'm sorry." She lifted her hands to show they were empty of weapons. Doe-Eyes was still on the other side of the house, sniffing at the trees and plantings. "I . . . I know this house and I was only trying to—I mean them no harm," she said, lamely repeating what she'd told Galina.

"A woman?" The man sounded surprised as he identified her gender from her voice. "Turn around."

Yeva swallowed and obeyed—and then stared. It was Solmir.

His hard gaze didn't flinch, and he eyed her suspiciously. "If you'll pardon me for saying so, madam, you don't look like someone acquainted with the ladies of this house."

Yeva's tongue wouldn't work. When she'd found that a year had passed while she was with the Beast, she'd assumed Solmir had long gone. He'd agreed to look after her family in exchange for her hand in marriage when she returned, and Yeva had taken it as certain that when she was given up for dead, Solmir would have politely and quietly withdrawn to search elsewhere for a wife.

But here he stood, a year later, clad in fine leathers outside Tvertko's home, protecting the sisters from the mud-soaked madwoman staring at them through the window.

When Yeva didn't speak, Solmir took a step toward her, then stopped. The tension left his body, arms falling to hang limp at his side. His brows lifted and his eyes grew round, and an expression strangely suspended between horror and hope touched his features. "I don't believe it," he whispered, face draining of color.

Unlike Galina, Solmir had seen through the dirt and the blood and the leanness of limb and face. He knew her at a glance, even as she was.

"Hello, Solmir," Yeva said weakly.

BEAST

Despair. Despair. Cannot. Must go. Cliff.
Water. Bleeding. Ending.

The animal does not understand, cannot
understand the need to end our existence but
I am here now, I control us. I have let it
take me for so many years, so very many long
years, but she has brought me back.

And I cannot descend again into that
madness, the in-betweenness of animal and
man, the combination of which leaves us less
than the sum of us, less than who and what
we once were. I cannot lose myself to instinct
now I remember . . . now I remember . . .

End, our heart cries. Stop. Empty. Please.

Let us die human. Let us die remembering
Beauty.

NINETEEN

SOLMIR DIDN'T MOVE, RECOGNITION petrifying him to the spot. He stared at Yeva as though she were the Firebird itself, myth turned real, magic become mundane and standing in someone's front garden. When it became clear he would not speak again, Yeva tried to clear her throat, and the sound interrupted whatever spell held Solmir and made him gulp for air.

"I'm alive," Yeva said, aware that this was a rather silly thing to say given that she was standing there before him.

But it seemed to hearten Solmir, who took a step forward, and then another, and another until he could reach out. His hand seemed uncertain where to rest, though, and after hovering by her shoulder, by her cheek, tracing the outside edge of a muddy lock of hair, it fell to his side again. "Yeva," he breathed finally. And there, at the edges of his eyes, Yeva saw something unexpected: sorrow. "I don't . . . I thought . . ."

Surely she must be imagining the sadness there—it was his confusion trying to steer him one way or the other. Yeva took the first of what she felt would be many long, steadying breaths. "I will tell you what's happened, and where I've been," she said. "And I will want to hear what has happened to you. But—but I would like to see my sisters first. And I'd like to tell you all at once."

She didn't think she could tell the story twice.

Solmir started, and the way he shoved his hand through his hair in sudden chagrin was abruptly so familiar to Yeva, and so completely human, that she felt a smile tug insistently at her cheeks. "Of course," he said, backing toward the door, as if loath to turn away from Yeva for fear she might vanish again. His face was so changed, so marked by emotions that Yeva could not interpret them all. Joy, disbelief, confusion, relief . . . and again, that conflicted flash of torment she could not place.

He groped for the latch and then disappeared, bursting through the house and leaving Yeva to trail after him, feeling strangely like a visitor in her own home, like she ought to wait by the door to be shown into the parlor. As if on cue a servant appeared, someone who had not worked for them before and who Yeva didn't recognize.

"May I take your cl . . . ," the maid began, then trailed off as she saw Yeva's warlike appearance. "Your cloak?" She paused, then hazarded, "Miss?"

Yeva gulped and reached for the clasp at her throat instinctively before thinking to point out that she was as muddy and wet beneath the cloak as on top of it, and it would do little good. But the maid was already gingerly taking the dingy thing into her arms, and rather than hanging it with the much cleaner—and more expensive—garments on the pegs by the door, she vanished into the next room.

She heard Asenka's voice firing off questions, growing nearer. "What are you saying? *She* who? Solmir, I don't understand. . . ."

Yeva turned to see Lena standing in the doorway to the front room, white-faced and frozen, and Asenka following, leaning on Solmir's arm to steady herself. Before Yeva could speak Lena screamed and fell back, half collapsing against the doorframe so that Solmir had to drop Asenka's arm or let Lena go crashing to the floor.

Asenka's eyes met Yeva's and clung there, round and dark, and, after a few long seconds, filling with tears. "I knew it," she whispered, so that Yeva could barely hear her over the sounds of Solmir attempting to revive Lena, who was still half senseless at the sight of her dead sister. "I knew you were alive." Asenka limped forward.

Yeva found she could not speak, could not even move, and it wasn't until she felt Asenka's arms go around her that she broke into a storm of weeping. Lena recovered herself and staggered toward them and threw her arms around them both, but her knees were still buckling, and after a moment of unsteadiness all three sisters sank into a heap on the floor, sobbing and hugging one another and all getting so muddy from Yeva's clothing that it was no longer easy to tell who was who.

By the time they made it to the sitting room before the fire, the rest of the household had heard the commotion, and word had spread that Tvertko's youngest daughter had returned from the dead. A few of the servants Yeva knew, for they'd been employed by their father and had returned. The cook screeched when she saw Yeva and then, just as loudly, announced she'd have the kettle on for tea. Others were new, and more confused about what was happening, for all they knew was that both the merchant and his youngest daughter had perished during the winter they'd spent at his hunting cabin.

Albe had stayed, too, but he was so bashful of Yeva—or

perhaps fearful of her, she could not tell which—that he hovered in the hall, peeking around the open doorframe at her whenever she spoke, and vanishing again whenever she looked his way.

Slowly, very slowly, with pauses for more tears and for explanations, Yeva learned what had befallen her family after she disappeared.

Solmir had faithfully continued to help feed and protect Albe and the sisters, monitoring the perimeter around the house for any sign of Yeva's return. After a little more than a week Radak, Lena's fiancé before their father's financial ruin, had appeared at the cabin, wild-eyed and demanding to see Lena. So flustered and distressed was he that he kept repeating his demand even after Lena stood in front of him repeating, "I am Lena! I am she! Radak, what is it?"

He had heard of her father's plight while traveling back from a business venture and had left his wagons and hired the fastest horse he could find, and arrived at the house in town to find another family living there, with no clue of Tvertko's whereabouts, nor his daughters'. Eventually he'd found a hunter who'd worked with the merchant long ago who knew the approximate location of the cabin, and from there he'd found Solmir's tracks, which led him to the door.

When Lena's voice brought him out of his cold and exhaustion, he dropped to his knees and asked her to marry him again, there in the open doorway of the cabin, soaked to the knee with melting snow and face chapped raw by wind and travel, and she had cried, and kissed him, and said yes. Radak, in possession of a fine new fortune as a result of his venture, had bought Tvertko's house back. They were wed immediately, so that he could bring her and her sister both to live with them—but they were unwilling to leave the cabin yet, hoping that Yeva and their father might return.

Yeva could not tell them about finding their father's body, her voice refusing to form the words—but when Lena's drawn face lifted and she whispered, "Father?" they could all see Yeva's answer in her eyes as they fell, in her hands as they twisted together, in the set of her lips as she turned her face away.

It was from that vantage point that she saw Solmir's hand twitch, a gesture she recognized as the urge to help, to touch, to comfort. And when she looked up, his eyes weren't on her, and her grief—they were on Asenka, who sat still as silent tears dripped from her chin and onto her folded hands.

Yeva was so caught by this that she was almost distracted from the reversal of her family's fortunes—but then Radak appeared in the doorway, having been fetched by one of the servants to come home and see Lena's long-lost sister.

"By God," he exclaimed in the doorway. He was a tall, thin man with terrible hay fever and a perpetually reddened nose that got chapped and flaky from the constant rubbing of his handkerchief. But he'd always been very kind, and after the story she'd heard of his devotion to her sister and to her family, Yeva thought that his face was perhaps one of the most handsome she'd ever seen. He joined them by the fire and kissed her cheek and then took Lena into his arms, wrapping them around her from behind, and it was only then that Yeva noticed with a jolt the curve of her sister's stomach.

She gasped wordlessly, and Lena, seeing Yeva's eyes go to her belly, grinned. "I did always like things to be prompt," Lena said, making Radak laugh softly in her ear. "The baby's no exception. He should be along in another four months."

Yeva gaped. She was still getting used to being a sister again, and now she would have to learn to be an aunt. "I've missed so much," she said, passing a hand over her eyes.

"Where *were* you?" Solmir burst out. He'd been quiet through most of the story, contributing only to dismiss the sisters' descriptions of his devotion to them during Yeva's absence with shakes of his head and flicks of his hand. He wouldn't look at Yeva directly, not if she was looking at him—he'd drop his eyes like a guilty man, as though his care and protection of her sisters was an act he ought to be ashamed of.

Yeva was slow to answer, at first because she was distracted by Solmir, and then because she could not think how to start. Each minute that she spent in her house, with her sisters, surrounded by the trappings of home, of wealth and security and all that had been stripped from her over the last year, made her life in the Beast's valley seem more and more distant.

Like it was no more than a fairy story, to be read in an old leather-bound book, from the safety and comfort of a warm bed.

Yeva accepted a cup of tea from the cook and blew on its steaming surface to buy herself time to order her thoughts. She took a sip to wet her throat, and began. "Do you remember the Beast Father spoke of, before he vanished?"

As the afternoon passed into evening and evening into night, Solmir left to return to the baron's household, where he was staying. As an eligible bachelor, it was hardly proper for him to stay too late in a household with two unmarried girls. The baron had been ailing from a chill caught over the last winter, and as his heir apparent, Solmir was a great comfort to him.

The servants brought dinner, and then tea, and then sweet-meats, and then cordial and brandy, all the while lingering a little too long in the sitting room as Yeva told her story. She imagined them gathering in the kitchen, each contributing what they'd overheard as they tried to patch together, thread by thread, the tapestry of Yeva's time with the Beast.

"I heard he was no Beast at all, but a man under a curse . . . ," one would say, while another would interrupt, "But I heard her say he had fangs and claws, and a roar so loud it shook the very earth beneath her feet."

At first her sisters, and Radak and Solmir as well, interrupted her with questions. But after Solmir was forced to depart, the questions grew fewer and fewer, and her sisters and her brother-in-law fell quiet, listening to the story. After its end they sat together there in front of the fire, digesting what Yeva had told them, and watching her with an even deeper, more profound disbelief and awe than when they'd first seen her, risen from the grave.

When it had been some hours since the last servant had appeared to eavesdrop, Yeva cleared her raw throat and stood in order to put another log on the fire, which was burning low in its grate. Radak had fallen asleep on the love seat beside his wife, head thrown back, breathing audibly through his mouth in deference to his hay fever. Lena threw him a fond look from where she sat curled in the now-limp circle of his arm, and nudged him gently until he settled to the side and his snoring ceased.

"He works too hard," she murmured into the quiet, the first anyone had spoken in some time.

Yeva sank down onto the rug before the fire, turning so that the coals warmed her back, and hugged her knees to her chest. "I knew he loved you for more than Father's wealth."

Lena's smile widened, and she sneaked another glance at the man sleeping next to her. "I had hoped. But that time was so awful, so full of unhappiness, it seemed all our luck had fled and everything that could go sour would."

"Our father died," Asenka said softly. "And with him, our little sister."

Yeva had always been closer to Asenka than Lena, in spirit as well as age. And it had always been Asenka to whom Yeva had confessed her heart. From the time Yeva could talk, Asenka had always been the one to listen to her when her little soul could no longer bear the weight of everything she wanted, the adventure and magic and the wide, wide wood, and all the things she could not name, that no one else seemed to understand.

Yeva's eyes stung, but she'd shed so many tears that day that none fell now, the well inside her dry. "If I could have sent word I was alive, I would have. I didn't think I would ever see any of you again."

"We waited as long as we could," Lena said, smile fading now. "But after summer ended, we knew we could not spend another winter in the cabin, not when Radak had this place for us again. And not with your new nephew on the way."

Yeva knew Lena was hoping for a boy, but she could hear a sound beneath everything else, a tiny, pulsing rhythm like the one she'd heard in the Beast's valley, and when she closed her eyes her sister's afterimage seemed to glow against her eyelids. And in that glow Yeva could see that the child would be a girl, though she could not have explained how she saw it. It was magic, and it frightened Yeva that she could see it even here, in town, as removed from the Beast's valley as it was from the far eastern sea.

Yeva watched her sister, and her unborn niece, and said nothing.

The quiet broke as Radak's breath caught and he harrumphed in his sleep, half waking. Lena took his hand and kissed his cheek and sent him off to bed and he went, only after she promised she would come soon.

"Yeva, this story . . ." Lena shook her head, her brows drawn in. "If it were anyone but you I would call her a liar."

"It's the truth," Yeva said. And yet there were pieces of the story she hadn't told them, fragments she kept to herself without knowing why: the way the Beast's voice changed when he said *I* instead of *we*; the way he smelled of spice and wind, except when snowmelt dampened his fur, when he smelled a little like a wet dog; how familiar the soft whisper of his paws on the stone floors had become; his eyes, as they met hers, right before she cut his throat.

She told herself it was because they would not believe those details, but in her heart she knew that wasn't the reason. Though she could not put the real reason into words.

"I believe you." Asenka slid from her chair onto the rug next to Yeva with a sigh, and stretched her feet out toward the fire. "But it will take some time before any of us understand."

"I know." Yeva's lips twitched. "I don't even understand yet. I just know that seeing you, and knowing you're here and safe . . . when I saw the empty cabin I feared something terrible had befallen you."

Lena had been avoiding Yeva's eyes—watching her, but looking away whenever her youngest sister glanced up. She finally let her breath out in a rush and bent over, face in her hands. "Oh, Yeva. I'm so sorry." She burst into tears.

Alarmed, Yeva glanced at Asenka, but she wouldn't meet her eyes either. "It's all right," Yeva said, sliding forward on the rug toward the love seat until she could take Lena's hands. "I'm fine. None of this was your fault."

Lena lifted her head, eyes brimming and face starting to redden and swell. "No, no—Yeva, I w-wanted to leave the cabin when spring came. I believed you were dead and I wanted to come home, and I was the one who told Solmir to stop. . . ." Her voice petered out, and she shook her head, unable to continue.

"You were the one who told him to stop looking for me," Yeva finished for her, gently.

Lena glanced at Asenka, then nodded.

"You did right." Yeva squeezed her hands. "You couldn't know I was alive."

"Asenka did!" Lena blurted through her tears. "She begged us to stay through the summer. She refused to believe you had died."

Yeva squeezed Lena's hands again and looked across the rug to Asenka, whose eyes were on the fire. Yeva bent her head and kissed her sister's hands. "None of that matters," she said firmly. "I don't think anyone can find the Beast's valley unless he wants them to—Solmir would not have found me if he had searched for a thousand years. Lena, you did the right thing. I'm so happy to find you all here."

Lena mumbled something and wrapped her arms around Yeva's neck, and they stayed that way for a time until Yeva told her to go join her husband, and sleep. She did so reluctantly, pausing on the third step to look back toward the fire, and the sister she'd thought she'd lost, before vanishing upstairs.

Yeva crawled back over by the hearth until she was near enough to Asenka to curl up as she used to do when she was a child, head in her older sister's lap, fingers grasping at her skirts as though they were a comforting blanket. Asenka bent her head and kissed Yeva's temple, and Yeva felt a tremble in her lips. She felt the patter of a tear hitting her cheek, and then another, but before she could look up, Asenka's hand began to stroke the dirty, muddy hair back from Yeva's face, and Yeva did not want to move for fear she would stop.

She fell asleep like that, and her last thought was of waiting to feel the next tear fall from Asenka's face to hers.

BEAST

I cannot continue.

The wolf is too strong. With her I could . . .
I was . . . but the animal within is angry and
his anger makes him strong. He wants us to
hunt, and feed, and run through the wood.
He wants us to exist as instinct and whim,
quick and brutal as winter. My thoughts
drive his mind as mad as his instinct poisons
mine. But I remember what I was, and it
makes me weak. My despair is mine alone,
and I am so tired.

Can't keep . . . no point. Curl up. Let
him. I'll fade.

Disappear.

TWENTY

YEVA ASSUMED SHE'D FEEL the itch to hunt, after it had become such a habit. That the town would seem crowded and dirty and loud, that the house would feel small after having lived in a castle. Instead it surprised her how easy it was to come back from the dead.

News spread through the town like the howling winter wind, so quickly that Yeva did not have to tell her story to anyone, because they already knew. Most of them had heard it entirely wrong, for the stranger the story, the more elaborate it became in the retelling—but she felt no urge to correct them.

And while her body was used to far more exercise than she could get strolling around town, it soon understood it was not being called upon to prowl through snow-covered forests or sprint after wild beasts, and settled.

She was not invited to rejoin the baronessa's circle of ladies, no doubt because no one quite knew what to make of her, whether she had spent the winter with an unmarried man under a curse or if she'd spent it in the bed of a wicked monster. Though neither was true, Yeva was hardly surprised that such doubts would prevent her from reentering high society. And since the baronessa's solarium was the one aspect of her life at home that she hadn't missed at all, that suited her perfectly.

After all, it didn't matter if the townsfolk were unsure about Yeva's honor, or whether her fantastical tale was the truth. She wasn't anticipating marriage proposals from any of them.

And then there was Solmir.

He visited daily, and though Yeva felt as fond of him as she'd been before her father's death, she also couldn't deny there was an odd gulf between them now. They'd grown close during their afternoon walks through the forest, checking Yeva's traps and talking about hunting, but he seemed stiffer around her, uncertain of himself. At first she thought it might be her new reputation making him ill at ease, and after a week she finally found the courage to ask him about it.

"Will you not tell me what's the matter?" Yeva burst out, after they'd sat in utter silence together under the peony tree, wrapped up against the autumn chill and watching the fire-gold leaves fall all around them.

Solmir started, looking for an instant like he'd forgotten Yeva was there at all. "What—what's the matter?"

"You're unhappy," Yeva said softly, and though it was the first time she'd used that word even to herself, she knew from the look on Solmir's face that she was right.

"No," he said swiftly. "I'm glad you're home."

"I know. But you can be happy about a thing and sad about it at the same time. Feeling one thing in your heart doesn't stop you from feeling another." Yeva pulled her cloak more tightly around herself. If her time in the Beast's castle had taught her nothing else, it was that anything—be it Beast or her own heart—could have more than one nature.

"I'm not unhappy that you're safe," Solmir said, so firmly he almost snapped the words. "Yeva, please. I'm only tired, and the baron is ailing, and I worry about him."

Yeva swallowed. "I know he once planned on naming you his heir. And I know the rumors that have been circulating about me. For you to be tied to such a woman would surely hurt your chances of—"

"Enough of that!" Solmir scowled at her, the first flicker of real, bright emotion beyond that distant melancholy she'd seen. "If you think I give a damn—sorry—about the silly rumors people whisper in the streets, you must not think very highly of me."

Yeva couldn't help but smile, for he was his old self again just then. But then her smile faded and she sighed. "I *do* think highly of you," she said softly. "I want you to be happy. Which is why—all I mean to say is that I don't intend to hold you to a promise you made a year ago. You believed I was dead. For all I know, you've begun courting someone else, some other girl in the baronessa's court."

Solmir's scowl smoothed, his face going blank. "You don't want to marry me anymore?"

Yeva's breath stuck in her throat, and as she saw hurt flickering behind that expressionless mask and her heart responded with a painful flutter, she realized she *did* love him. She loved him like she loved her sisters, like she loved Albe. She loved his heart, and his kindness, and the devotion he'd shown her family even after they all believed her dead. She didn't love him as a wife loved a husband, but she knew she could learn to do so, that she could be happy with him. If it would make him happy.

"You saved my family," Yeva said. "You helped my sisters

through the winter even after you thought I was dead and would never fulfill my end of the promise." Greatly daring, she reached out and took his hand. "I'll do anything you ask of me."

Solmir stared at her, his boyish face suddenly haggard. Weakly, his fingers squeezed hers back.

Yeva smiled. "Including releasing you from our engagement if that is what you want. You have your own reputation to think of, and I know that."

Solmir was silent, watching her. Beyond him and around him the peony leaves fell, drifting to and fro like feathers on the wind. *Yes,* Yeva thought. *I could love him.*

But though she struggled not to, she found herself listening with all her might for the tiniest glimmer of a song in him, of the magic the Beast had taught her to hear. All she heard was the sighing rustle of a breeze through the branches, and the crunch of leaves as Doe-Eyes and Pelei frolicked in the back garden, and the distant ring of the blacksmith's hammer in town, echoing back through the buildings.

And then Solmir's voice, saying, "I want nothing more than to continue keeping your family safe, as I promised." He squeezed her hand again, and this time there was strength to his grasp, and his smile was warm. "You are one of the most remarkable women I've ever known, Yeva, and it would be a fool who would let you go." He lifted her hand, and Yeva's heart flickered, and she waited for him to turn her palm over and kiss the inside of her wrist as he'd done that day in the forest. But he just brushed his lips against her knuckles, and then helped her to her feet and led her back inside.

Yeva dreamed that night of the peony tree. She was kissing Solmir beneath its branches, and its leaves fell around them like a rain of fire. His arms were around her and his palms pressed warm against her back, and all through her body ran a burning torrent she felt might consume her at any moment.

Solmir ducked his head to kiss her throat, then behind her ear, breathing in the scent of her hair and pulling her closer against him. Her head tipped back and she opened her eyes, and gasped.

The leaves falling all around them were not leaves after all, but feathers, feathers of red-gold fire. Yeva knew that if one of them touched her it would be too much, that just that tiny spark of heat would be enough to push her over the edge into the fire and she would burn. Her mind filled with the song she'd been searching for, and she felt magic in his pulse, and in the rhythm of his breath, and in her skin everywhere he touched her.

Then Solmir lifted his head and she saw his eyes, and they were gold, gold like the Firebird, gold like the feathers swirling around them in a blizzard of fire. His face wasn't Solmir's after all, but one she'd seen only once, and only by the faint light of a dying fire. But his eyes . . . those eyes were as familiar to her as her own heartbeat.

"Beauty," he whispered, tracing his fingertips along the contours of her face.

She woke gasping as if from a nightmare, but her body felt flushed and feverish and the pounding of her heart was not telling her to flee. Her thoughts flooded with regret, and for an instant she wished more than anything that she could return to that dream, for never in her life had she felt so awake.

Abruptly she realized three things: that she was sweating, that the window had blown open in the night, and that she was shivering. The heat and longing of the dream vanished and she groaned, sliding out of her bed and hurrying to the window. She was about to pull it closed when she heard something that made her stop.

It was still well before dawn, and the town was silent. She ought to hear only the noises of the night and the wind, but as she strained, she caught the faintest sound that made the fire of that dream sweep over her again.

She thought she heard distant music.

song

fire

beauty . . .

TWENTY-ONE

GALINA HAD COME TO visit Yeva a few days after word had spread through the town that Tvertko's youngest daughter had returned. She'd figured out the identity of the strange, wild-looking woman who'd accosted her in the street, and came full of apology and embarrassment that she hadn't recognized Yeva at once. But after a few visits, Yeva had managed to convince her that the lack of recognition was hardly Galina's fault. And since Galina was one of the few women around Yeva's age who didn't avoid her and her reputation like the plague, Yeva was glad for her company.

Aside from her sisters, who were all too eager to pretend nothing had changed, and Solmir, who responded to any mention of Yeva's absence with visible distress, Galina was the only other person who didn't turn every conversation into a stream of questions about the Beast. She'd talk about her new husband, a tailor on Market Street who had shyly designed a beautiful gown for her to wear at one of the baronessa's parties. She'd talk about how exhausting and frustrating her pregnancy was, as she was currently suffering through an endless run of mornings where she could not eat a bite without throwing it back up again. She'd talk about the current fashions, and the other ladies, and who was leaving for the city and who was moving into the vacant house on the eastern edge of town, and whether there would be an early frost to damage the harvests.

Perhaps it was *because* she didn't ask about the Beast that Yeva wound up speaking of him herself.

They were strolling through the marketplace, where the vendors were pressing their wares on passersby with renewed vigor, determined to sell as much of their stock as possible before winter shut the marketplace down for the year. Galina found that walking eased her nausea, and Yeva was all too glad to stretch legs that had been accustomed to long days of running through the woods.

"Yeva, is something the matter?" Galina's voice was soft, a change from the laughter with which she'd been talking about her husband's latest experiments with brocade.

Yeva lifted her gaze from the ground, where she'd been separating and categorizing the layers upon layers of footprints in the dried-mud street. "What? No, I'm merely feeling quiet today." But when she saw Galina's face, gentle and concerned and entirely without artifice or anything hidden, she sighed. "I've been dreaming about him."

"Solmir?" Galina asked, eyebrows lifting.

Yeva shook her head. "The Beast."

Galina was quiet, stride not even pausing. Yeva waited for the standard reassurances—*oh, the nightmares will fade, you've been through such a trial, give it time and you will learn you've nothing to fear anymore*— but Galina just asked, "What kind of dreams?"

Yeva felt her face warming despite the chill in the air and
kept her eyes down. "They aren't bad dreams. In fact, I . . . I
like them. They're nice dreams. They make me . . ." She stopped
before she could finish the sentence, unwilling to utter the words
she was about to say.

They make me miss him.

Galina nodded toward the square up ahead, and claiming
weariness, suggested they sit on the rough-hewn fountain over
the well. It wasn't the most private of places, but just now nobody
was fetching water, and the blur of activity about the town offered
its own cloak of anonymity.

Yeva sat, feeling the cold stone seeping through her layers of
skirts. She'd been thinking of the Beast's valley more and more
as winter approached, and though there'd been no frost yet, she
wasn't sure if she'd be able to see the town blanketed in snow
without longing for the forest and its music.

Galina let her breath out in a rush as she sat, and watched
people moving to and fro for a time before she spoke. "I have a
cousin in Kiev," she said finally, "who got married very young,
because she wasn't wealthy enough for a large dowry and her
parents didn't know if she'd ever get another offer like the one
she'd received."

Yeva wondered if Galina had forgotten about her dreams,
and nodded.

"Her husband wasn't a good man. He hit her when she didn't
do everything exactly to his liking—if the bread was burned,
or if the house wasn't spotless, or if he thought she'd looked too
long at another man. He always hit her where it wouldn't show,
until one day he lost his temper and blackened her eye and her
brother recognized what was happening. But when he prepared
to deal with the husband, to bring the matter to the magistrate

and get the marriage annulled, my cousin begged him not to. She defended her husband and said he only had a terrible temper, that he was so loving and so apologetic afterward, and that no other man could possibly make her feel so special, so loved. She said that without her he'd be lost, and that he needed her."

Yeva listened in silence, her own thoughts troubled. She'd known other women who'd formed attachments to men who were cruel to them, though she'd never known any in such dire situations. She'd always thought them foolish, weak, lacking in the self-assurance to know they were better than the men whose backhanded compliments made them flush so. But perhaps they were simply in love. Perhaps their hearts had betrayed them, and not their courage.

Galina leaned back. "I tell you this because I wonder . . . I wonder if something like that has happened to you."

Yeva bit back a quick reply, forcing herself to absorb the story, and closed her eyes. "He never hurt me. Well, he did once, but to be fair, I had shot him with an arrow and was about to kill him with an ax."

Galina's expression flickered, but she managed not to blanch too visibly. "Maybe not, but you were his prisoner. That's a different kind of hurt, but hurt nonetheless."

"And I wanted to kill him," Yeva said, "when I was his prisoner. It was my whole reason for existing, surviving. I didn't fall in love with him because he hurt me—the idea is absurd."

Galina's eyebrows shot up. "In *love* with him? Heavens, Yeva, that's not what I meant at all. Who could even imagine such a thing?"

Yeva's face burned hot. "I thought—I mean, you were talking about your cousin—"

Galina shook her head quickly. "Good lord, no." Now she

was watching Yeva closely, voice dropping despite the noise of the bustling streets. "You care about him."

Yeva blinked hard, the words ringing in her ears, words she'd never dared say even to herself, even in the deepest, quietest parts of the night when she woke sweating and longing. "I—I feel for him," she whispered. Her eyes burned at the admission, and she looked up, barely able to meet Galina's eyes. "What does that make me?"

Though she tried to hide it, Galina's expression held the tiniest glimmer of horror, and it made Yeva shrink. But Galina drew a breath and when she let it out, her reply came in a sigh: "Human."

Yeva balled up her fists and ground them against her eyes, punishing them for their betrayal, making sure there'd be no more tears. "I hated him. I hated him more than anything, like I've never hated before. I didn't know I could hate until I hated the Beast."

"So what changed?"

Yeva had to pause to breathe until her voice steadied. "I found out he was a prisoner too," she whispered. "And that he was as lonely as I had been."

"Lonely?" Galina echoed. "But Yeva, he was the reason you were lonely, cooped up all alone in that old castle—"

"No," Yeva interrupted. "I was lonely before. I was lonely in the cabin, with my sisters. I was lonely here, with the baronessa."

Galina bit her lip, eyes dropping. Too late, Yeva realized she was saying that even her friendship with Galina in the past had left her lonely, but it was the truth, and she couldn't take it back.

"I was always lonely, and I never knew it until I met the Beast. The real Beast, the one beneath the fangs and the claws and the rage. The one who reads, who listens to fairy stories, who comes alive in the forest, who hears music. . . ."

"Music?" Galina frowned.

Yeva started. "No, I just meant—I don't know what I meant."

"But Yeva . . . he held you prisoner. He threatened your family."

"I know." Yeva's eyes crept up toward the hill, and though she couldn't see her father's house from here, she could imagine it just on the other side of the ridge. "And I took advantage of his trust and tried to kill him. We have both hurt each other."

"What makes you think he wouldn't have kept trying to hurt you if you hadn't escaped?"

"Because I didn't escape," Yeva replied simply. "He let me go."

Galina's face was troubled. "Give it time," she suggested softly. "You have your sisters, and me, and you have Solmir. Think of Solmir—you won't be lonely here, Yeva. You're surrounded by people who love you."

Yeva knew she was right. She thought of Solmir, and of his warm eyes, and of the tremendous kindnesses he'd shown her family. She tried to ignore the bite in the air as she and Galina stood and began the walk back to her home. It smelled like snow.

Asenka still spent most of her days at the leech's shop, helping to nurse the sick. The leech himself was good enough at treating illnesses, but he was an arrogant, officious man with no patience or interest in people—his passion lay in disease itself, in making endless lists of symptoms and treatments and linking them together. So it was Asenka, and her smiles and her unflinching sympathy in the face of horrific injury or disease, to whom many of the townsfolk quietly attributed their recoveries whenever they fell ill.

Yeva came now and then to share the noonday meal with her. Though Asenka was given lunch by the leech, it was more often than not cold meat on cold bread, so when Yeva brought hot stew from home, the change was more than welcome. Asenka's little corner of the upstairs loft in the shop was quiet, and unless the leech had patients so ill as to need full-time care, the beds in the loft were empty. It was a respite from the bustle of town, and even from their own home, which was full of servants, and Radak and Lena. Yeva had come to understand why Asenka enjoyed her time here so.

Sometimes they talked about the Beast. Sometimes they talked about Lena, and how increasingly irritable she was becoming due to the baby growing in her womb. Occasionally they spoke of their father, but most often they simply ate together quietly, enjoying the rare, precious company of silence shared.

It was the latter Yeva was hoping for when she decided to wrap up a tureen of dumplings in mutton broth and cabbage and walk down to the leech's shop. Lena was overseeing the redecoration of their sewing room as it was being converted into a nursery, and Yeva felt she might shout at her if she were asked one more time to choose between two nearly identical tapestries to cover the walls.

But as she climbed the stairs to the leech's upstairs, she heard voices.

"I asked you to go." Though Asenka's voice was quiet, the pain in it carried easily down the stairs and made Yeva stop short.

"I don't believe you mean it." It was Solmir. Yeva stifled her breath of surprise with her hand, and though her conscience told her she ought to creep away again, she couldn't help but stay to listen. Solmir sounded every bit as sad and hurt as he'd seemed lately, and she'd do anything to discover the cause.

"You can't keep coming here," Asenka said, voice rising. "It's improper. Someone will see you, and talk, and our family's had more than its fair share of rumor and gossip lately."

"What do I care?" Solmir burst out, with that same passion Yeva had come to find endearing.

"It's not you!" Asenka cried, making Yeva teeter on the stairs in surprise. She couldn't remember the last time Asenka had raised her voice to anyone. "*I* care, Solmir. Lena and Radak care. Yeva cares."

Solmir let out a frustrated, wordless sound, and Yeva heard his boots clomping first one way, then the other. "Asenka," he said, more quietly now. "Asenka, please. We must tell her the truth. If we don't, you'll be miserable, I'll be miserable—no one will be happy if we go through with this."

"Yeva will be," Asenka whispered.

"Asenka—"

"Go."

"No, I won't—"

"I said *go*." Asenka's voice held such steel as Yeva never knew she possessed, and Yeva ended up gawking at the empty landing ahead of her. It wasn't until she heard Solmir's slow, leaden footsteps heading for the stairs that she started and hurried away as quietly as she could.

That night Yeva waited until the household grew silent, and all the servants had retired and Radak and Lena were asleep. She crept out of bed, shivering as she pulled on a pair of woolen stockings, and then took up the quilt on her bed to wrap around her shoulders before slipping into the hall. She padded down to Asenka's room, where the door was open a crack as it always had been when Yeva was a child, and crept inside.

When she was young Yeva would crawl into Asenka's bed to tell her about her dreams of fairy-tale monsters and wicked spells, as thrilled and excited as she was frightened. Tonight her heart quickened as it used to, and for a moment she thought her throat wouldn't work until her whisper burst out: "Asenka?"

Her sister mumbled unintelligibly, then sat up. "Yeva, what is it?"

"Can I come in?"

"Always." Asenka slid sideways to make room for Yeva on the bed.

Yeva darted over and under the covers, warmed by Asenka's body heat. She turned on her side and wrapped her arms around her sister, pressing her forehead against her shoulder. "I need advice," Yeva said.

"About what?" Asenka tilted her head to the side until her temple rested against Yeva's hair.

"Solmir."

Asenka's body stiffened—so close, it was impossible for her to hide it from Yeva, and she knew it. "Please," she said eventually, sounding tired. "I can't."

Yeva's arms tightened, and she reminded herself that she needed to know what was happening, even if asking made her sister unhappy. "Something is wrong. I want him to be happy, but he's not, and he won't tell me why."

"Why would you think I could answer, when you can't?" Asenka's words were careful. She was never able to lie well, and certainly not to her own family.

"Because," Yeva said. "Because I think you're still in love with him."

Asenka's breath tangled in her throat, audible with Yeva so close to her. For the first time Yeva could remember, her sister pulled away from her and sat up, retreating to the corner of the bed and drawing up her knees. "Yeva," she gasped, anger tinting her voice. "He's your fiancé. I would never—it was a girlish whim, a childish fancy I set aside long ago."

Yeva's heart ached, because she could see the lie even in the dark, shining from Asenka's eyes more brightly than the moonlight from the window. "Asenka—has he fallen in love with you, too?"

Asenka's eyes flashed. "Of course not," she spluttered. "He loves you, he's marrying you. He wants to spend the rest of his life with you, he always has, since he met you."

"Even when he thought I was dead?" Yeva asked gently.

"It doesn't matter!" Asenka's voice was suddenly fierce. "I never believed you were gone. I knew you were alive. I knew you would come back, and I knew he must be here, waiting for you, when you did."

"Oh, Asenka." Yeva reached out, groping until she found her sister's hand. "If you love him, and he loves you, you must accept that. I won't be the one who comes between you."

"No," Asenka snapped, her voice as steely as when she'd sent Solmir from the leech's shop. "He was meant for you."

"I don't want him." Yeva spoke as gently as she could. "Oh, I care for him—I care for him very much. I can never repay all that he did for us. But Asenka, I've realized . . . he wasn't doing all of it for me. He was doing it for you."

Asenka had begun to cry, and was shaking her head again and again. "No," she said, voice thick. "Yeva, you are my sister. I love you. I love you more than anything. You and Lena are the most important things in all the world." She finally squeezed Yeva's hand back, swallowing audibly. "I would give up a thousand Solmirs for you."

Yeva crawled forward and slid her arms around Asenka's waist. "I know. But I'm not in love with him. Not the way you are. Asenka, I want you to be with him. I want it for you both."

Asenka's tears overflowed and she gave a wordless sob. A memory hit Yeva, the force of it robbing her of breath: a single sob, lost in the darkness in the back of the hunting cabin, the night Solmir had come to propose to Yeva and Asenka had seen where his heart lay. Yeva pulled her sister close, and they sat that way, rocking together, bound and twisted up in the bedclothes and murmuring to each other.

Finally Asenka's tears slowed, and she lifted her head. Yeva brushed her hair from her eyes and touched the tears from her cheeks, just as Asenka used to do for her when Yeva would come crying to her for comfort.

"But you must marry Solmir," Asenka whispered, her eyes intent.

"Why?" Yeva shook her head, unable to think why her sister was so insistent.

"Because if he doesn't hold you here, you will go back." Asenka reached up to lay her hand against Yeva's cheek. "Back to the Beast."

Yeva's heart twitched and leaped, and she caught her breath. "What? Don't—don't be absurd. Why would I go back?"

But as they sat there together, and Yeva held Asenka until she drifted off to sleep, her sister's words echoed in her mind over and over, until they settled into place, like a missing piece that filled the exact shape of the hollow in her heart she'd been trying to ignore.

Back to the Beast.

BEAST

We run. We hunt. We feed.
*   *We are of the forest and of magic, and we*
have always been. We glory in the kill.
*   *We are the Beast,*
*   *and we will always be.*

TWENTY-TWO

THAT NIGHT YEVA'S VISION of the Beast was a
nightmare. She dreamed she was the deer, and that the Beast was
stalking her through the wood. She could not see or hear or smell
him, but some deep-rooted instinct knew he was there. She knew
she was prey.

But when she woke gasping, it was not the thought of being
caught and consumed that echoed in her fear-muddled mind.
All she could see were the Beast's eyes, red and fixated on her,
full of bloodlust and nothing more. They held no humanity, no
sense—not even the careful cunning of a predator. The eyes were
simply mad, like those of a rabid animal. They were not the eyes
of the creature, man or Beast, she'd come to know in the castle.

She rose before any of the servants and stoked the fires in
the sitting room and the kitchen, and put a kettle of water on to
boil for tea. The tasks reminded her of her life in the hunting
cabin with her family, and she felt a twinge of loss as she stood
warming her fingers and toes before the flames. She knew her

sisters would remember those few months as a time of terrible hardship and fear, but Yeva couldn't help but see them as the start of a journey that would change her forever.

For she *was* changed. Yeva knew that to live here, among her family and the townsfolk and the bricks and mortar and steel and bustle, would require diligence and focus. She could not think of the forest, of Lamya and the music and the things she'd seen deep in the castle valley, of the thrill of that other world. She would not remember how alive she'd been when she was the animal, focused on nothing but the hunt.

Because Asenka was right. Without Solmir, without the knowledge that she must keep her promise, that she must make him happy to repay him for all he'd done, that she must make herself happy and pretend that this life still held a place shaped for her to slip into . . . without all that, what her heart most wanted was to return. Her nightmare needled her, a gnawing worry for the Beast himself. Though it was only a dream, she could not shake the fear that there was some truth in it—that without her, the Beast's humanity was slipping away.

She could not banish the thought that the Beast needed her.

By the time the rest of the household had woken, Yeva had packed a few meager possessions into a bag. Her father's bow, which had been unstrung since the day she'd returned, stood next to it, string dangling from one notched end as if in invitation. She'd brought her fletching knife, some day-old bread and apples and dried meat, flint and tinder, a new cloak to replace the torn and muddy one Lena had insisted on burning. She brought only what she thought she'd need on the journey back to the Beast's castle.

Except for one thing, which served no practical purpose: she'd brought a book, one of the few volumes her sisters had managed to track down and buy back from the townsfolk who'd purchased Tvertko's possessions before the family departed a year ago. It was the book of fairy tales that her father had read to her when she was very small, so small that it was his voice telling her stories that colored her very earliest memory. She remembered perching on the sill of her bedroom window with the pane opened a crack so she could let the winter in, and she remembered letting it sting her nose and wash over her until she was shivering and blue.

"Ah, my little Beauty!" her father had cried when he lowered the book and saw her. "You'll be frozen to the core! Come away. What are you doing?"

"I'm listening for the Firebird," little Beauty had replied, voice shaking with cold. "Can't you hear it, Daddy?"

Her father set the book aside and strode to the window beside her. He wrapped her up in his warm arms, but rather than close the window and bring her back to bed, he stood listening too. And after a moment, she felt his whiskers scrape at her cheek as he nodded. "Aye," he said gravely. "I hear it."

"How sad it sounds," little Beauty said.

"Why is it sad?" her father asked.

"Because it is lonely."

Her father stayed quiet for a while, then sighed. "Perhaps we will give it some company. When spring comes, how would you like to come with me to my cabin? I used to live there, before I met your mother and we were given you girls. It lies deep in the forest, and I can teach you all about the things that dwell there."

"Does the Firebird live there?" Beauty had asked, brimming with sudden excitement.

"The Firebird, aye, and many other wonders. Would you like that, my little Beauty?"

Beauty had squealed and turned from the window and thrown her arms around her father's neck, making him laugh and fall back as though she'd been a wild beast whose weight had driven him to the floor. She was five years old.

Now, Yeva shivered despite the fire surging back to life before her. *How sad it sounds,* she thought, remembering the Beast's low, somber voice. *How lonely.*

Pelei, while overjoyed to see Yeva again, had nonetheless developed a quick and surprising preference for Radak. Lena said it was because of everyone, Radak had been the least generous with his affections for the dog, which seemed to make Pelei work all the harder to win him over. Though Radak protested he cared nothing for the creature, Lena privately confessed that most nights it was Radak who covertly invited the big shaggy scent hound up on their bed, to fold himself up in the hollow behind Radak's knees.

Doe-Eyes, however, still rarely left Yeva's side. It was Doe-Eyes who woke with her when Yeva bolted upright out of her dreams, and it was Doe-Eyes who padded downstairs with her when she woke early or wandered the back garden aimlessly.

And it was Doe-Eyes who lay across the front door now, trying to look easy and relaxed, but watching Yeva's every movement with an intensity that betrayed her. Even as servants stirred and began the morning's tasks, Doe-Eyes didn't move. Yeva wondered how she could possibly know this morning was different from any others, how she could possibly read Yeva's heart, but her time with the Beast had taught her how a creature could shout its intentions to the sky without ever making a sound. She knew Doe-Eyes could see Yeva meant to leave.

"If you wish to come," Yeva whispered, crouching down by Doe-Eyes and laying her cheek against the top of the dog's warm head, "then I will be glad for the company. But here you'll be warm and fed, and there I can't guarantee what we'll find. He might be—we might be on our own."

Doe-Eyes heaved a great sigh, blowing hot, wet air across Yeva's neck, and didn't shift from her spot guarding Yeva's belongings by the door.

"What are you doing up?" Lena stood at the bottom of the staircase, rubbing at her eyes. She was wearing a dressing gown over her nightclothes, and her hair was flattened on one side from her pillow.

Yeva searched for the words to tell her sister that she was leaving, that she was afraid for the Beast, but could find none. But after a few breaths Lena's sleepy eyes widened, traveling from Yeva, to Doe-Eyes skittering urgently from side to side, to the pack at Yeva's feet.

The sleep left Lena's face and she stumbled down the last few steps toward her sister. "Yeva! Where are you going?"

Yeva shook her head mutely, and gathered the cloak in her arms more tightly against her chest.

"No." Horror colored Lena's voice. "No, you *can't*. He's a monster."

Yeva closed her eyes. "I know," she murmured. When she opened her eyes again Asenka had emerged, drawn by the sharpness of Lena's tone, and stood on the stairs watching them. "He is a monster. But I believe he's a monster because of something that was done to him. I believe I can save him."

"You don't owe him anything!" Lena cried. "He's done nothing but hurt you!"

Yeva shook her head. "He let me go. And if I return to him now, we'll be on equal terms. I won't be hunting him, and he won't be hunting me."

"Why would you *want* to go back?"

"I . . . I can't explain it." Yeva sighed. "But . . . the Beast is not the monster. The monster is what he's become. He took me because he thought I could free him, and I mean to find out why."

"You mustn't." Lena, stubborn as always, stalked across the floor and snatched up Yeva's pack, as if she might prevent her sister from leaving if she could take away her supplies. "This makes no sense."

"Yes, it does." Asenka's voice came quietly from where she'd sunk down to sit on one of the steps leading to the upstairs. Her eyes never left Yeva's. "She's going to rescue him."

Lena stared from Asenka to Yeva, spluttering. "R-rescue? Yeva! You're no knight from an old story, and he's certainly no maiden in distress."

"No," agreed Yeva, fighting back the irrational urge to smile. "But I mean to try, nevertheless."

Lena's expression clouded. "You left us once before," she said intently, well aware that she was resorting to unfair tactics. "If it weren't for Radak and Solmir . . ."

Her sister's words cut. She had abandoned them in pursuit of revenge. But it was different this time. "But you have them now, for always," Yeva said gently. Her eyes flicked toward Asenka, whose face flushed, guilt and longing mingling in her features. "Solmir was never for me, Lena."

Lena, too, glanced over her shoulder at Asenka. Yeva knew from the look on Lena's face that she'd been right to release her fiancé from his promise.

Lena drew a shaky breath. "At least stay one more night," she begged. "One more dinner, one more evening before the fire. Please?"

Yeva hesitated, but even Asenka's expression was pleading, and her resolve crumbled. "One more night," she agreed, then turned for the door.

"Wait! Where are you going?"

"I must speak to Solmir." Yeva didn't have to look at Asenka to know what she'd find on her sister's face. "I promise, I'll come back. Here," she added, when Lena didn't look convinced. "Take Father's bow. I wouldn't leave it behind."

Lena took the long, curved staff of the unstrung bow in hands that were unused to holding weapons of any kind, and cast Yeva an uncertain look. "One more night," she repeated.

"I promise."

The baron's manor house stood on a rise on the other end of town, and Yeva took the long path that circumnavigated the busier streets. Though she often preferred to avoid the crowds who still looked at her like she was half spirit, half saint, today she simply wanted the time to gather her thoughts.

The Beast had been waiting hundreds, if not thousands, of years to break his curse. One more day would not be the end of him. And yet Yeva's heart felt tight and uncomfortable, and her feet itched for the soft give of the forest's carpet of leaf mold instead of the hard-packed mud of the town streets.

The gates of the baron's estate stood open, as they almost always did, and Yeva was not stopped until she reached the manor itself. The doorman showed her inside; Solmir must have given the staff instructions in advance. She was brought to a sitting room hung with tapestries—one of the baron's rooms, and not one she frequented as part of the baronessa's retinue—and left to wait.

She couldn't help but compare this room to those of the castle in the valley. Though this room had no hint of mildew or age, nothing worn or cracked or shabby, there was an obvious grandeur that Yeva found off-putting. The pieces in the room had been selected to show off the baron's wealth, and whoever had done the selecting lacked the taste of the castle's decorator, whoever he'd been, all those centuries ago.

She was inspecting the books displayed prominently on one of the shelves when Solmir appeared in the doorway. Last year, whenever he arrived to accompany Yeva on her walks through the forest, he'd appear disheveled and out of breath, eagerness flushing his face and quickening his steps. Now, she couldn't help but notice his face was grave, his steps unhurried.

He inclined his torso a few degrees when Yeva turned. "Good morning," he greeted her, crossing the room to take her hand and lead her to one of the couches.

She thanked him and sat, then abruptly found that everything she'd planned to say on her walk here had vanished from her memory. She stared at Solmir dumbly.

He stood by the fire, leaning one elbow on the mantel and looking exactly like a painting, a single frame from a story of lost love and tragedy. When Yeva didn't speak, his brows knit, concern coloring that grave face. "Yeva? Are you all right?" His eyes widened. "Is it your family? Is something wrong?"

"No," Yeva was quick to reassure him, finding her tongue again. "No, everything's fine." She hesitated, then glanced around the expansive room. "I've never been in this part of the manor," she said finally, "only in the baronessa's wing and the grand hall. It's . . . big."

At that, Solmir grinned, some of his stiffness relaxing. "Coming from you, I'm pretty sure that's not a compliment."

Yeva's smile came out in response, and she chuckled. "You know me too well."

"Well, you are to be my wife," Solmir replied, the grin softening and easing away. "I should know you well."

Yeva's throat tightened. "That's what I came to talk to you about."

"The baron's told me in confidence that I will be his heir." Solmir said it without much surprise, or pleasure, and Yeva could see the grief there. The baron was dying, and Solmir truly did care for him—far more than for the riches he would inherit. "He wants me to marry before he announces it publicly. He feels the people will be most comfortable if the new baron is taking steps to produce an heir, so that this period of uncertainty won't repeat itself."

Though the words were mercenary, even callous, Solmir's hollow voice said everything Yeva needed to know in order to be finally, utterly certain that she was right.

"Solmir," she blurted, "I know you're in love with Asenka."

Solmir's face froze, then drained of color as his lips thinned. "I'm not—that isn't what—I won't sit here and . . ."

Yeva wouldn't look away, though he squirmed under her gaze like a schoolboy being taken to task for misbehavior. "Solmir, I'm glad. I'm *glad*, you understand? I want you to marry her."

Solmir's face tightened further, and his voice was strained. "Yeva, I made a promise to you."

"And I to you." Yeva got to her feet and crossed to the mantel. "But why hold to a promise that benefits no one?"

Solmir's expression flickered, the boyishness peeking through his newfound gravity, before he shook his head and looked down. "It doesn't matter."

Yeva felt a flicker of annoyance. Asenka and Solmir were both so determined to be miserable—she shouldn't have to fight this hard to make them see she wanted no part of standing between them. "If it doesn't matter to you, then it certainly matters to me. I have no interest in being married to a man who's in love with my sister."

"I love you," Solmir said fiercely, as if he could make it so by saying the words with enough force behind them.

Yeva took his hand. "And I love you." She leaned forward, rising on her toes enough to press her lips to his cheek. "And want nothing more than to call you brother."

Solmir's face crumpled, and he pulled back, striding from the fireplace and shoving both hands into his hair. "It doesn't matter," he repeated. "It doesn't matter, because she won't have me."

Yeva stopped short. "What?"

"I asked her." Solmir turned, and Yeva could see guilt in every line of his face. "I asked her to marry me, months ago, when we believed—" His voice caught.

"When you believed I was dead," Yeva whispered.

Solmir nodded wordlessly.

"And she refused?"

Solmir cleared his throat, then cleared it again when the words still wouldn't come. "She told me she wouldn't marry me because she knew you were alive, and that you'd come back to us, and she wouldn't betray you."

Yeva's eyes closed, heart swelling. She didn't know whether she wanted to throw her arms around her sister or pinch her for being so stubborn. "You must ask her again."

Solmir glanced at Yeva, face agonized, so moved by feeling that Yeva almost felt music in it. "I couldn't bear to hear her refuse me a second time."

"Solmir," Yeva said gently. "Ask her again."

❋ ❋ ❋

That night Lena threw an elaborate dinner, conspiring with the
cook to create a feast far beyond anything they'd eaten before,
even at the height of their father's wealth. Though she said it was
to celebrate Asenka's engagement to Solmir, Yeva suspected it was
in no small part an attempt to keep her there. She'd promised
Lena she would only stay this last night, but it was obvious they
would be having the exact same argument all over again in the
morning.

As it turned out, Lena was not the one she'd have to fight.
Asenka and Solmir barely seemed to notice the rest of the family,
or indeed the food. Solmir stared at her so dreamily that at one
point he put his elbow into his bowl, and only noticed when
soup soaked through his coat and burned his skin. And Asenka
sat still as a statue, barely eating, flushing beet red each time she
glanced up to meet his dreamy stare.

It was at the end of the meal, when Yeva was offering the
last of her stew to Doe-Eyes under the table, that Asenka finally
drew a breath and broke away from Solmir's gaze. "We're to be
married in a week," she said, interrupting a conversation about
the spring planting to come after winter's end.

Yeva started. She couldn't think when they'd had time to
decide upon the date, but there they were, Solmir nodding
eagerly and Asenka beaming down the length of the table at her.

"The baron wants a swift marriage," Asenka went on
hurriedly, "so he can announce Solmir as his heir. Otherwise we
wouldn't be so hasty."

"There's no need to explain," said Yeva, feeling a warmth
inside her that hadn't come from the stew.

"We all know why you're pushing for a swift wedding,"
Radak added, laughing and earning an elbow in the ribs from
his wife.

Asenka ignored this, her gaze on her little sister. "You must stay," she blurted, her normally soft voice peaking with urgency. "I know you planned to stay only one more night, but—Yeva, you have to be at my wedding."

Yeva glanced from Asenka to Lena, whose wedding she had missed, and her heart ached. That itch in her feet, the hollow in her soul that called for the forest and the valley and the Beast's song swelled. The animal ferocity of the Beast in her nightmare tugged at her heart. Autumn would soon become winter, and once winter came, it'd be too perilous a journey to attempt in the bitter cold and the waist-deep snow. But, gazing at her sisters, surrounded by her new brothers and the warmth of her old home and the dog at her feet, she found that the music seemed more distant than ever, more like a dream than a memory, and she found herself nodding.

"Of course," she whispered, and Asenka's eyes filled. "Of course I'll stay."

BEAST

He is gone forever now.
I am the WOLF.

TWENTY-THREE

THOUGH BOTH ASENKA AND her betrothed would have been most pleased with a small ceremony, Solmir's new status as the baron's heir required a certain degree of festival when it came to his wedding. Yeva found herself so occupied with preparations that she had little time to think of the Beast, nor his valley and how she could break his curse. There were holly branches to weave into garlands, dishes to arrange for the feast, gowns to fit, dignitaries to greet.

Yeva continued to dream, but each day kept her so busy that the nightmares seemed to vanish like morning mist in the sun. She still had time; the days were long, and though they grew gradually shorter, they hadn't yet seen the first frost to herald the start of winter. And after her sister was married, she was so exhausted from all the preparations that she convinced herself that she needed rest before she set out. Her sisters said nothing, though she knew it was on Lena's mind, for her father's bow had vanished from its corner, no doubt hidden away to avoid reminding Yeva of what she'd intended to do.

Asenka moved into Solmir's quarters at the baron's manor, and one week to the very hour after their wedding, the baron died. His funeral was a grand, solemn event, for he'd been a good landowner, and his people had prospered under his guidance. The last of the autumn leaves fell in a sorrowful shower of red and gold as Solmir spoke to the gathering across his predecessor's coffin. The shower of color reminded Yeva of . . . something. Something she couldn't quite pin down in her mind.

Though the baron's young widow made motions to move out of the wing of the manor that had been her home, Asenka wouldn't hear of it. She insisted that the former baronessa stay, and that as the new baronessa, she only needed a few small rooms for herself. Yeva came daily to visit her sister, and found the baron's widow often at Asenka's side, the two of them becoming fast friends. It was after such a visit that Asenka confessed to Yeva that she'd underestimated the baronessa, judging her from Yeva's descriptions of lavish parties and court gossip, and that the baronessa had done much of the governing while her husband had been ill. She was proving to be a valuable advisor for Solmir, who was considering throwing tradition to the winds and adding her in an official capacity to his council.

Asenka and Solmir set aside a suite of rooms for Yeva, asking her to come live with them, for Asenka had little interest in hunting and Solmir remembered his walks with Yeva as fondly as she did. Now the looming prospect of their marriage was gone, Yeva found her friendship with Solmir to be one of the closest she'd ever known.

Lena insisted that Yeva stay with them, in her old room, and Lena even stopped scolding Yeva for allowing the dogs up onto her bed. She said nothing when the laundrywomen complained of the difficulties of getting dog hair out of the linens.

Radak, surprising Yeva by showing her he knew her at least as well as her sisters did, quietly offered to purchase Yeva her own little cottage by the northern edge of town. It would ordinarily be an act of social suicide for a young, unmarried woman to live alone in her own home, but Yeva was such an odd figure in the town as a result of her time with the Beast that it wouldn't cause too many ripples.

She'd so longed to come home, but now that she was here, and with a flood of different homes to choose among, Yeva could not banish the twinge of discontent inside her. She no longer dreamed of the Beast, having managed to train herself to wake at the start of the nightmares when they came. But the town had no song, not like the forest or the Beast or his castle. And she was restless.

Lena's belly grew rounder each week, and Asenka's happiness was so infectious that Yeva couldn't bear the thought of leaving them. *A few more weeks,* she told herself, stubbornly watching the weather and telling herself winter was still far away. She had plenty of time to make it back to the Beast's valley before the snows came and made travel impossible.

And so Yeva, choosing to remain in her old room in Radak and Lena's house, threw herself into work. She helped prepare the baby's room. She went out riding with Solmir. She managed the household staff so Lena could rest. She had Radak teach her how to understand the family's finances.

Radak had gone on a spree when Lena first accepted his proposal, buying back the things Tvertko's family had sold to pay their debts. Not all of it had found its way back into daily use. Some of it had been tucked up in the attic crawl space to be dealt with later, but later had never come. There were books, and flatware, and linens, and trunks of old dresses long out of fashion. Yeva decided to sort through it all, keeping what still held meaning for them, and giving away the rest.

The hour was late on a chilly, windy night when Yeva crept into the attic storage space to sort through the dust-covered piles of belongings. She'd found that if she wore herself out, it was easier to go back to sleep after dismissing one of the Beast's nightmares, so she was awake long past the time the rest of the house had gone to sleep. She was rummaging through the trunks of clothes when she found a dusty roll of burlap tucked behind one of the chests. She tugged it free, choking on the dust and trying to stifle her coughs.

She unwrapped the cloth and discovered that it was concealing her father's bow.

It rested unstrung in her hands, feeling heavier than she remembered, and unfamiliar. And yet as she closed her eyes and curled her fingers around the grip, she found that her hands remembered its shape well, and found the touch of its smooth wood to be a comfort.

Beauty.

A shiver ran down Yeva's spine. The word had come to her mind so abruptly, and in the Beast's voice, that for an instant she thought he was behind her and speaking her name aloud.

Startled, her hands let go of the bow. Before it hit the ground, Yeva opened her eyes and found herself standing in a snowy wood. It was the clearing where the Beast had first laid his trap for her, and he lay with his back to her where he'd been before, side rising and falling with each breath, the snow around him churned up and trampled.

Yeva shivered, for she was wearing only a thin wool dress, and the snow was soaking through her stockings. "Beast?" The breathing caught and halted, and Yeva knew he'd heard her. "Beast, did you call for me?"

He didn't answer, and Yeva crept closer. The familiar sense that all this had happened before kept tingling at the back of her mind, along with alarm. *It's a trap,* her memory told her. *He's hunting you. Run away.*

But she knew the Beast now. And he knew her. She knew he wouldn't harm her. She reached out until she could bury her hand up to the wrist in his fur, the soft gray fur that smelled like spices.

The instant she touched him, the Beast leaped. He whirled, snarling with rage and bloodlust, and his eyes locked on Yeva. She scrambled back but then stopped herself, fighting the instinct to flee. "Beast, it's me!" she cried. "It's Beauty. You know me."

There was no response, not the tiniest flicker of recognition in the red, empty eyes. He took a step closer, his body moving like that of a predator stalking its prey. His lips curled back to bare his teeth in a wet, slavering growl.

Beauty felt a sudden stab of fear. This was not her Beast. This . . . this was a monster.

The Beast's muscles bunched, rippling under his long coat as he crouched. He launched himself and Yeva screamed, clasping her arms over her head and dropping into the snow.

Her knees struck wood and her eyes flew open. She was in the attic again. A heartbeat later, the bow she'd dropped clattered to the floor. Her stockings were dry, and though her body shivered with the memory of cold, she found she had no gooseflesh, no reddened fingers, nothing to suggest she'd left the warmth of the attic at all.

Her breath came like a sob as she staggered to her feet. The attic had no windows, only a vent at either end of the house to allow the air to circulate in summer. Yeva stumbled to one of the vents and tore the shutters loose, too rattled to work the clasp. The night air poured in, wrapping Yeva in cold and leaving her shivering in her autumn dress. Her nose tingled with the bite of frost, the first frost.

It was only after she'd been standing there for some time that her eyes adjusted to the darkness outside, and she saw that it had begun to snow.

Yeva threw the necessities she'd chosen all those weeks ago into her pack, hands trembling with urgency. Doe-Eyes jumped down from the foot of Yeva's bed, where she'd been waiting hopefully for her mistress, pretending to sleep while listening as she moved from room to room. More than ever, Yeva could read the dog's heart in her movements, and Yeva paused to grasp at Doe-Eyes's chin. "Yes," she whispered. "We're going." Doe-Eyes gave a sideways prance and then stuck her nose into the pack, smelling dried meat.

Yeva considered leaving a note for her sisters, but told herself she couldn't waste those few precious moments. In truth, she had no idea what to write. That she'd had a vision of the Beast, showing him as the monster they feared him to be, and for that reason she had to return? That finding him and breaking his curse was what she'd been born for, what she'd been yearning for all her life? That she'd never feel content here, in the home full of people who loved her?

No. Better to slip out now. They would wake to discover her room empty, and Lena would run to the attic where she'd hidden their father's bow. She'd find it missing, and see that Doe-Eyes was missing too, and she'd know Yeva was gone.

She put on her old leather leggings that Asenka had made for her at the hunting cabin, and then two woolen dresses overtop, and then her cloak for warmth. She strung the bow, bracing it across her leg and trying not to flinch at how her muscles shook at the effort. She strapped her supplies to her back and slipped the bow over one shoulder.

Yeva paused, bracing against the inside of the door as she stared down the entry hall into the sitting room. She could see her father there, in the claw-footed stuffed chair by the hearth that still bore the worn indentation he'd made over so many long years of sitting in the same spot. She could see him doubled over, his head in his hands. She heard his voice the night he learned of his caravan's fate, the voice that had become so sad, so broken. "Oh, Beauty."

She closed her eyes, groped for the latch at her back, and then slipped out into the night.

TWENTY-FOUR

THOUGH YEVA NEVER WOULD have been able to pinpoint the location of the Beast's valley on a map, nor describe to someone how they might find it, her heart knew exactly where to take her. She thought about renting a horse in one of the villages she passed after dawn, but decided against it. She'd found her way out of the valley on foot, and some part of her, the part that knew the rules of fairy tales like she knew down from up, was certain that she must be on foot to find her way back.

Doe-Eyes, too, seemed to know the way. For all she'd been wary, even frightened, of the Beast at first, she'd grown accustomed to living near a predator, and Yeva had the strangest feeling that the dog was excited to be returning. Though Doe-Eyes had spent every evening with Yeva's family stretched out in front of the fire with her head upside down and beaming in the heat of the coals, there was a spark to her now, a sort of life that had been missing in town.

With every step, Yeva felt lighter. Each league she closed

between her and the Beast made his pull all the stronger, as if she were a needle drawn to a lodestone. Her heart had grown so used to hating him that she couldn't make sense of how her feelings for him had changed, but she knew that just now, in this instant, this crossroads of her life, she was meant to find him. She could not tell what would come after, but she hadn't felt such certainty since the very first time she'd held her own bow in her hands.

She would find him. She would free him.

The snow that had sent her out into the night stopped later that first day, and the pale autumn sun was enough to melt it on the roads. But once she left the road for the forest, the snow lay beneath the trees in cool white swaths that marked out intricate patterns of shadow where the sun never penetrated the branches above. Each one seemed to point onward, north, illuminating her path.

Her sleep, when she paused in the pitch-blackness of night long enough to get some rest, was dreamless. The days flew as though the magic was pulling her onward, summoning her home.

The air shifted when she reached the river where it passed out of the southern border of the Beast's valley. She stopped at the water's edge, gazing down the glittering expanse. The river glittered in the afternoon sun, burbling against the rocks a few paces from her boots, and Doe-Eyes pranced over to lap at it noisily. Here the water was lively and dancing swiftly through its carven course, but a league upstream Yeva could see that it was frozen. The deep winter that froze time itself in the Beast's valley hadn't changed.

Yeva ran, throwing wisdom and endurance to the wind in her haste. Doe-Eyes let out an uncharacteristic, joyous bark and sprinted after her, falling into step at her side and breathing noisily. The air once again singed her lungs with cold.

The castle burst into view, looking as it had always looked, nestled in a cradle of ice and snow where it straddled the river that flowed beneath it. The sound of Yeva's pounding footfalls changed as she hit the stone of the bridge, which she'd once crossed so gingerly. She went first to the den, veering from the castle doors and sliding in her haste down the trodden path to the cave. Despite the violence of her nightmares, she felt no fear—she knew that if the Beast could see her, if he could only know she'd come back for him, the wolf would release him.

The den was empty. Gnawed bones littered the shadowy recesses of the cave, and she could smell him, but his scent was faint and seemed fainter with every breath. Yeva took a step back and looked down, and saw that her tracks were fresh and new but that they were the only ones that had broken the crust of an old snow. No one else had come this way in weeks.

Yeva whirled and made for the castle doors. One of them stood slightly ajar, as if in invitation. She hurried across the dusty marble of the great hall, past the room full of shattered windows, and into the one with the blue velvet divan and the table with books propping it up and tapestries covering the high windows to keep out the drafts.

It was dark and cold, and empty. Her heart ached at the sight of the hearth, which had always been burning bright or glowing with hot coals—she'd never realized how often the Beast must have laid the fire for her until now. She'd taken that warmth for granted, as though the fire had simply lit itself for her each day by magic.

Her legs refused to run anymore, and the ache in her heart began to spread. For the first time an icy trickle of fear lifted the hairs at the back of her neck.

Where is the Beast?

She moved back out into the great hall. Doe-Eyes, panting from the headlong flight through the valley, took one look at the stairs and dropped onto her belly before them. She cast Yeva a baleful look, and Yeva told her to stay before heading up the wide curving stair.

The library was empty, and the master bedroom too—but she'd expected that. It was the tower room she sought, the tower room where she knew she'd find the Beast. She pulled back the tapestry to find the secret door unlocked.

You may come here any time you wish, the Beast had told her. But Yeva's memory of his offer could not quite touch the rising fear in her heart that she refused to look at directly.

She climbed the steps two at a time, calling breathlessly, "Beast? Beast, it's me. Your Beauty." There was no reply, and Yeva imagined him so shocked that she'd return that he could not speak.

But when she burst through the second door at the top of the spiral stair the tower room was empty. The fire in the hearth was unlit, and when Yeva drew nearer and put her hand out to the ashes, she found them ice cold. The carpet crumbled and stank under her feet, and she saw that nothing had been cleaned, dried blood still staining the floor.

The Beast was gone.

Yeva could not think, could not move. She had been so certain she was meant to return, so certain that her whole life had been steering her toward this place, this time, this task. She knew that in it she would find everything she'd ever wanted, everything she'd ever imagined she could be. Instead she'd found an empty castle, as cold and dark as the winter in the valley surrounding it.

Yeva stood in the center of the room, shivering, her eyes seeking anything that might ease the blow.

The knife she'd used to slash the Beast's throat still lay on the floor where she'd dropped it. The smear of blood her leggings had made as she scrambled from him still streaked the stones by the wall. The book whose pages had been spattered by . . .

But wait, where was the book?

Yeva frowned, scanning the room again. That night was so intimately carved into her memory that she could see in her mind's eye exactly where the book had been: by the daybed, lying open as though the Beast had been reading it. She set her bow down and crossed to the far side of the tower room, where she crouched low and saw the faint outline of a rectangle where the book had lain, shielding the ground beneath it from the Beast's blood.

The Beast had moved it.

She summoned up that night once more, ignoring the sting of guilt in order to compare the memory to the room where she stood now. There, on the table by the window, illuminated by the pale winter sun slipping through the cracked shutters, lay the volume she sought.

It was closed. She picked it up and found a guinea fowl's feather between its pages like a bookmark, and she let it fall open there.

The handwriting inside was cramped and slanted, not penned by a scribe like most of the other books. Yeva could not read it. She flipped back a few pages and the writing changed, and then changed again, written by many different people. Past the page the Beast had marked, the vellum was blank. Yeva leafed back to the start and a series of numbers, more easily read than the cramped writing, leaped out at her. They were dates.

The book was a history. And as the occasional word emerged from the tangle of ancient lettering—*land, kingdom, tithe, heir, drought*—she realized it was the history of the family who'd once lived here and the land they'd ruled.

Yeva hurriedly flipped back to the spot marked with the feather. The language was so archaic that she could barely understand any of it, but she saw enough to know that the writer was describing a royal family. A king, his queen, his three sons, princes all. The feather marked the last entry in the book, with nothing to tell of what had happened to this land all those centuries ago, nor the family that had ruled it.

It was the name of the youngest prince that drew Yeva's gaze, but a speck of the Beast's blood had landed on it, making it difficult to read. She leaned close to the page, holding it under a shaft of sunlight.

Eoven, she read.

You may call me Ivan, the Beast had told her once, after she'd told him the story of the Firebird.

Eoven. Ivan.

With trembling fingers, Yeva picked up the feather that had marked the page with the prince's name. She'd thought it a feather from a guinea fowl, but it was stiffer than that, a tail feather from a bird far better suited to flight. She blew on it, dislodging decades or centuries of dust and grime, and ran a shaking fingertip along its spine to knit the disheveled barbs together. She reached out to hold the feather in the light.

The instant the sunlight touched it the feather seemed to burst into flame. Yeva gasped and almost dropped it, but her fingers felt no heat. She tilted the feather this way and that, watching as the sunlight caught and danced, turning the dull browns into fiery red, gold, and orange. Like the leaves in her dream of kissing Solmir, of kissing the man the Beast had once been, the leaves that had turned into a rain of feathers.

The Beast, before vanishing to wherever he'd gone, had left this book here for her to find. And though he could not tell her the origins of his curse, he could leave her clues to discover it herself. Yeva drew the feather close and heard, very softly, so softly she didn't dare breathe for fear she would drown out the sound, the tiniest pulse of music as it brushed her skin.

Her Beast was Prince Ivan. And the quarry he needed her to hunt in order to break his curse was the Firebird, the creature from her father's stories that Yeva had always loved the most.

To save him, she would have to kill the thing she'd longed for all her life.

Yeva picked up her bow.

TWENTY-FIVE

YEVA LET THE MUSIC of the wood wash over her. At first she didn't try to understand it or separate its pattern into individual threads of song. She stood in the center of the clearing, with snowflakes drifting around her like dust motes in a sunbeam, and listened.

When a familiar rhythm asserted itself, tugging her northward, she opened her eyes again and turned in the direction of the song and followed it. Doe-Eyes trotted next to her. The song was elusive, moving this way and that, and Yeva's instincts urged her to move more carefully, to stalk her prey as she'd learned to do. But she was not a hunter today—at least, not the kind of hunter she'd been before.

"Lamya," she said softly, when she sensed the song she'd been tracking was coming from all around her now. "Lamya, I need your help."

There was no reply, but the rhythm of the song changed, like a heartbeat quickening.

Yeva tried again, licking her lips. "Do you remember me? My name is Yeva. I've seen you here, and you've seen me."

Again there was no response, and Yeva's heart tightened. Without the help of one of the strange creatures that lived in this place, she'd have no idea where to start, no clue as to where to find the Firebird in the wood that stretched on forever to the north, to the edge of the world.

"It's for the Beast," Yeva burst out, voice ringing loud in the cold air. "It's for Eoven."

A gust of air nearly knocked her from her feet, the sound of massive wings shattering the quiet and blinding her with snow flung up by the wind. When Yeva had wiped the melting snow from her eyes there was nothing there—but then Lamya emerged from behind a birchling far too slender to have concealed her. She wore nothing but her long, black hair, which fell over her shoulders. "For Eoven?" she asked, her voice velvet.

"He told me he asked you to help him once before."

"He wanted to die," Lamya said dreamily, moving through the snow without stirring a flake, her bare feet perfect and white and showing not a hint of cold. "I have helped many that way."

"He said you couldn't kill him."

Lamya's black eyes swung round to meet Yeva's, and Yeva had to fight the need to shiver with all her might. "The Beast cannot be killed."

"I know," Yeva said, trying not to show her impatience. "I need to—"

"But Eoven can die," Lamya went on as though Yeva had not spoken.

Yeva froze, chilled as though she were as naked as Lamya. "What do you mean?"

"The world of men," Lamya murmured, "is so strange." She

rubbed her body against a rough-barked tree with a little sigh of pleasure. A normal woman would have been left scratched and bleeding, but Lamya's skin only shone all the brighter. When she continued moving, inscribing a wide, lazy circle around the clearing, Yeva saw a glimmer of scales left behind on the tree's bark.

Lamya continued. "For you all things have one nature. Winter is cold. Death is a tragedy. But even in the world of men, this is not true. Your warmest memories are of winter, and the times spent near hearth and home. For the sick and the old death can be a gift. And yet you insist on seeing only the faces of things. I am a woman. I am a dragon. I am these things all the time, and I am never one but not the other."

Yeva's impatience grew. She couldn't afford to alienate Lamya, but the urgency in her heart made it almost impossible to stand and listen. "Please. Tell me what this has to do with Eoven. I've had dreams that he's lost himself, that the animal within him has taken over, and I need to—I need to know that he's all right."

"The Beast was a man and a wolf," Lamya said. "As I am a woman and a dragon. But the day I saw you with him in the wood, he was no longer those things. He was a man only. The face of him still spoke of the wolf, but his nature—the truth of him—was Eoven and not the Beast. You did that to him."

Yeva blinked. "How can that be? He was the Beast when I first came upon him in the woods. He was cursed long before I was even born."

"The Firebird made him a being of two natures," Lamya went on. "You changed him into two beings grappling for a single heart."

A little trickle of horror shivered down the back of Yeva's neck. "You're saying I . . . I caused the wolf to take over?"

"You let the man take over," Lamya corrected her, "and give his heart to you." She lifted a languorous hand and combed her fingers through the long length of her hair so that it fell slowly, carving out the shape of a dragon's wing in the air. "Now, without it, Eoven has no more strength to exist alongside the wolf."

Yeva's eyes burned. She slipped her hand into the pocket at her waist so she could curl her fingers around the feather there. "It was the Firebird that cursed him. And it's the Firebird that can free him. I must find it."

Lamya paused, surprise halting her sinuous movements for the first time since she appeared. "The Firebird?" she echoed. "No one has seen her for many years."

"You must have some idea where to find her," Yeva pleaded, desperation rising. "If I'm the one who did this to the Beast then it's all the more important that I fix it."

Lamya's brows drew together, and her eyes caught Yeva's. All at once their blackness called to Yeva, becoming not an empty abyss but the warmth of a soft, velvet bed. Yeva wanted nothing more than to stagger to Lamya's side and drown in those eyes. "I can help you," Lamya whispered, and her lips were as soft as her eyes. "I can free you from the pain in your heart. Winter does not have to be cold. I can show you heat. . . ."

Yeva found herself aching, found the sharp edges of her thoughts fraying. She was so tired, after all—tired of fairy tales and magic and empty castles, tired of wanting so intensely that she didn't know what she wanted.

Perhaps Lamya could be what she wanted. It would be so easy. . . .

"The Firebird, Lamya." Yeva held up the feather in her hand, her face flushed despite the cold. "Please."

Lamya's lashes fell, and as soon as her gaze left Yeva's, the spell vanished like smoke. "North," she said softly. "I have never seen the Firebird and I have wandered here since the first time the sun ever rose." Her soft voice held a deep sorrow, a longing that touched Yeva so deeply her eyes stung with tears. Yeva was not the only one for whom the Firebird was a symbol of wanting. "You will not find her here. Go north into the next valley, and the one beyond. What you seek can only be north."

Now that Lamya's heat had left her Yeva's body ached with sudden cold. She wrapped her cloak more tightly about her body. She discovered that Doe-Eyes was some distance behind her, belly low to the ground and ears back, her large round eyes fixed fearfully on the dragon-woman. Yeva backed up until she felt her dog's warmth press against her calves.

"Thank you, Lamya," she whispered. Then she ran.

Yeva had barely traveled a few leagues into the next valley before her exhaustion began to catch up with her. She'd slept so little in her haste to return to the Beast, her body now ached, and her eyes burned and itched in the dry, icy air.

She touched the feather in her pocket again. A fortifying warmth began at her fingertips and trickled slowly up her arm, spreading through her body and letting her blink away the exhaustion weighing her down. She could not be sure whether the feather's warmth was magic, or if it was hope that surged through her, urging her to push aside her desire to rest.

When she passed for the second time a gnarled tree, blackened by a strike of lightning, Yeva realized she was walking in circles. The innate sense of direction that had guided her this far had left her, and when she stopped, confused, Doe-Eyes halted too. The dog cocked her head, puzzled by her mistress's sudden lack of direction, then turned and trotted off through the trees.

Yeva called out for her, but for the first time since she'd been a puppy, Doe-Eyes didn't come running at the sound of her voice. Letting out a weary oath, Yeva dragged herself after her pup.

She broke out through a dense, icy thicket and found herself at the river's edge, the same river that passed through the Beast's valley below. Doe-Eyes was drinking from a hole in the ice, lapping at the water greedily. The sun briefly broke through the thick gray clouds and its glare on the river ice jolted Yeva from her weary confusion. Her eyes traveled upriver, and she saw that its course led through a pass between the mountains surrounding the valley she was in. The sun beamed down on Yeva's right cheek before vanishing behind the clouds again, and Yeva realized that the river flowed north to south.

"Thank you, Doe-Eyes," Yeva whispered. She'd found her road north.

Yeva discovered as she walked that she no longer had to listen for the magic of the wood—in fact, she began to feel deafened by it. Though the forest was silent, lacking even the little noises of a hibernating wilderness, her ears rang with music. When darkness fell she made a little camp, and huddled close to the fire with Doe-Eyes sharing her warmth under her cloak.

The magic swelled, and when Yeva looked up, she saw the song for the first time with her eyes. The clouds had cleared, and the sky was dancing. Ribbons of pale green and peach shimmered above her, robbing her of breath until her very heart seemed to beat in time with the magic. She leaned back against a tree so she could fall asleep looking up, and the dancing sky grew brighter and brighter until it burned red and gold and spread wings of flame and sang the Firebird's song.

Yeva woke with a longing in her heart so strong that she leaped to her feet and kept moving north without banking the

fire or packing up her belongings. She left behind her food, her
flint and tinder, the goose fat she'd been using to protect her lips
and cheeks from the icy chapping of the wind. All she brought
was what she'd fallen asleep holding: the feather in her pocket,
the book of fairy tales tucked inside her cloak, and the bow in
her hands with a single arrow to its string.

The sun was high and pale in the vast crystal-blue sky when
a flash of brilliant rust red made Yeva skid to a halt. It had
been days since she'd last seen even a set of tracks that wasn't
hers, much less an animal to leave them. And now a fox appeared
ahead of her, sitting primly in the snow with its tail wrapped
around its haunches.

"Borovoi?" she asked, her voice hoarse from disuse.

The fox grinned at her, showing a row of pointy little teeth,
and inclined its angular head. "That's one question spent."

Yeva drew a breath to retort, but paused, and instead
inspected the little fox. Almost as she'd seen the ribbons of magic
dancing overhead, she could see in the fox's face the grizzled,
mossy beard, the hollow cheeks etched in bark, the ancient eyes
of the leshy spirit she'd glimpsed that first day alone in the wood,
before she met the rusalka. "You tried to kill me."

"I gave you what you asked for," said Borovoi the fox, the
leshy. "I do not lie. Ask what you will."

Yeva could not take her eyes from the creature, caught by its
dual nature, the eyes of the ancient forest spirit in the frame of
its sharp-cheeked fox face. "I came here to . . ." But the song of
magic and the roaring in her ears made it hard to concentrate.
Yeva swallowed. "I seek the Firebird."

Borovoi grinned again. "Don't we all?"

"I must find it," Yeva said, throwing all her feeling behind
her voice. "It's the key to everything I've ever wanted."

The fox's head tilted the other way. "What will you do if you find it?"

Yeva stared at the fox, exhaustion and confusion and magic tangling her mind so that she couldn't think straight. "I . . . I just want it. It is my destiny."

"The Beast can never find the Firebird himself, you know." The fox lifted one paw and chewed a bit of ice from between its toes. "The bird must come to him. That is why he believed he needed a hunter—someone to trap the Firebird and bring it to him."

Yeva stared at the fox. "The Beast?" she asked slowly, stupidly, her mind full of dancing ribbons of red and gold and a song she'd first heard one winter when she was five years old, sitting by a window and listening to her father read her a story.

"Has her song gotten to you already?" the fox asked, sounding surprised. "I would have thought you'd last longer."

"The Beast," Yeva echoed again. Somewhere in the back of her mind, the word *beast* meant something to her beyond bears and boars and other dangers of the wood her memory conjured. Her hand crept into her pocket by itself, and her fingers touched the soft, worn barbs of a feather. "The Beast!" she cried, remembering. "Yes. I need to find the Firebird for the Beast."

"Go north," said the fox.

"I've *been* going north," Yeva protested, aware that at any moment her exhaustion would catch up with her and she'd be able to travel no farther. "I've been going north for years."

"That's because the Firebird is always north of you," the fox replied. "No matter how far you go."

Yeva stumbled on through the forest, and only by reaching out and finding Doe-Eyes's warm fur with her fingers could she remind herself that she was real, that this was real, that it was no tale from the book tucked close by her breast.

There would be a third, she knew. First Lamya the dragon-woman, then Borovoi the leshy, and now there would be one more. In stories there was always a third sign, a third test, a third bit of wisdom to urge the hero onward. Three wishes, three princes, three feathers, three hearts, three . . .

But Yeva walked, and walked, and found only the next valley, and the one beyond, and the one beyond, and the river she followed grew narrower and narrower until it was nothing more than a stream. She staggered up hills and climbed rock faces and eventually found herself beside a frozen waterfall that emerged like a crystalline blossom from a hidden spring in the rocks. The river's source. The end of her north road.

She saw pale green and peach reflected in the waterfall's frozen folds, and when she blinked and looked harder, she saw red-gold and fire.

She stepped out onto the frozen river, ignoring how it cracked and groaned under her weight. Dimly the sound made her think of some half-lost memory, another time she stepped onto ice that had not held her, but she could not quite remember what it was. Doe-Eyes stood on the bank and watched, and though she whined and cried and paced this way and that, it seemed she could not follow her mistress. And so Yeva walked on alone until she reached the waterfall.

The ice moved, the frozen sheets curling and parting like Lamya's hair, like falling snow before the wind, like autumn leaves from the peony tree. The curtains of ice opened for her like the massive doors of a castle she once knew, revealing that behind the waterfall lay a hidden cave. Yeva would have hesitated to go inside, but the cave was unlike any she'd ever seen, for the inside of the cave was brighter than the daylight where Yeva stood, as though it contained its own tiny sun.

Yeva stepped inside, and the moment her boots touched the cave's stone floor, the ice folded back into place behind her. She could not be afraid, however—in fact, she barely noticed she'd been sealed inside at all.

For before her, asleep with its wings wrapped round its body like a cloak, was the Firebird.

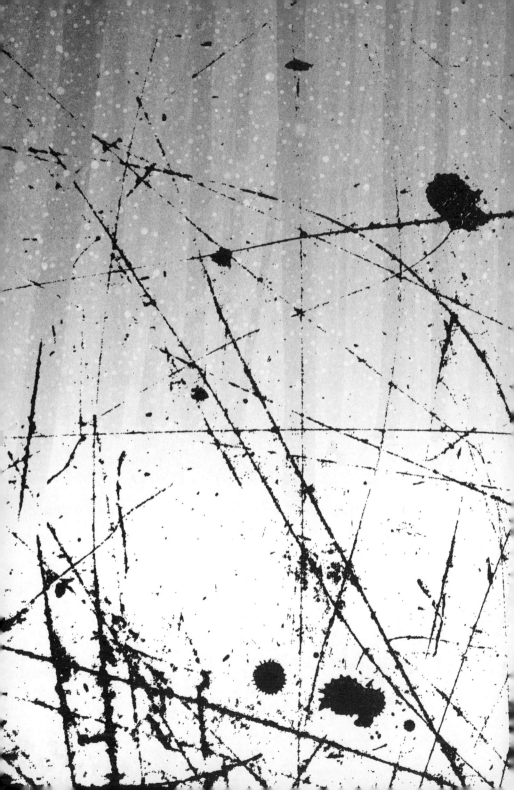

TWENTY-SIX

YEVA FELL TO HER knees. The sound of her body hitting the stone floor woke the Firebird, who lifted its golden head and looked at her. It looked at her like nothing in her life had ever looked at her—it looked at all of her, every inch of her heart, every shadow that had ever darkened her soul, every wrong thing she'd ever said or done or felt. It looked at her and bowed its head.

"Welcome, Beauty," it sang.

Yeva was crying, and not from grief or even joy, but simply because she was too full to contain herself. "I have been looking for you," she said.

"I know." The Firebird unwrapped its wings and stretched them, and Yeva saw they were like a falcon's wings, wide and broad and made for soaring, and their tips brushed each end of the cave though Yeva could have lain down across it many times over.

"I've been looking for you my whole life." But even as Yeva said it, something tiny and quiet stirred deep inside her. Something that, for the first time since she'd picked up the feather in the tower room of the castle, shook her certainty.

"Everyone is," the Firebird said. "But most stop searching. Most tell themselves they have found me in their mates, in their children, in their fields and in their gods."

Yeva's eyes blurred. "The fox," she whispered, trying to sort out memory from dreams, reality from story. "The fox told me you were always north of me, that you'd always be north of me."

"The fox has never found me," the Firebird said. "And he is jealous."

"What are you?" Yeva felt the Firebird's song in that hollow space in her heart, the space that had always known she wanted more than what her mundane life could offer her. "Desire?"

The Firebird spread its wings again, throwing back its head and showing its fiery, breathtaking plumage in a display that dazzled Yeva's half-blinded eyes. "I am the goal. The reward at the end of the quest. The end of the story."

Yeva put her hand into her pocket and touched the feather. Only then did she see that one of the Firebird's tail feathers was missing, and she started. "Eoven," she breathed, struggling to remember. "I'm here for Eoven."

"Who is Eoven?" the Firebird asked.

"I . . ." Yeva stared, bewitched, into the Firebird's knowing eyes. "I don't remember."

"I am what you seek," the Firebird said. "I am the conclusion of your journey. All you've ever wanted. Magic. The music of the forest. Forever. You are home, Beauty."

Yeva's eyes had begun to close, the Firebird's sweet voice warming parts of her she'd long ago forgotten. But her name, the word *beauty*, it rang in her thoughts and her eyes flew open. For a moment she saw not the Firebird, nor its crystal cave or the sky ribbons dancing at the edges of her vision, but a pair of gold eyes, and the rumble of a warm voice, and the feel of a blue velvet divan beneath her cheek.

She saw her Beast, and felt the lonely weight of his gaze, and heard the soft sound of his paws by her door, and smelled spices and wind and, just a little, the smell of wet dog—she remembered.

"You are not real," Yeva said, gasping. "It's as Lamya said. Nothing is in itself only one thing. You can't be all I've ever wanted because I've never wanted only one thing."

The Firebird's eyes narrowed, then softened. They held such acceptance, such knowledge of her. "I am everything," it said.

Yeva forced her hands to tighten, intending to drive her own fingernails into her palms to jolt herself from the Firebird's spell. Instead she found one of her hands was full, and when she looked down she remembered she was still holding her father's bow.

"You're right," Yeva whispered. "You are everything I want. Because you are what will save my Beast. You are the third test."

She raised the bow and fitted the arrow to the string and drew in one motion, so practiced and swift from her months of training with the Beast that it happened all in the quiet between one heartbeat and the next. The Firebird's chest swelled, its wings still outstretched as if daring her to shoot, as if certain she could not.

Yeva's fingers trembled.

I will call you Beauty, said the Beast. *For that is what you are.*

She loosened her fingers and let the arrow fly.

fire

snow

beauty

TWENTY-SEVEN

THE FIREBIRD'S LIGHT WENT out the instant the arrow would have struck it, and Yeva found herself in darkness so complete and solid that she cried out, dropping to the ground so she'd have something to touch, something to tell her she was alive and real. She groped around ahead of her, expecting to touch blood and feathers and the still-warm carcass of the creature, but all she found was a single feather it had left behind, like the one the Beast had left for her to find.

It glimmered at the touch of her fingers, just enough for her to make out the outlines of the cave. The ice curtain had sealed her in, and this time when she approached it, it did not part. It was as solid and as cold as stone. Her arrow had struck the far wall and sunk halfway up its haft into the rock. She couldn't pull it free, and without the sharp edge of the arrowhead, she had nothing with which to chip at the ice sealing the cave's entrance.

Fear surged through her like a winter wind, and like a winter wind, it left her teeth chattering. She was cold, colder than she'd ever been in her life, as though she'd been exposed for weeks but was only noticing it now. Her stomach ached with hunger, and she couldn't remember the last time she'd eaten. She felt dizzy, weak, lost in the dark.

I'm alone, she thought. Her father had taught her that she should never try to comfort herself by lying about her situation. *No heat, no food, and no way out.* She wedged herself in between ice and stone, trying to trap what little body heat she had left, instincts still fighting for survival despite what her senses told her: that she would die here in this cave of ice and darkness. Yeva couldn't help but cry, and it was only some time later, when they began to freeze against her cheeks, that her tears ceased.

If only the Beast were here, Yeva thought, her numb heart warming just enough to ache. *I would tell him I don't care that he's the Beast. I would tell him the Firebird doesn't matter, that he doesn't need to be cured. I would tell him my choice, that I would stay with him forever, and teach him how to find Eoven again, and keep him safe for as long as I live.*

She'd been so sure she was destined to save him that she'd left him to fade away.

The only warmth she could feel came from the feather clutched in her hands, and she lifted it up so she could see its pale light. A lick of flame danced along its edge and then whispered out, too tiny to generate any lasting heat, but Yeva could not stop staring at the afterimages before her eyes. The cave was empty, but with a jolt, Yeva remembered the bow in her hands and the book nestled against her breast.

She had fire. She had wood. And she had kindling.

Her hands began to work before her thoughts had caught up, before she could think twice, before she could stop herself. Who was she without stories, without the promise of the wood she hunted in and the gift her father had given her, to see the quiet, hidden tales the forest held? What was she without the restless wanting that drove her?

She ripped the pages from the book of fairy tales without hesitation, then tore them into smaller pieces. She took her father's bow and wedged one end into a fissure in the stone wall, and then heaved with all her might, crying again even before the great splintering crack rent the silence of the cave.

She set the torn fairy tales and the pieces of her father's bow at the foot of the ice wall, and then picked up the Firebird's feather. She held it in her cupped palms, feeling its light bathe her face one more time. Then she settled it down in the nest of kindling and wood, and let it burn.

Yeva dozed, huddled close to the tiny fire, waking now and then to blow on a failing coal here or tuck a splinter of her father's bow back into the flames there. The fire's heat was melting the ice, but slowly, far too slowly. Yeva wiped at the trickles of frigid water with the edge of her cloak so the moisture wouldn't swamp the fire, and rocked, and waited, and hoped.

She could not be sure how much time had passed when a change woke her with an urgent sense of dread. She automatically leaned for the fire to check it, and found it had dwindled to little more than a few faint coals, coated with thick white ash. She grabbed for the book of stories but all its pages were gone now, and the fire was too low and cold to burn the leather binding.

Yeva staggered to her feet and slammed her shoulder into the ice curtain with all her weight behind it, straining to hear some groan or crack or sign that her fire had thinned the door of her prison even a little—but even her imagination heard nothing. Stifling a sob of panic, she began ripping strips from the bottom of her cloak, finding the driest sections to add to the fire.

No, her thoughts screamed, as she tried again to budge the ice, throwing every ounce of strength she had left against the unyielding wall until her body ached with bruises. *The story doesn't end this way.*

But if her experience with the Firebird had taught her anything, it was that even here, at the edge of the world, life wasn't a story. If she died here no one would tell about it. She'd be one more soul lost to the wilderness, and the Beast would be left forever to run through the trees and hunt and feed without ever looking up, without ever seeing the dancing sky. Yeva slammed against the wall one more time and then stayed there, the side of her face against the wet, too-slowly-melting ice, its cold so shocking that it made her gasp.

And then, with her ear against the ice, she heard a sound. At first she thought it was the ice settling, but when it came a second time, and more loudly, she recognized with a new jolt of terror the roar of a wild beast.

The wall beneath her cheek shuddered, and Yeva lurched back. A chunk of ice fell from the other side of the wall, casting dim, pale-blue light into the cave. The creature roared again, and suddenly Yeva's heart filled. She knew that voice, would know it anywhere, whether it was whispering her name or roaring in fury.

"Beast!" she cried, renewing her efforts and slamming into the wall again—this time her efforts rewarded her with the faintest of splintering sounds. "I'm here!"

There came a great screeching as the Beast raked his claws down the wall outside, then another shudder as his whole body weight came crashing in against the wall. Yeva staggered back, sense reasserting itself and reminding her that he outweighed her many times over, and that trying to help him break down the barrier would most likely end with her crushed under an avalanche of shattered ice.

The growls and roars grew louder as the Beast carved away more and more of the wall. Beauty could see his shape behind the ice, silhouetted by the sun. It took only moments for the entire frozen curtain to fall in a shower of crystal fragments. The Beast burst into the cave in a brilliant glare of sun, blinding Yeva and making her throw up both arms to shield her eyes.

"Beast," she gasped, struggling for breath through her relief. "How did you find me? How did you know to look?"

But when there was no reply, Yeva lowered her arms and squinted through the sudden glare and saw the hulking shape of the Beast circling, head low, each step meticulous and calculating. His lips were drawn back in a snarl, and when she met his red, red gaze she saw no hint of the man she'd come to save.

She took a hesitant step toward him, and the creature's entire body tensed, the muscles in his shoulders bunching, his haunches readying to attack. Yeva froze, hand half outstretched, her mind going blank. She had no weapons anymore. Every bit of gear she'd packed, she'd left behind in a magic-induced haze.

Except . . . the age-worn feather the Beast had left for her was still in her pocket.

She started to reach for it, but the monster stalking her saw the movement and let out a snarl that rattled her very bones. Yeva had only an instant before he leaped at her, and she thrust her hand into her pocket and drew out the feather as she threw herself backward, shielding herself with both hands, instinctively, waiting to feel the Beast's crushing weight, the rending of her body with his claws, the cruel snap of his jaws.

They never came.

When she managed to open her eyes, Yeva saw the Beast looming over her, still snarling, panting with bloodlust—but his focus had narrowed to the feather clutched in her fingers. Compared to the soft, gleaming thing she'd used to start her fire, this feather was dull and dirty and bedraggled, battered by the centuries until it was barely recognizable. But the Beast stared at it, snorting steam into the frigid air, muscles trembling as if he were being held back by invisible bonds.

Yeva scrambled back, lifting the feather like a talisman, heart pounding painfully and fear leaving her mouth bitter and dry. But as the Beast moved to take a step after her, she found her voice and blurted the first words that came to her lips.

"Let me tell you a story!" she cried out. The Beast froze, though his gaze never flickered. Yeva had to draw three breaths before she found her voice again. "I will tell you a fairy tale."

BEAST

Story. Lie. Words. Meaningless. Empty.

She smells of something more than fear and blood. She smells like sky.

We snort and flex our claws until they grind on the stone but she holds us. We could devour her in one leap but she huddles there in her torn clothing and she holds us like no creature ever could.

She is magic. And we will wait for her spell to falter.

TWENTY-EIGHT

"ONCE," YEVA BEGAN, HER voice shaking, her whole body shaking, "there was a man. A king. With three sons." She couldn't push aside the fear that made her want to run for the mouth of the cave, to lunge for freedom. So she closed her eyes instead, and tried with all her might to fool her body into believing she was back in the Beast's valley, in a cell below his castle, speaking to someone on the other side of a locked door—her invisible ally, her friend, the man called Ivan.

"The elder sons begged him to name an heir, each of them wanting the power and wealth they knew would make them content. But the youngest son was different." Yeva's voice steadied a little. "He didn't want his father's throne, had never wanted the life spelled out for him by his birth. What he wanted, he couldn't name. All he knew was that he *wanted*, and that he'd never truly be home, never truly content, until he found all that he longed for.

"His father, the king, had a beautiful garden with a beautiful orchard that was his pride and joy, but every night an invisible thief had been stealing the golden apples from his most prized tree. He gathered his three sons and told them that whichever prince could catch the thief would be named heir. The elder sons were so eager to catch the thief that they fought and grappled with each other all night and missed the thief entirely. It was the youngest prince who, despite having little interest in his father's throne, caught a glimpse of the bandit.

"He came to his father in the morning and told him he'd seen the Firebird, the most elusive of all magic things, stealing the king's golden apples. The king sent his sons out into the world to find the creature, and though the young prince couldn't care less about the throne, the moment he'd seen the Firebird he knew it was all he'd ever wanted."

Yeva's voice, dry with fear and tight with cold, caught in her throat. She heard the Beast draw breath, and for a terrified heartbeat she thought he might leap—but instead he let out a long, low growl.

"Speak." His snarl was barely a voice at all, but there was a word in it, and it made Yeva open her eyes.

The Beast was crouched low, and stared at her with a red gaze that pinned her to the spot, like a serpent staring down a mouse it intends to devour.

Yeva shivered. "Th-the young prince set out to find the Firebird but before long a great gray wolf came out of the forest and demanded the prince's horse. The prince begged him not to eat his horse, but the wolf could not restrain his hunger, and soon had devoured the horse whole. But when the prince explained he sought the Firebird, the wolf took pity on him and offered to carry him to the next kingdom, whose king had boasted of owning the Firebird as a curiosity.

"The prince explained to this king that he needed to bring

the Firebird back to his father, and the king told him that he would give him the Firebird if Ivan would travel to the next kingdom and bring him the thing *he* most coveted, a horse with a golden mane. So the young prince went back to the wolf, who agreed to carry him to the next kingdom and the next king.

"The prince told his story again, and again the king took pity on him and said he'd give Ivan the horse with the golden mane if the prince would go into the next kingdom and bring back Yelena, the most beautiful maiden in the world, with whom the king had fallen madly in love. So the young prince and the wolf traveled on to the next kingdom, and there they found Yelena the Beautiful locked away in a high tower."

Yeva had left the original story, the one her father had read to her from the book she'd turned to ash, behind her. She knew she couldn't possibly guess the truth of Eoven's life, or how he had come to be cursed, or even what had driven him to seek the Firebird. But she'd seen the longing in her own heart reflected in his, in the loneliness of his castle and in the hope on every page of the storybooks he'd kept safe in the tower room all these long centuries.

The truth of his life was that it was Yeva's life, too. And there was a reason she'd always loved and hated the story of Ivan and the Wolf, and the Firebird that sent them out into the world. She'd just never known it until she met the Firebird herself.

The prince's curse wasn't arrogance or cruelty, as it was so often in fairy tales. His curse was wanting, always wanting. And so was Yeva's.

"The young prince went to the king of that land and asked him to release Yelena, but this king was older than the others, and he'd seen more of the world, and he warned Ivan to stay away. He said that no matter how much the young prince wanted Yelena, the satisfaction of desires sated was short and pale compared to the dream of wanting.

"The prince ignored his warning and went back to the gray wolf, who turned himself into a rope stair so that the prince could climb the high tower and take Yelena for himself. They returned to the king who'd asked for her, but when they reached his castle the young prince looked at Yelena and decided that he wanted her for himself, because love would make him happy, and he begged the wolf for his help. The wolf took Yelena's form and the young prince brought him to the king, who was overjoyed to have his heart's desire at least. He gladly gave the prince the horse with the golden mane. Once the young prince was beyond the kingdom's borders, the wolf escaped the castle and ran back to meet him and carry him to the king who'd asked Ivan for the horse.

"But when they reached the castle gates and Ivan looked at the horse with the golden mane, with Yelena on its back and a beautiful golden bridle draped with silk over its neck, he realized he didn't want to part with it, because freedom would make him happy. He begged the wolf to help him again, and the wolf turned itself into the spitting image of the horse with the golden mane. The king was so filled with happiness to have the horse with the golden mane that he told Ivan to go into his menagerie and take the Firebird. He warned the prince, however, not to take the solid-gold cage that housed the Firebird. But when the prince went into the menagerie and saw the Firebird, he saw the cage as well, and he thought that if he could take the cage too, he would have wealth, love, and freedom, and he would finally be happy.

"But as soon as the young prince touched the cage, its golden door opened and the Firebird sprang free. Ivan leaped to capture it, but he was able to catch only a single feather from its tail before it was gone, vanished forever into the north.

"When the wolf escaped and rejoined the young prince, he found him sitting at a crossroads with his head in his hands. The wolf asked him how he could be so unhappy, when he had the love of the most beautiful woman in the world, and the freedom of the swiftest horse in the world, and a golden cage worth enough to buy him any luxuries he could wish for."

Yeva thought of her home, her sisters, her friends Galina and Solmir—she even thought of the Beast's castle, and the books there she hadn't had time to read, and how beautiful the river would have been to walk along in spring. *If only I could break the Beast's spell,* she thought bitterly, *then I could be happy.*

"The prince confessed," Yeva went on, "that the last king had been right, that the dream was what he'd longed for, and he'd never be happy until he found the Firebird and everything he'd ever wanted. None of the things he'd found along the way would ever make him happy."

Her voice petered out, for there the story should have brought the prince home triumphant, to marry Yelena and inherit his father's kingdom and use the golden cage to establish a stable full of mounts sired by the horse with the golden mane, which would be so prized that they'd bring his kingdom a century of prosperity. But there the fairy tale ended, and Yeva lifted her face to find the Beast still watching her. The force of his stare had eased, though, and now that she'd fallen silent, he was starting to stir where he lay against the stone and rumble with discontent deep in his throat.

"How does this story end?" the Beast growled.

Yeva swallowed hard, clutching the old feather in her hand. "I don't know," she whispered. "The wolf and the young prince were cursed to stay together for the rest of their endless lives so that neither could ever be truly content. And only if the Firebird, the one thing the young prince had always wanted more than anything in this world, came back to him on its own, would his curse be broken."

The Beast's claws flexed, and as Yeva watched his face, the gray brows drew in a fraction and he dropped his gaze in confusion. "How do you know this story?"

Yeva's breath caught. "Because it's my story too," she whispered. "Because I thought I wouldn't be happy until I left town to live in the wood, and then I thought I wouldn't be happy until I could hunt every day, and then I thought I wouldn't be happy until I avenged my father's death. Because I spent a year in an old castle with the young prince and the gray wolf and I thought I couldn't be happy until I killed them both, and when I did, I wept harder than I ever have in my life. Because I thought I couldn't be happy until I went home, and then I thought I couldn't be happy until I came back."

The Beast's features flickered, and Yeva's heart began to pound, because there in the red, senseless, animal depths, she thought she saw the faintest glimmer of gold. Greatly daring, she crept forward, her every sense on alert for the slightest sign the Beast's animal nature might take over and cause him to strike.

"Because I thought the reason I'd always felt so restless was because I was meant for magic," Yeva said softly. "That if I could fix the story, that if I rescued the young prince and the gray wolf and I found the Firebird and I held in my hands everything I'd ever wanted, I would live happily ever after."

"How does your story end?" asked the Beast, his voice easing back toward the velvet bass Yeva had come to know so well.

Yeva gazed back at him, all her answers gone. A thousand

fairy tales flashed through her memory, full of quests and dreams and wishes and rewards. But the path ahead of her was blank, as empty as the leather binding of the book of stories she'd brought with her.

"I don't know," she whispered. "I think maybe it doesn't end." She inched forward again and lifted a hand, but the Beast didn't pull away, and he didn't snap at her. Her fingers crept into the soft fur at his chest, and his warmth banished the numbness of the cold. She felt the beating of his heart beneath her hand, and below that, the pulse of the magic binding man and wolf that sang as strongly as ever. Her eyes filled. "I'm so sorry."

The Beast's chest rose and fell under her hand in a sigh. "For what?"

"I was so close," Yeva replied. "The Firebird was here. I almost had it, but I was . . . slow. I could have saved you, and I failed." She lurched forward until she could lean against him, burying her face in his shoulder and feeling his warmth spread through her, chasing away the bone-deep chill the Firebird's cave had left her with. He smelled as he always did, and the familiar scent of wind and spice swelled inside her and she knew she had the answer to the Beast's question. She knew how her story ended.

In a rush, she blurted, "I would give up a thousand happy endings just to go back with you to your valley, and live as we did. I'd give up every fairy tale I've ever known just to hear you say my name again."

The Beast's warmth wrapped around her and the wild song of him swelled, and she could hear the ice curtain melting and dripping and saw in her mind's eye the crystal droplets falling like autumn leaves.

Then a voice whispered, "Beauty," and the warmth tightened, and she felt lips touch her temple, her cheek, the line of her jaw. She realized there were arms around her, and she broke away, gasping. Tears blurred her vision so that when she looked at the Beast she saw only a shimmer, the same shimmer he had when he saw her smile, or unlocked his room full of books, or lit her a lantern to keep the dark at bay. She blinked and blinked and finally her eyes cleared, and before her was a face, a human face. She'd seen it only once before, and a thousand times in her dreams.

"But," Yeva said, "how? I failed. I didn't bring you the Firebird."

The Beast knelt before her, seemingly unaware of the icemelt soaking into his clothes, which were of a fashion Yeva had never seen, from a time so long ago it predated even the oldest paintings and tapestries.

"Yeva," said the Beast, and though there wasn't a hint of a snarl in his voice, it still rumbled, still echoed in her heart and her bones, still warmed her from within. "We were both wrong."

He reached out and took her hands, folding them between both of his and drawing them up so he could press them against his chest, where the same heartbeat sounded, the same magic that called to her, only it wasn't magic, for the man before her was real, more real than the ice or the cave or the ancient feather, which she'd dropped somewhere in the slush, and forgotten.

"Don't you see?" the Beast went on, pulling her close so that she could breathe his scent, feel his hair brush her skin as he pressed his forehead to hers. "You are what I want most in all this world, and you came back to me. Yeva . . . *you* are the Firebird."

Yeva felt dizzy, confused not by the strangeness of this man she couldn't know, but by the fact that he wasn't strange at all. His touch was as familiar to her, and as certain, as the curve of a bow fitting in her palm. "This is a dream," she whispered. "Magic. A fairy tale."

The Beast smiled, and for the first time Yeva saw that he had a dimple, a little crease in his perfect face that made him imperfect, and that his nose was a little crooked, and the gold eyes were more hazel than gold. "Yes," he agreed. "And it's real."

A wolf and a man. A woman and a dragon. Hunter and hunted. Nothing in this world has only one nature.

The Beast's eyes fell to her lips and he bent his head, but there his movements faltered a little. The sudden uncertainty in the tilt of his mouth toward hers was so completely, so utterly human that Yeva felt she might laugh, or cry, or both. So instead, she leaned forward and kissed him, and he let go of her hands so he could wrap his arms around her and pull her body in against his. He was warm and solid and real, and Yeva felt as insubstantial as smoke that might drift away like the ashes of her bow and her stories.

She gave up trying to understand and just kissed him, there in the Firebird's cave. And though Yeva knew she would always long for tomorrow, and for what lay in the next valley, and for what colors she would see in the sky in the years to come, the kiss was, for that single instant, everything she wanted.

EOVEN

It is strange, to be whole. To know every thought and want is from my own heart. That every memory and instinct is mine.

Because I do remember another life. And not the life of the wolf, not the hunt nor the kill, nor the endless hunger. I remember a life before that was good, but not the one I wanted. I remember feeling as though nothing and no one in this world could ever understand the way I wanted, that pang that rings deeper than flesh and bone.

My longing for something else, beyond, into magic and dreams and the things everyone else seemed to leave behind as children. For something I knew I could never truly find.

It's the wanting that brought me here, to

her. To another soul as empty as mine, and yet not empty at all, because it's so full of everything I thought only I ever felt. Her soul against mine feels like music, like a heartbeat, like magic.

Like beauty.

EPILOGUE

EVENTUALLY YEVA WOULD BRING Eoven to the town where she grew up. She would tell her family as best she could what had happened, and they would not understand, but they would welcome Eoven anyway because of the way he looked at Yeva. They'd stay there for a long time together, and Eoven would tell Lena's daughter stories, and teach Asenka's twins to hunt when they were old enough. They'd stay sometimes at the baron's household, and sometimes in Yeva's old room in Radak and Lena's house, and sometimes in a little cottage at the edge of town with a garden and a peony tree and shelves full of books.

Her family would ask them eventually when they intended to be wed, and Yeva and Eoven would look at each other and realize that it hadn't occurred to either of them. Perhaps someday they would marry, and perhaps they would tell *their* children stories and teach them to hunt, and perhaps they'd live at the edge of town and add room after room onto the little cottage.

Or perhaps they would live in the forest, and never speak to another soul again but the trees and the beasts, and they'd tell their stories only to each other.

Or perhaps they'd journey to the far eastern sea and strike out for the edge of the world, where there were dragons, and women with hair like wings, and birds that caught fire when the golden sun hit them just so.

Perhaps they would do all these things.

But before any of it, Beauty and the Beast walked together back along the river leading from the Firebird's cave, with Doe-Eyes trotting at their side. They traveled through each mountain pass and saw that winter was fading away with every step, and when they arrived once again in the Beast's valley they found spring had come and that the windows in the tower room looked out over a meadow filled with wildflowers that bloomed in every shade of red and gold and brilliant fire orange.

And from somewhere past the mountains that separated the Beast's valley from those beyond, behind them, always to the north, the Firebird's song drifted in the air, and called to them, and waited.

A NOTE FROM THE AUTHOR

I dedicated this book to myself.

I've been writing Hunted since I was a child. In my head, in my dreams, in every retelling of Beauty and the Beast that I could consume. In gazing out the window on long car trips, in traveling the world, in those indescribable moments of completeness after reading a particularly beautiful book.

I wrote the beginning of this manuscript at the start of my career, as I waited to find out if my first book would catch a literary agent's attention. (It did. Thank you, Josh Adams.) When that first book became a trilogy, Hunted was put on a shelf to gather dust.

It stayed there for five years while I wrote my other books and navigated the new, unknown waters of being an author. It's an awesome job, but it can be all-consuming. It's easy to start drowning without realizing what's happening.

Fortunately, along came Kristen Pettit. My editor's whip-smart advice, along with my agent's encouragement, convinced me to dust off Hunted and really look at it again, and that's when I realized that I'd left Yeva in limbo—much like I'd left myself. Neither of us was finished yet.

Though I've never lived with a cursed Beast in medieval Russia, this is my most autobiographical novel. Yeva's dissatisfaction with her life was mine; her guilt over her restlessness, her tendency to pour herself into a single focus to the exclusion of everything else, her inability to fit into the world, her confusion about what she wanted and why she felt incomplete—all the things I'd carried with me the last five years.

So, to quote a favorite musical, I wrote my way out.

I'm blessed with an amazing network of friends, family, and fellow writers who gave me the courage—and, occasionally, the figurative kick in the butt—to keep going.

I owe an unpayable debt (for so, so many reasons) to my best friend and soul sister, Amie, who was this book's first champion and who remains its biggest fan. I'm also forever grateful for my family, who've always encouraged me to tell stories, and my extended family of neighbors and friends, who were among my first fans. I can't express how much support I got from my early readers, especially Cait, who's been asking for this story since we were in high school together, and Stephanie, who has helped me immeasurably as a friend, confidante, and fellow writer. I also must thank everyone who helped me research this book, especially Erin, whose expertise in Slavic folklore was invaluable, and Grimm, who, when I wanted to interview him about archery, put a bow into my hands instead and introduced me to a lifelong passion. And to everyone at HarperTeen, I am so happy and grateful to be a member of your team.

It's hard to admit that despite this network of support, it's difficult to let go of this book and send it out into the world. This book is me, and I've kept it to myself for a long time out of fear. But stories change you, if you let them, and *Hunted* has changed me.

So while I dedicated this book to myself, it's also dedicated to you. Male or female, young or old, if you're reading this book, then you're also that child reading by flashlight and dreaming of other worlds. Don't be scared of her, that inner Beauty, or her dreams. Let her out. She's you, and she's me, and she's magic.

There's no such thing as living happily ever after—there's only living. We make the choice to do it happily.

You are the Firebird. And above everything else, I'm most grateful for you.

JOIN THE

Epic Reads

COMMUNITY

THE ULTIMATE YA DESTINATION

◀ **DISCOVER** ▶

your next favorite read

◀ **MEET** ▶

new authors to love

◀ **WIN** ▶

free books

◀ **SHARE** ▶

infographics, playlists, quizzes, and more

◀ **WATCH** ▶

the latest videos